I'M
THE
GIRL

Also by Courtney Summers

Cracked Up to Be

Sadie

The Project

For a full bibliography, visit courtneysummers.ca

I'M
THE
GIRL

A Novel

COURTNEY
SUMMERS

WEDNESDAY BOOKS
NEW YORK

First published in the United States by Wednesday Books,
an imprint of St. Martin's Publishing Group

I'M THE GIRL. Copyright © 2022 by Courtney Summers. All rights reserved.
Printed in the United States of America. For information, address
St. Martin's Publishing Group, 120 Broadway, New York, N.Y. 10271.

www.wednesdaybooks.com

The Library of Congress Cataloging-in-Publication Data is
available upon request.

ISBN 978-1-250-80836-3 (hardcover)
ISBN 978-1-250-87993-6 (international, sold outside
the U.S., subject to rights availability)
ISBN 978-1-250-80837-0 (ebook)

Our books may be purchased in bulk for promotional, educational, or business use. Please contact your local bookseller or the Macmillan Corporate
and Premium Sales Department at 1-800-221-7945, extension 5442,
or by email at MacmillanSpecialMarkets@macmillan.com.

First Edition: 2022

10 9 8 7 6 5 4 3 2 1

I'm the Girl is dedicated to my sister, Megan,
and our mother, Susan.

This might be the only page in one of my books
where they wouldn't be afraid to see themselves.

Thank you both for all you have and
—thankfully—
haven't inspired.

PROLOGUE

spera.

It comes to me on my knees in the back of one of the mall's storerooms, its gray concrete walls dappled with early morning light. I close my eyes and there's a memory there: I was thirteen years old and I'd gone missing just a little while. Ended up on a dirt road outside of town. It was summer then too, the kind of heat that sours you, and I was angry with my mother, the kind of anger that changes the way you look at the world and makes you understand, for better and worse, the way the world's looking at you. I remember my body as it was then, caught between fading adolescence and aspiring womanhood. I didn't yet fully grasp my burgeoning chest or bee-stung lips turned suddenly suggestive. I was dizzy, dried out from the weather, and I wasn't sure how far I'd walked when the car pulled up beside me, its window rolled down.

A man inside.

Are you the girl? he'd asked.

And I'd felt like I'd been saved from something, but I didn't know what.

Until now.

Now: I open my eyes, letting my gaze drift from the man

standing over me, to the transom window in the corner, to the view outside. I know the mountains are that way.

Aspera is too.

A revelation.

"We doing this or what?" he breathes.

"I want to see the pictures again," I say.

He makes a noise, his face red and strained with his unattended hard-on, but he gives them to me. I hold the glossies in my trembling hands, a young white girl stretched across the top photo's length. I take in her long, perfect legs reaching for the smooth plane of her perfect stomach, extending toward the soft swell of her perfect breasts. Her perfect blond curls spill over her shoulders, haloing the peaches-and-cream complexion of her perfect face. Her pretty little lips form a perfect pink *o*.

Oh: the most beautiful girl I've ever seen in my life.

It's me. I'm the girl.

He calls me a stupid little cunt as I leave, says I have more beauty than brains.

What he was offering, he tells me, was more than I was worth.

I leave the mall behind, the photos carefully stowed in my messenger bag. Aspera is beyond the city, and I'll have to ride back through my neighborhood to get to it. My bike's tires hum against the road as the sun continues its slow rise up the horizon, stirring this sliver of world awake, the air cool and damp with last night's rain. I pass houses that could all be my house: the same missing shingles on the same weathered roofs, the same flaking blue siding, the same week's worth of trash at the curb. Tyler will be up by now, glancing at my closed bedroom door, believing I'm inside before leaving for work. He hasn't spoken to me since last night when he found out what I fucked up—what I did to him—in the name of myself. Our mother always told me, and only me, *it's more important to know who you are than who you think you're meant to be,* as though she could see this betrayal taking root. But if she did, it's only because she planted the seed. So whose is it in the end—hers or mine?

If my mother thought Aspera was the one place in this world I didn't belong, it was only because she didn't imagine me in that storeroom, threadbare carpet digging into my knees while the man above me fumbled with his fly.

I pump my legs harder and before long, Ketchum is behind me, giving way for the lush sun-shimmered green lining its either side. When I finally turn onto the road leading to the resort, a car comes tearing down it out of nowhere and seems to have me in its sights. I swerve in the last-second moment I realize it won't, that it'll run me over if I don't, and it clips the back end of my bike. The violence of it untethers me, and the brutal impact of my return to earth rattles my skull, forcing the breath from my lungs and a different kind of untethering . . .

I turn my face to the road.

The car is coming back.

I cough, choking my way to consciousness, my lips against gravel, the taste of metal in my mouth. I press my hands into the dirt, gasping as my left arm gives out under my weight. There's something wrong with it. The agony of that discovery washes over me before I try again, letting my right take on the burden, forcing myself to my feet.

Once I'm standing, I clench my jaw, steeling myself against the involuntary sway of my body. My bike is gone, my bag road-killed at the shoulder, four thousand dollars' worth of photographs of me crumpled inside. There are faint impressions of footsteps where I lay, circling me. Blood on me where skin and road connected. I try to get a hold of myself, breathing slowly in through my nose and out my mouth, clutching my left arm to my chest, my head pounding. I limp my way forward. Aspera is far, but it's closer now than home, but even if I was hurt bad enough I should turn myself around—I wouldn't.

I couldn't.

This is the closest I've ever come.

Aspera. A 12,000-acre members-only resort hidden away in the mountains. What God couldn't put a price on—all that wild beauty ever-reaching for the limitless blue sky—its owners, Matthew and Cleo Hayes, surely would. There are always whispers about the latest rich-and-famous hiding there to escape themselves, and when my mother worked housekeeping, everyone would ask me for her dirt. I'd beg any little detail, but she wouldn't talk about the place—at least not in any way I wanted to hear. They call it the heart of Ketchum, but she always said it was its diamond and *it's not shining for you.*

Before she died, she tried to make sure of it.

Today, I'll find out if the promise it made me is greater than the one she broke.

I put one unsteady foot in front of the other, and for the longest time it's only this until a flash of pink catches my eye. It has to, it's such an aberration. Not the kind of pink you find in nature. I squint to be sure, and once I am, I move brokenly to it, heading down the ditch, shoes sinking into soggy earth, wet grass tickling my ankles. I wince at how difficult it's become to do this simple thing. The sunlight overhead is fading fast, devoured by the trees, making it even more impressive, or impossible, that I saw it at all. I press farther on to claim my prize, and the glimpse of color blooms larger the closer I get, slowly taking form.

A girl pressed against the ground.

At first I wonder if we both got hit by the same car.

Her white skin is mottled red, her right leg turned inward, its knobby knee pointing toward the left. Her right arm lies rigidly beside her, the crook of her elbow stained purple, hand palm-up as though awaiting someone to place something inside it. Her left hand is rested against her chest, her stiff fingers reaching toward her throat. Her bright pink shirt is smeared with dirt and her frayed denim shorts are unbuttoned and splayed open, revealing no underwear, revealing the most intimate part of her, a bruise.

Her eyes are open, cloudy.

"Hey, kid," I whisper. "You all right?"

Her fine blond hair fans over the ground, a strand of it crossing her porcelain face, finding its way into her open mouth. Her lips are pale and chapped.

A fly traces the outline of their delicate pout.

Ashley James. That's who it was.

The road should be somewhere ahead and I know what's behind me, but the trees feel endless, everywhere . . . sunlight skitters over my feet through their leaves, world skittering with it, and I fall once, twice, three times, but I get back up each, moving forward until the ground rises and finally meets the road, and it's like breaking the surface after so long underwater.

She's thirteen years old.

I collapse, my legs splayed in front of me, a bitter taste at the back of my throat, a cold sweat breaking out on the back of my neck. I think of her body out there, think of all the things that can no longer happen to it, and then I need to know if I can still bleed. I dig my fingers into the torn skin of my knees. A buzzing fills my head, a thought reaching me on a long delay: *call for help.* I slip my hand into my pocket and it's empty.

My phone is gone.

Lost? Taken?

I turn my face toward the road.

A car is coming.

I wave my hand weakly until it gets close and then my

arm drops to my side. The car eases to a stop next to me, and I stare at the blurry edge of the driver's side door as it opens and a beige heel descends to the ground.

I follow it all the way up to the woman it belongs to.

Oh.

The most beautiful woman I've ever seen in my life.

An aura of light surrounds the curves of her body so perfectly, I can't help but wonder if she's real. She crouches in front of me, her eyes a pale blue, their sweet concern offsetting the devastating angles of her breathtaking face. Her white skin is summer-tanned, glitter-flecked, rays of sunlight threading themselves through the short strands of honey-blond hair hanging loose at the nape of her neck. She looks like something out of a magazine, her beauty almost defiant in the face of everything that's put it before me, refusing to be less than what it is even though there's a dead girl out there right now, rotting.

I need to go to Aspera, I tell her.

There's a body in the woods.

Ashley James.

The deputy sheriff's little girl.

The woman makes some calls and then everything she says after that seems to end in my name, but I don't remember telling it to her. Something about the gentle persistence of hearing *Georgia, Georgia,* over and over again keeps me from floating too far away. And then we're in her car and it's the nicest car I've been in in a long time, and I shiver against the cool leather seat, my head lolling against the window.

Every time my eyes drift shut, she says my name.

Georgia.

The view changes and there's a gate in the distance stretched across the road. Even from here, I can make out the gold lettering across its top, sparkling in the light, declaring itself:

ASPERA
PRIVATE. NO ADMITTANCE. MEMBERS ONLY.

"What if they don't let me in?" I manage.

But the gate opens before we even reach it.

My pulse quickens as the lodge slowly appears on the horizon, only to unmake itself before I can get a closer look.

"You're already in," the woman tells me.

I finally realize who I'm sitting next to.

"Georgia," she says, alarmed, stopping the car as my head falls forward. Her hand comes to rest against my cheek and carefully turns my face to hers, as though she wants to be sure she's the last thing I see.

"Was I at Aspera?"

The shape of my brother stands at the window, staring out at the hospital's parking lot view. I don't realize I've asked the question aloud until he moves to my bed, reaching for the cup of water on the stand beside it. Ice rattles against plastic as he brings the straw to my lips and then: a cold miracle against the sandpapered insides of my throat. Beyond my room, the soft sounds of doctors and orderlies moving down the corridor, beds being rolled from one place to another, beeps from machines I wouldn't know the names of . . .

Tyler comes into focus slowly, his thick brown hair knotted in a bun at the back of his head. The cold white glow of the room's lights casts the lines in his light brown face in sharp relief. He works construction all day, every day, the wear and tear of the job belying his thirty years. Mom had him when she was twenty-seven and then I came along, an accident when she was forty-one. He got the benefit of her youth and the heart that body housed, and I got—something else. We don't look the same. Different dads. Mine was a fuck-and-run, the way Mom told it, but Tyler's is Tony Ruiz. Lives down in Roanoke. Tyler visits him sometimes, but mostly keeps him at an arm's length, like if Mom couldn't make it work with him, he shouldn't either.

That loyalty to her is the difference between us.

"Sheriff Watt's going to come down to the house tomorrow to question you," he says. "I might put him off a little longer. Doc Abrams says it's important you rest."

"I'll be okay tomorrow."

"Tell that to me when you're not hooked up to the good stuff."

I breathe in, the chemical clean of the hospital coating my tongue.

"What's he going to ask me?"

"I'm sure he'll want to know anything you can tell him about the car that hit you, its driver . . . the body. Maybe what you were doing out on that road."

I close my eyes and some of what I see there is more than I want to see, but the rest is like an overdeveloped negative, details all blown out. I can't remember the car, can't conjure the face belonging to the person driving it.

Footprints around my body.

My bike, my phone, gone.

I open my eyes.

I suddenly feel like I survived more than I realized.

"He thinks it's connected?"

"I don't know. I don't like how it's looking."

I stare at my IV line. The painkillers keep me from my concussion, my broken arm, from skin turned raw meat and all my newly stitched together places. I wish it would keep me from other things too. I'm not as numb as I want to be.

I'm more awake than I'd like. Tyler sits in the chair next to my bed and leans forward, his shoulders slumped.

"Just heard this morning about the James kid. She was missing a couple days. Can't fuckin' believe it took this long to reach our side of town . . . white girl, cop's daughter." He lets out a breath, his fingers twitching, itching, I know, for that pack of Camels he keeps lovingly tucked in his shirt pocket. They'll kill him one day, just like they did Mom, and I don't want to be around for it when it happens. "Ashley James, goddamn. She's not much younger than you. Her sister in your grade or older?"

Nora. "Older. Seventeen. She just graduated early." I close my eyes and there's a memory there: "She invited me to her birthday once . . . Mom wouldn't let me go."

"Right," Tyler says slowly. "I remember that."

When I was thirteen . . . and I got so angry, I ran away from home . . . all the way out to a dirt road . . . and a car pulled up beside me . . .

"Ashley the one always getting into shit?"

I blink.

"Yeah. Ashley."

There are stories about her, but people are always careful in their retellings, just in case Justin James ever finds out who's been saying what about his baby girl. Ashley James: a wild little thing. Ashley James: paints ten years onto her face every day and sneaks out every night. Ashley James: always on the lookout for the kind of trouble she one day won't be able to get herself out of. Ashley James: dead.

God.

"What the hell were you doing out there, George?"

I shift, the crisp sheets painful against my tender skin.

"I went to the mall to get your money back."

He scrubs his hand down his face. The pull of his skin makes him look even older and even more exhausted in this light. "I said I'd take care of it."

His voice is tight, still mad at me, and my chest gets just as tight at the thought of him trying to "take care of it."

"There's nothing to take care of. He wouldn't give it to me. But I was thinking." I hesitate. "I could earn it back instead."

"Yeah? And how you gonna do that?"

"Aspera."

He looks at me. "You kidding? That's where you were headed?"

"I could be an Aspera girl."

"No."

"I'm sixteen," I say, and he rises angrily to his feet. "I could work there now. If they took me on, I could make back half what I owe you in *one* summer—"

"Mom would roll over in her grave," he hisses. "That place killed her—"

"It didn't."

"She had no *fight* left in her—where do you think it went?" I wince, and he lowers his voice but it doesn't do much to soften it. "What do you think you're going to prove, huh? What's got into you? Some man at a pop-up shop tells you you can be a model, so you steal four grand from me for a photoshoot and now you're begging a job at Aspera after what they did to Mom? You want to earn back what you owe me, Mac's Convenience is hiring—"

"I'm not working *there*."

"If I don't get my money back, George, you might not have a choice."

I press my knuckles against my forehead, tears pooling at the corners of my eyes, and let out a shaky breath. Tyler sighs.

"You thirsty?"

I nod. He gives me another drink of water.

"We shouldn't even be talking about this now." He sets the glass down. "You're—you need rest. So do I. It's been a long fucking day."

"Yeah," I say.

He rests his hand on the top of my head, his thumb lightly stroking my forehead as the warm hold of the drugs takes over. The hard lines of his face smooth as I drift, and as I drift he keeps his hand there. I know I'm not an easy person to love, and the times I really feel it are the times I'm asking it of him the most.

"Besides," he says quietly as my eyes close, "you forget the part where the Hayeses don't want to see an Avis pass through that gate ever again?"

I struggle to stay awake. It's a losing battle, but I have to know. Because the road, the car, and the body feels like it happened today, but everything after . . . her . . .

"But I was there. Wasn't I?"

Feels like a dream.

"Yeah," he finally answers. "You were."

When Nora James shows up at my door a week and a half later, her sister's death is on her, everywhere.

I'm not used to seeing her so undone. Nora is a girl who lingers in the corners of your mind, a mean kind of pretty, bordering on unapproachable. If she looks like she has time for you, it's likely a trick of the light, but when it's not and she means it—nothing more important could happen to you. At least not in the halls of Ketchum High. She was one of the most popular girls before she graduated. Captain of the volleyball team. She's tall, lean up and down, with strong shoulders, skin taut around muscular arms and legs that call attention to how hard she trains. She's always been so sure of herself, but she seems so small to me now. Her chin-length black hair is tied into a baby ponytail that reveals her undercut but doesn't hide the tangled, unwashed state of it. Her pointed face is pale white, dark circles under her wide hazel eyes.

"Watt says you don't remember most of it," Nora says—as close to "hello" as I'm getting, I guess. "But I want to know what you do. Show me where you found her."

"You know where I found her." Everyone does.

"Show me where you found her," she repeats. "And tell me everything."

She drives us to the road. I tell her I can't be out long.

"Why? Where else you got to be?"

I don't answer. Before she showed, I was making myself sick waiting on Tyler to come back from the mall, the modeling agency. I begged him not to go, told him to forget about it. He wasn't going to get his money back *so let me see about Aspera,* and it was the wrong thing to say. I keep thinking of the flash of worry I saw in his eyes before he left, the possibility of coming home empty-handed too great for him to ignore.

I keep thinking about how I'd rather him come home empty-handed.

"Should Sheriff Watt be telling you what I do and don't remember?" I ask Nora, but now it's her turn not to answer. "How's your dad?"

She keeps to her silence. All she's got is her dad. Motherless, her and me. Nora's mom left when she was thirteen. It was one of those hard leavings too. The kind that doesn't call. Doesn't check in. The kind that makes you wonder if you ever had a mother. I can't help but wonder if I got the better deal, mine six feet underground. I glance at Nora's hands on the steering wheel, fingers clutched around it so tight, it looks like they could snap it in half. The fervor of those first few days following the discovery of Ashley's body has settled into an uneasy, open wound. Tyler drove down that road right after, said there was yellow tape everywhere, reporters and cameras, a little wooden cross planted in the ground, people laying flowers when all they really wanted was to gawk. It rained that first night, he told me. Whatever evidence they didn't gather, washed away. I want to tell Nora that; that where she thinks she's taking me now is gone, just like her sister.

The funeral's soon.

"How are you?"

She gives me a withering look and I wonder what my mother would make of the two of us in a car together. She was no fan of the Jameses, especially Justin, who, like every cop at the sheriff's department, is welcome to enjoy Aspera's golf course as thanks for doing his job. *They only care about their own, and that's not us.* But that's what my mom felt about anyone higher up the food chain—which to her eye was everyone. And it wasn't always true.

Because when I was thirteen, Nora invited me to her birthday party.

I almost want to remind her about that now, tell her how circular all this is, how fated it's starting to feel, but I don't think she'd want to hear it.

I turn to the window and the closer we get to familiar things, the more my body rebels against this whole idea. My pulse races and my palms sweat, my throat tightening, my lungs constricting. I try to remind myself I won't—can't—discover Ashley there a second time, but the moment we step out of the car and face the woods, I feel like I could. I look up at the sky, wincing at the glare, and hope against a headache because every day since, there's been one, bad ones. Doc Abrams said it's normal—the consequence of bashing my skull off the ground. If Nora's noting these little signs of my distress, she doesn't care. Unlike her sister, I'm here to feel them.

I point down the road behind us.

"Back there. That's where I got hit."

"You see the license plate? The driver?"

I shake my head. "I blacked out."

"And then what?"

"When I woke up, my bike was gone. And there were footprints around me."

"He do anything to you?"

". . . What do you mean?"

I know what she means.

"You know what I mean."

"He just took my bike," I say. "I got up, walked, and then I got here and I saw—"

The woods there, empty now. The sun seems to stop at the edge of the road, marked by a pile of withering bouquets and water-soaked votives set in front of that small cross, a pink ribbon tied around it. Pink. I stare past it, into the darkness, and I have no idea how I ever saw that flash of color in the first place, and again, I have that thought about the way the universe is working, but I still don't say it aloud.

"What did you see?"

"Well—Ashley."

"Show me."

"Nora, I don't—"

"Show me."

I lead her down the ditch and into the woods. It's an easier trip this time. At first, the sameness of the area, the lack of Ashley as its marker, makes me worried I won't find the exact spot she lay, but that moment of discovery is burned in me and it stops me in my tracks. I let out a slow breath.

"Was it there?" She nods a little off center to where her sister was.

I shake my head, pointing.

"There."

"Show me."

"Nora—"

"Please."

When I turn to her, there are tears in her eyes.

A light breeze pulls my hair from my face and rustles the leaves in the trees. And then, the faint trilling of birds I can't see, singing their sweet songs to one another. I think of Ashley out here alone, the world moving around her, without her, and it makes me dizzy enough that I sit down where she lay in the end anyway. I stare at the gaps of sky through the trees. A whole world in front of her wide-open eyes, as unreachable to her as she to it.

"Just like that?"

"No."

"Show me how it looked."

"Jesus, Nora."

"I need to see it."

"Why?"

She presses her hands against her eyes.

"Just do it, okay? Maybe you'll remember something."

I do as she's asked. I lie on the ground, tilting my head back, my chin pointed stiffly upward. I turn my right leg toward my left and I pin my right arm beside myself, realizing how uncomfortable a position it all actually is. My sore body protests it. Nora makes her way to me, standing over me while I complete the pose. I rest my left arm against my chest, feeling the added weight of my cast, and let my fingers reach for my throat. I swallow, feel the jump of movement there, and it's suddenly obscene, to have all this.

Hey, kid. You all right?

Nora takes me in.

"You think it means anything, he put her like that?" Her voice splinters. "Does it feel like it means anything?"

"I don't know." I pause. "It feels uncomfortable."

"She was raped."

I close my eyes. "I know."

"She was drugged first. Died of an overdose while he was raping her, they think." My stomach turns. She touches the crook of my elbow. "There was an injection bruise there."

She was thirteen.

"She was messed up so bad, my dad can't even get out of bed, and he's seen a lot." I open my eyes and she's above me, blocking what little view there is of the sky, her expression cold, and more than that—angry. "And you couldn't even get a look at the guy driving the car."

Nora reaches her hand out to help me up and I slap it away. I try to get to my feet, first on my bad arm, which elicits a pained yelp, but I'm successful the second time, fumbling away from her with what little dignity I can muster. She calls after me, "Avis, hey—Avis," and I flip her off over my shoulder, nauseous and sweaty, dirt and grass and leaves stuck to my clothes. I make my way to the road, the ghost of my escape on me—but this time no one's pulling up to help.

"It's not your fault." Nora emerges behind me.

"I don't need you to tell me that."

"But do you know what it means?"

I turn to her, holding out my arms.

"What does it mean?"

"It means he's anyone. It means he's still out there. It means I'm going to find him. I'm gonna find the fucker that did that to my little sister."

"And then what?"

"What do you think?"

I don't know what to say to her, and the way she's looking at me wants me to say something.

"It was Cleo Hayes picked you up, right?" she asks after a minute, and I nod. "What do you think your mom would think of that?"

"I'm sure she'd just be glad I was okay."

But I'm not. Not really.

"Let's get out of here," she says. "Since you can't be out long."

In the car, Nora seems steadier, surer of herself. An evolution of grief taking place before my very eyes, like she just needed to say out loud to someone what she planned to do. I feel like less of myself in the exchange, some part of me still out there in the woods because I saw the question when she stood over me; if there was some way, some world, where this could have happened to Ashley and me with the roles reversed. I'm tired, the kind of bone-deep fatigue that comes with healing. The sun sears my eyes through the windshield. I pull the visor down. Nora asks what my problem is.

"You," I tell her.

She takes me back home.

I slam the car door and that's a mistake; the sound burrows into my skull. I stand on the curb with my back to her until I hear her pull away, and then I slowly make the walk to the screen door, where I press my forehead against its cool metal. After a long moment, I pull it open, fumbling for my pocket, to get my key. The cast makes it nearly impossible. I'm reaching across myself with my good hand to get it, the pressure building behind my eyes, when Tyler flings the inside door open and says, "You couldn't *text* me?"

I hadn't noticed his truck in the driveway.

"I don't have a phone," I remind him, edging past.

"Then leave a *note*, George!" he snaps. I wince and rest my hand against the kitchen table. "And—sit down before you fall down. Jesus."

He grabs the painkillers under the window at the sink, then goes through the cupboards for a glass, which he fills with water. I sit as he sets both in front of me.

"You've still got a concussion, you know that? You're not supposed to be running around doing—" Now he remembers what he was pissed at me for, and he asks his next question with no small amount of wariness: "Do I even want to know?"

I down the pills and tell him about Nora. He listens, grinding his teeth back and forth. When I'm finished, he lights one of his Camels to relieve his tension, blowing the smoke toward the nicotine-stained ceiling. "That family . . ."

"What?" I ask.

"Nothing." He shakes his head. "I'm sorry for 'em, but we got enough of our own problems."

He takes another deep drag from the smoke, the cherry electric orange. He's nervous and that makes me nervous, makes me afraid to find out what happened at the mall.

"How did it go?" I ask in a small voice.

He purses his lips, contemplating another drag before putting the cigarette out in the sink. He stares out the window before finally turning to me. "I gotta ask you something and I'm not going to be mad, but you gotta be honest."

"Okay."

"Okay," he echoes. "Uh, these pictures you took with this photographer—what kind—" He clears his throat. "What kind of pictures were they, George?"

The silence stretches uncomfortably between us.

"What do you mean?"

"They weren't anything . . . special, were they?"

"What do you mean?" I ask again.

His hands go up, his fingers reaching for something, but I don't know what. "Okay, so you had your clothes on?" I cross my arms and look away, my eyes and face burning. "I'm sorry. I hate asking, but when I went down there, this guy was so obviously . . ."

"So obviously what?"

"What kind of pictures were they, George?"

"They were just—" I wipe my eyes. "Modeling shots. Professional."

He exhales, says, "Okay," and then tells me how it went at the mall: the guy's willing to return a portion of the money in exchange for the prints because you can't expect a refund without bringing back the goods.

"So you got 'em?" Tyler asks, and my stomach flips, my mind frantic until I remember the last I saw the photos, I was shoving them in my bag, and the last I saw my bag it was crumpled on the side of the road. I left it there.

"No, no, we got it," Tyler says, when I tell him. "It's in the hall closet."

He moves to get it, but I head him off, the sudden rise to my feet wreaking havoc on my throbbing head. My bag is stowed next to the shoes, stained and tattered, dirt and grime embedded into its cloth, rough against my fingers.

The thing is, I don't want to give the photos back.

I want to keep them.

They *are* special.

They're me.

"George?" he calls.

Maybe they'd just settle for some headshots. I fight with the buckle, a little crushed now. When I finally manage it open, the photographs are gone.

Taken.

. . .

It scares Tyler enough he calls the sheriff about it.

I sit on the living room couch with my palms pressed against my eyes, wishing that shock of pink had caught anyone else's notice.

That anyone else had found her on that road.

"Useless motherfucker," Tyler mutters after he hangs up.

"What did Watt say?" He doesn't answer. I lower my hands. "Tyler."

"He says that if nothing's happened yet, it probably won't, but I gotta tell you, I don't love the idea of some sick fuck who raped and killed a little girl holding onto your picture—"

"Tyler, come on—"

"And maybe getting in their head they need to come back for the real thing—"

"You're freaking me out!"

"That's because I'm freaked out!" He pinches the bridge of his nose, taking a good minute to weigh all this new and terrible information. "Okay. You know what. If Watt says it's fine, it's probably fine." But I can tell he doesn't believe it. He glances at the bag on the table, then his phone. The door. "I could only take the morning off. I gotta go back to work—"

"Then go."

"So I gotta trust you to be smart."

"Nothing's going to happen to me."

But something already did.

His eyes meet mine.

"I gotta trust you to be smart," he says again, slowly.

"Is that because you think I'm stupid?"

"Don't start. I'm locking the door behind me." He opens one of the drawers under the sink, grabs a fresh pack of Camels and tears the plastic wrap off it, tucking it into his pocket. "Don't go anywhere else today."

"I won't."

"I *mean* it." He snatches his keys off the counter. "I'm gonna call the house. And I'm not going to tell you when. And if you're not here to pick it up, George, I swear—"

"I'll be here." I pause. "What are you going to do about the pictures?"

"I'm gonna stop at the mall when I clock off," he answers and then cuts me off mid-protest. "I will figure it out. And if I don't, a summer job's not going to be the worst thing for you. At least I'll know where the hell you are." He grabs my bag. "Watt wants this."

"Will I get it back?" I don't know why this is the thing I ask.

"I don't know." He stares at it, then snaps himself out of whatever road his mind is trying to take him down. He gestures to the door. "Keep it locked, okay? Stay inside. Call if you need anything. And wait for my call."

"I will."

He hesitates one last time and then he goes. After I hear his truck pull out, I get up and move to the door, touching the lock, turning it back and forth, listening to the *click* and release. Locked—unlocked—locked. I close my eyes and feel the road against me, pebbles and dirt scratching my scalp, getting in my hair . . .

Unlocked.

The car coming back. Wavering, indistinct, formless, a

shadow, no color or license plate or driver, but it had all of these things. I don't remember letting go and this is what terrifies me the most: to be so acutely in my body one minute and then, suddenly, not there at all, and then, just as suddenly, returned, someone else's story writing itself in my gaps.

I think of footsteps around me, carving a path.

Locked.

And now, something else: hands rooting through my messenger bag, finding my photos and leaving with them, the hands of someone who killed a girl . . . and did he always decide to kill her, to use her body like that and let her die in the same moment?

What makes you decide to kill a girl?

What makes you decide not to?

He has my photos.

Unlocked.

Knock-knock-knock.

I jerk away from the door. The lock. *Fuck.* I reach out quickly to lock it and the loud *click* of it gives me away. I fumble back when I hear my name—or I think I do.

"Georgia."

Cleo Hayes.

She stands in front of me as real as she's ever been and even more beautiful for it, though I'd thought her shattering out there on the road when she was no more than the hazy, angel outline of someone who would save me. She's taller than I realized. Her blond hair is slicked from her face, making the lines of her jaw and cheekbones even more distinct. Her lips, cherry red. She wears a wide V-neck shirt revealing her collarbone before its long plunge down, hinting at her impressive chest. There's a gentle intensity in her blue eyes as they take me in, and that intensity makes it easy to forget she's only twenty-five. She occupies a space between delicate and sharp, and every part of her body feels like an imposition on the place it inhabits, a demand to be recognized on its own terms. It sends a shiver through me.

She tells me she was worried. She's called to check on me a few times, but Tyler wouldn't tell her anything, and said no when she asked if she could stop by. So forgive her, please; she decided to take matters into her own hands. She was driving down my street when she saw Tyler leave, hoping what she did next would bring her to—me.

"I don't make a habit of showing up where I'm not welcome," she says. "But you were in such a state when I saw you last, I had to be sure you were okay . . ."

"I didn't know." The thought of her worrying over me is almost too impossible to grasp. I can't believe Cleo Hayes has been calling and Tyler didn't tell me. It's shameful after what she did for me, us—picking me up, getting me to help. If it had been Matthew, I could maybe understand, but Cleo's only crime is being his wife. And I've never thought either of them guilty for what happened with Mom. They were only looking out for what was theirs.

"Is it all right if I sit down?" she asks. "Or would you rather I leave?"

"Stay," I say quickly.

She doesn't belong in this room, in this house, on this side of town, but I watch as she moves around the kitchen with ease, like the mess of this life belongs to her. She turns a chair out at the table and sits, crossing her legs. I trace their slender path up until our eyes meet, and look away, blood rushing to my cheeks.

But she stays looking—at me.

"I keep thinking how . . ."

"What?" There's nothing more I want than to hear what she's thinking.

"Matthew and I seem to have a habit of finding you when you need it the most," she says. My heart leaps at this; that she knows that story from so long ago, that he told it to her. And then there's nothing more I want than to hear how it was told. "How are you, Georgia?"

"I didn't know you called," I say again, my shame sharpening into something else. Hurt.

Tyler kept that from me.

"You didn't answer my question."

"I'll be okay."

"It's shocking something like that could happen here. Ashley was . . ." Her eyes grow distant as she tries to find the right words. "She was thirteen. And he stopped the car after he hit you, is that what I've been hearing? That you got a look at who did it?"

I grimace at these awful details finding their way into Ketchum's collective consciousness without my permission. Imagine the blame of the whole affair somehow landing on me because I'm Katy Avis's girl.

Because if you're Katy Avis's girl, where else would it fall.

"No . . . I passed out. When I woke up, my bike was gone, and my phone. There were footprints around me." I clench the fingers of my good hand, thinking of Nora's accusing eyes. "All I had to do was look at him, and I couldn't even manage it."

"Maybe that's what saved your life."

"I thought that was you."

She smiles faintly, and we stare at each other, the space between us holding so much unsaid . . . the longer I look at her, the less I understand why.

"I was at Aspera." But it sounds like a question.

She inclines her head. "You were. We waited for the ambulance outside the lodge."

"I don't remember it."

"I'm not surprised. You were barely holding on."

"I've always—" My voices catches. "I always wanted to see it."

"Your mother never brought you, did she? Not even for a visit?" she asks. I shake my head. "Maybe I shouldn't say this . . . but I'll never understand why she hated us so much."

"I do," I say. "I mean, I think I do."

Cleo leans forward. "Would you tell me?"

I never get to tell anyone what I think about what happened with Mom and Aspera. It's a line Tyler won't let me cross, says there's too much I don't know. But there's things I know that he doesn't. I've gone over it again and again, and I think I'm closer to the truth of it than anyone.

Just because she's dead doesn't mean I'm wrong.

"I think . . . it's that she was afraid of her own dreams, and some people, they don't know how to have dreams . . . so they decide to live in a world where they just can't ever come true." That was my mother: a woman who didn't know how to do the type of work she did in the type of place she did it in and come home to our kind of house and live our kind of life. "It makes them bitter and that bitterness makes them . . . well. You know what she did."

Cleo nods, slowly scanning the room, the dirty window over the sink, the hole in its screen that lets bugs in through the summer, the stained walls and ceilings and grimy tiled floors.

"This house feels familiar. I didn't come from money either. Did you know that?"

It's hard to imagine.

I shake my head.

"And I know what it's like to dream—in a place like this." She tilts her head as she regards me. "And I know how dangerous that can be to do, if you're not strong enough."

"She always used to tell me it was better to know who you are than who you think you're meant to be. And then she'd tell me—"

And then she'd tell me who and what, exactly, I wasn't.

"No," Cleo says sharply. "It's *always* better to dream."

Something uncoils inside me.

"That's what I think too . . . so I was headed to Aspera that day."

"Is that right? Why?"

Because when I was thirteen years old, I'd gone missing for just a little while. Because I was angry with my mother, and it was the kind of anger that puts one foot determinedly in front of the other as though it has some specific destination in mind. Because Nora James had turned fourteen without me there and the next day at school made me understand exactly what it was that I'd lost. Because she was surrounded by girls, girl-stars turned into one great girl-constellation, and there I was, staring up at them from the gutter. Because I should have been a star. Because when I was past the point of turning around and each step forward didn't feel as certain as the last, I stopped and a car pulled up beside me. Because when its window rolled down, there was a man inside: Cleo's husband, Matthew Hayes.

Are you the girl? he'd asked.

My skin prickles, like something big is about to be decided about my life, like that day at the mall. My gaze drifts to the window and I can't see Aspera from here—

But I can See it.

"Georgia," Cleo says. "Why?"

"Because I'm not afraid to dream."

I'm sorry, Mom, but I can see it.

PART ONE

. . . .

I sit on the front step as a steady stream of cars drive down our street, all of them making the same left at the corner, all of them headed to St. Mary's just to watch Ashley get put in the ground. This beautiful summer day, the final insult. I catalog all of them: her remaining surviving hours spent drugged, raped. Her body dumped in the woods. Her body found twisted, a feast for the earth. Her body bagged, processed for evidence. I think of that, think of faceless people—men—pulling her even further apart for trace evidence and then stitching her back into as much a little girl as this world never let her be. I rest my chin in my good hand, my injured arm to my lap, before I realize the looking is going both ways. Everyone knows I found her, and in the exchange of all our meeting eyes, I can no longer tell if I've come out for this grim parade or it's come out for me.

I wait for Tyler's call because I know I've got at least ninety minutes before he'll call again. After we hang up, I go to the cemetery because I feel like I should. By then, the sun is an electric gold line on the horizon. The fresh laid dirt of Ashley's grave is visible from the road—at least those parts of it not covered in flowers. Her headstone is bad; salmon-colored granite carved into the crude shape of a heart with a quote about little girls becoming little guardian angels, but why, after all this, should she look out for us?

I wonder about it, this pink rewriting of Ashley's life when everyone knew she was all fury and grit, raw and wide open. I don't know who this false memory is preserving, but it makes it feel like she's even more lost to the world now.

I bow my head because it's another thing I feel like I should do, but I don't know the thing I should do after that. I remember a different funeral, over a year ago, Tyler and his dad and me standing coffin-side, only us and nothing to say. I'd cried for my mother for the first and only time that night. I think it was a relief for Tyler that I could. It was quick, the cancer. I'd never known it could be so quick. A cough one day, then the next, her lungs full of tumor. Tyler told me it's like that sometimes. Those last few months of her life were uneasy between us. I kept my distance, worried whatever anger I might inspire—because we always seemed to make each other angry—would steal her last breath from her.

"What are you doing here?"

I turn, the voice too familiar now to be a surprise. Nora has materialized from somewhere I'm unsure of, in what could only be her funeral clothes. A rumpled black dress shirt and black slacks cling to her sweaty skin. Her eyes are puffy and red, her hair limp, strands of it stuck to her neck and cheeks. She looks feverish.

"Paying my respects. What are you still doing here?"

"You think I should just leave her alone?"

The question unravels her. She closes her eyes, her hands

turning into fists, and, after a struggle back to herself, she opens them again.

"I heard killers sometimes go to the graves of their victims. Gets them off."

"Really?"

She nods. I look around at the tidy rows of graves, the cemetery's path wound around us. It's half-enclosed by trees that stretch into undeveloped land I wandered into once when I was a kid, after my grandmother's funeral. I went as far as the light reached, stuffing my pockets with flower petals and plastic leaves that had drifted away from their headstones.

"People act like it was inevitable," Nora mutters, drawing my attention back to her. "They don't say it, but I know it's what they're thinking."

I stare at the stone again, at her name etched, unforgivingly, in it.

ASHLEY JAMES

The cloying scent of wilting flowers at my feet.

"It wasn't her inevitability," I say. "It was his."

"Yeah? That's what you think?"

"If it hadn't been her, it would've been any other girl."

It was almost me.

"Have you been out here since it ended?" I ask. "This whole time?"

She's suddenly embarrassed, eyes glistening, tears just this side of spilling out. I feel so bad for her, I step closer and hold out my hand.

"Let me walk you home, Nora."

But she doesn't want to go home, at least not right away, so I get us slushies at Mac's Convenience, and we meander in the direction of her house, the sickeningly sweet drinks staining our tongues and teeth cherry red. She tells me Monday, she's going down to the sheriff's office to find out everything she isn't supposed to know about their investigation.

"I figure," she says, turning the straw in her cup, loosening the ice, her voice thick and numb from the slush, "they'll feel bad enough for me, they'll let something slip." I almost tell her about my photographs, but there's too much there I don't want to explain. I ask about her dad instead, if he's working the case. She looks at me like I'm a fool and says, "He couldn't even dress himself for the funeral. And that's him when he's sober. He's on leave."

"Who's looking after you?"

She turns a shade of red that makes me think I'm the first person to ask, and her lack of answer doesn't sit well with me.

"Any word from your mom?"

"We don't even know if she knows," she says flatly. "That's why we waited on the funeral. Thought maybe she'd see the news or something."

So nobody's looking after her.

"I'm sorry, Nora."

She squints ahead; her place isn't too far from us now.

"What's the point in being sorry."

We continue in silence, and I notice how empty the neighborhood is, houses standing sentry, their long shadows cast over the road. Usually this time of night, this time of year, kids don't go down until the sun does, burning off inside them all there is to burn, their laughter and shrieks echoing street by street. I listen for it, but there's nothing, the suspension of normal life only hinted at in the toys scattered across certain lawns, in want of small hands.

I ask Nora if there's a curfew.

"Not officially. But everyone around here agreed no kids out past seven."

She rubs her eyes, and I try to imagine the day she's had. Greeting each individual mourner and rubbernecker, every single one with their own suppositions about Ashley's death, and thanking them all alike. And no one's looking after her. I have an impulse to touch her but I don't. She looks at me like she could sense it and lowers her hand.

"You wanna come down to the sheriff's office with me Monday?"

The question catches me off guard, and even though everything that inspired it is wrong, I feel like I did when I was thirteen and she marched up to me in the hall and handed over a torn piece of paper because she didn't have my phone number. Date and time. *You're invited.*

Proud.

Like I passed some kind of test.

"I can't. I gotta see about a job."

She doesn't hide her disappointment. "Where?"

"Aspera."

She stops and I do too.

"That's a joke, right?"

"No."

"How the hell does a thing like that happen?"

It happens because when Tyler went back to the mall, the man was gone. It must have been his plan all along: send Tyler home for the photos to buy enough time to skip town. When he told me, I felt some small sense of relief at the fact that we'd both been taken, that even Tyler can fall for something he wants to believe in. But with that, he could no longer deny the reality of what I'd done, and he told me where it left us money-wise was *really bad, George.*

And then I told him Cleo Hayes stopped by.

"What do you mean by that?" I ask.

"Your mother—"

"I'm not my mother."

"So what kind of work is it?"

"You tell me, you seem to know it all."

We face each other, and I await her verdict. Cleo only said she wanted me to come down to the lodge to "explore the possibility of a future at Aspera" out of the wreckage of my mother's past—but she didn't say what kind of job they'd give me.

There's only one thing it could be, though.

I want to hear it out of Nora's mouth.

Her eyes travel over my body. I try to see it as she's seeing it. My head tilted sweetly to the side, my breasts always, a little, preceding me. I'm wearing cutoffs today, and they hug my hips, coming up a little shorter than they should, and my peach tank top might be tighter in the same vein, though I don't know at what point it all becomes inappropriate. This is how clothes wear me.

"Jesus," she says softly.

"What?"

"You're blowing me off for *Aspera*. There's a killer on the loose. He knows who you are. Do you get that? Do you get how close you came?" She nods at my cast. "He dumps Ashley's body and then he *hits you with his car*. He gets out of that car and—"

"I don't want to think about it," I say over her.

"Ashley didn't die so you wouldn't."

"That's a fucked-up thing to say—"

"You know you don't have to act like a brain-dead fuckin' blow-up doll just because you look the part," she says, and I feel it like a slap across my face. "Or maybe that's not an act if they want you working the resort."

She storms away and I storm after her, fighting the urge to grab her by the hair and pull, and I only restrain myself because she buried her little sister today.

"I remember Ashley—" Her body steeled against the world, her flinty mouth an unsmiling line across her face, her eyes older than they had any right to be, and the soft apples of her cheeks letting everyone know just how young she really was. All of her, a vessel for a certain kind of chaos. She was constantly moving like she was on borrowed time, and maybe somewhere deep down, she knew she was. Nora comes to a halt and I do too, staring at the hard, tense line of her broad shoulders. "—And I *saw* her, and what you think you know from our little Play Pretend doesn't even come close—"

"Avis—"

"So what do you want from me, huh? Why are you acting like I owe you something? It's not my fault I didn't see him—you *said* that." My voice gets louder, a quaver in it I wish I could keep her from hearing. "And I guess you hate me for it, but I don't care because not seeing him probably saved my life, and my life is worth something too. So, no. I don't want to think about it. And if you'd seen her yourself, you wouldn't either."

That bruise.

It's dizzying, thinking about what it would take to make— to do that . . .

Nora keeps walking, and we finally reach her house, which is nothing like my house, on a side of town that is nothing like my side of town. It's nice, and if it's not, at least it can pretend to be. A modern brick two-story with a beautiful green lawn before it, American flag hung beside the door, waving back and forth in the wind. Nora stops abruptly, and I follow her gaze to the front picture window, and there, standing in it, is her father.

When I think of Justin James, I think of a uniform pressed to perfection against a hulking body. He used to come to the elementary school to sell us kids on the idea of the law and all the good men and women of it, but by then, I knew about cops from my mom, who wanted me to understand from a very young age the way the world really worked. I could see it for myself in the way they roamed our neighborhood, looking to create trouble they could never find, and which people they created it for. He'd pick up Nora and Ashley at the last bell at that same elementary school, and they'd tumble into his open arms, but that was before his wife left and his daughters outgrew him. I'd never known a father, but for the longest time, that brief moment after school offered what felt like a defining glimpse of them—there, and happy to see you.

There's no suggestion of either Justin James now. Not the cop, not the dad. He's still funereal, suited up, with dead eyes and a slack, dummy mouth. There's a sway to him, like he's been drinking. When his empty gaze lands on us, I take an unconscious step back.

He lists out of view.

After a minute, the front door opens, and there he is.

"Inside," he says tonelessly to Nora.

"You just notice I was gone?" she asks and he winces. Satisfied, she turns to me, raises her half-drunk slushie with a wan smile. "Thanks for this, Aspera girl."

"My friends call me George."

She goes inside, brushing past her father without a backward glance. He stays where he is, staring at me. I should say something but I don't know what to say.

"You." It's sudden and sharp out of his mouth. And then, again: "You."

Me.

I turn, his eyes on me as I go.

There's a wash of twilight over everything now, spring peepers crying out to one another in the night. When I reach the end of Nora's neighborhood, headlights break the dim, brights on and staying on as a truck comes closer. I narrow my eyes against their glare, tensing at the way it slows when it passes. When I'm halfway down the next street, there's another pair of headlights from another truck, and then I realize I don't know if it's the same one. I cross my arms and pick up the pace. By the time I reach my front door, I'm out of breath. I keep my back to the street, house key shaking in my hand.

When I'm safely inside, I lean against the door.

Locked.

I kick off my shoes.

This is what I want to think about: *Aspera girl.*

That's what Nora called me.

I close my eyes and there's a memory there: I was in the bathtub, hunched forward, my chest pressed against my knees, the water turning murky gray as the last of the road washed itself off me. I ran my hands up and down my prickly legs while beyond the door, my mother sat in the kitchen, chain-smoking through her fury, my missing hours dug into her. She wanted me to answer for them but *clean yourself up first.*

I wasn't ready to meet her yet, though. I was too busy meeting myself. *Aspera girl.* I leaned back, my hair floating around me, and pushed the outside of my legs against the sides of the tub, taking in as much of myself as I could beneath the surface. The view wavered with the water, but the most important parts, I could see. The curve of my hips. My breasts, which I'd had mixed feelings about, but only because I somehow got it in my head I shouldn't leave them all to pride. I slipped my hand between my legs and snaked it back just as quickly, and then I sat there, my heart thumping, while the water cooled. It was the first time I saw the truth of myself. I saw it because Matthew Hayes had made note of it, told me to make note of it, and told me, always, to remember it: beautiful.

I was beautiful.

It was such a relief.

F

uck."

The shocks on Tyler's truck are worn out. Every time we go over a rough patch of road, he swears under his breath. He needs to get them fixed and not so long ago, he would've had the money for it. I gauge our closeness to our destination by his tightening grip on the wheel. He rolls his shoulders as if that'll make the suit he's in any easier to wear. It's not that he's wearing it—it's why. He feels my eyes on him and says, "Don't look at me like that. We're just checking this out. I was talking to Stu Weary down at Mac's and he'll take you any time."

"And it'll take forever to pay you back."

"Is that something you should've thought of before you stole from me?" he asks, and I turn back to the window, stung, trying to swallow past the guilty lump in my throat. He clears his own, a little bit of apology in it. "I just don't like the idea of Aspera girls, all right?"

"That's because you don't know anything about them."

"Really? Who do you think I heard it from?" *Mom*, the word fleeting and sharp across my heart. "Hiring based on looks, serving 'em up to members."

"That's not how it works, Tyler." I smooth my hands over

my yellow sundress, the nicest dress I own. I hope it's nice enough.

"And how would you know?"

I know because I learned all I could about them as soon as I realized I could be one, and I learned it from the same person—only I could see past the bitterness she filtered it through. Aspera girls. A select group of girls who work the resort, attending to members, girls who can make more in a week than Tyler earns in a month. And while it might be true being beautiful is an unspoken requirement of the job, Mom didn't understand that had to mean those girls probably work hardest of all because Aspera's members know beauty better than anyone, fleeing from the beauty of their lives to even more of it. So if, in spite of all that, the richest, most influential people in the nation can't deny you . . .

You might be the most important person in the room.

"If you really thought it was like that, then why would you take me?" I ask. "Why would you even *think* about letting me work there?"

"We can't afford not to—"

"And you're just saying it because Mom did. You only hate it because she hated it."

"Well, one of us should." After another mile of bad road, he says, "She'd clean up after those people, George. Clean their bathrooms. Wipe up their piss stains. She'd tell me about it. They only saw her when they decided she wasn't doing something right. Richest people in the world, wanting for nothing, bitching out the woman who wipes up their piss because they can't even hit the bowl. You know what that does to someone? There's something to going to a place like that, day after day, and knowing nothing about it can be yours. You can make its beds, mop its floors, scrub its toilets, but you can't have any of it for yourself. She'd stop at my apartment after late shifts, and she'd just be—it broke her. Do you get that? It broke her."

"I still don't have to hate it because she did." I pick at my cast. The skin itches underneath. "That man at the mall—"

"What about him?" Tyler asks sharply.

"When I asked for the money back, he—" There's something about the way I get stuck on that word—*he*—that puts Tyler's eyes on me. "He called me stupid."

"First of all, if I ever see that motherfucker again, I'm going to beat the shit out of him. But you're a good kid, George . . . even when you fuck up, you're a good kid, and you're always—*always* my sister, okay?"

"Then stop treating me like I'm stupid."

We look at each other. There's a little hurt in his eyes or maybe they're just reflecting what's in mine. He turns his attention forward, rounds a corner, and then we're on the road to Aspera, or is it Ashley's road. I don't want to see it so I close my eyes, but I end up seeing it anyway. Her. Tore up, bruised. She's all I see until Tyler reaches out and touches my shoulder.

"George," he says.

I open my eyes.

The lodge was designed to evoke the mountains.

Its sharp, dignified lines rise from the ground as we pull up to meet it, and, like the mountains, the closer you get to it, the more impossible it is to grasp—but everything's starting to feel that way these days. The light sparkles off its rustic exterior, a mix of harvest gold wood and stone that frames the ground-to-ceiling windows making up its front and reflecting the view. As Tyler navigates the winding road up, I see members strolling along the terrace and lean forward, tips of my fingers to the glass, trying to imagine who they might be.

My heart pounds.

When we reach the lodge, the world seems to move to us; staff ushering us from the truck, valet at the ready, the doorman guiding us to the doors he wouldn't dream of letting us open ourselves, welcoming us to Aspera as he does it for us. That's what he says: *Welcome to Aspera.* The words almost float past me, but I catch them, clutch them, bury them as deep inside me as they'll go. This is what my mother worked so hard to keep from me.

But I'm here, now, in spite of her.

I'm here.

We cross the threshold, and I reach for my brother's arm, steadying myself as the lodge builds itself around us. That fine mix of stone and wood is as golden here as the outside, but it's almost as if the light works differently. I feel its glow across my skin, and if I could see myself, I know I could see it too—the whole place would be on me. I raise my eyes to the vaulted ceiling, where a magnificent chandelier made of entwined stag antlers hangs at its center, bones clawing upward in either our victory or their defeat. Their shadows spread across the walls and it's so dizzying, I fumble back, catching Tyler's foot against my own.

"Relax, George," he murmurs.

He takes in the place like it's any place, no wonder or overwhelm in his eyes—if not for the sights in front of him, at least for the fact that Katy Avis's kids are the sight in front of it. I want to ask him how he's not feeling this because there's something about wealth, *real* wealth, that's less what is seen and more what is felt. A viscosity, almost. I have a sense of moving through it as we make our way even farther into the lodge.

Both sides of the main floor offer windows with that to-the-ceiling view. Outside, a patio and firepit survey the golf course, and beyond it, the mountains, everything gorgeous and verdant in the morning light. Members sit at marble tables outside, drinks at hand, the sun on their faces. One table is being waited on by a young woman, and I crane my neck, trying to tell from here if she's an Aspera girl.

"Mr. Avis," a deep voice calls, "Miss Avis."

We turn; a man who must be in his late twenties or early thirties stands next to the concierge's desk. It's stunning, antlers carved into its front.

"Welcome," he says.

He's everything I expect of someone who works here and somehow, more. He's suffused with Aspera's cool sophistication, and I wonder if that's who he's always been or what this place turned him into. I wonder what it could turn me into. His midnight-black hair is tousled just so, his deep brown eyes warm and inviting. The neat lines of his blue designer suit complement his rich olive skin, perfectly tailored to his muscular frame. I realize my dress *isn't* good enough. Dulled by its surroundings, its second-hand origins now painfully apparent. I spot an errant thread hanging from the hem.

He rounds the desk to meet us, extending his hand to Tyler.

"Kel Allred," he says as they shake. "I assist Mr. Hayes and oversee executive. It's a pleasure. He's waiting. I'll take you to him."

"Are we late?" I ask.

Kel smiles at me in a way that's both reassuring and uncomfortable.

"You're right on time."

He leads us out of the lobby, down one corridor, and then another, Aspera's exquisiteness unfolding before our very eyes, everything I glimpse suggesting more magnificence beyond what I've already seen. The longing I've carried with me for years intensifies. I want an even closer look than what I'm getting, and I know that if I somehow leave here today without the promise of ever coming back, it will break me.

"The rotunda." Kel brings us to a stop outside a set of heavy wooden doors, antlers carved across them, a theme . . . I only just manage to stop myself from reaching out and tracing my fingers along them. "Reserved for this meeting. Mr. Hayes thought it would be best."

Kel assesses me one last time before opening the doors wide and enfolding us into the silent room. Chairs and tables are angled away from one another, dedicating themselves to the curve of windows, that, as ever, take advantage of the natural view. But the view here feels more like a secret, capturing a small stretch of woodland the sun only just manages to penetrate. It reminds me of a pretty piece of a much larger painting.

And standing in the middle of it—Matthew Hayes.

When Matthew Hayes is not in front of you, he ceases to be a man. He becomes Aspera itself, all its sparkle and flash. To be confronted with him in the flesh is startling, pushes his wealth back into the body it inhabits, creating a whole new picture. Not less of one—more. The first time I witnessed it, it was powerful to know one person could hold the world in the palm of his hand. But the world was so much smaller to me then.

It's even more powerful now.

Matthew Hayes is tall and lean, has a thick neck that follows his gently sloping shoulders down to ropey, muscled arms. His chest is broad, his pale blue dress shirt tight across it. A sheen of sweat overlays his tanned white skin, and his dirty blond hair has a light curl that sweeps his forehead with casual perfection. Crow's feet, more than were there last I saw him, line the corner of his brown eyes, softening his slightly overhanging brow. When he smiles at us, I don't know what to do. I remember his smile when it was for me and me alone, and back then, I couldn't help but return it. Everything in me wants to do that now, but I don't want to hurt my brother.

And then I notice who's missing.

"Is Cleo—is Mrs. Hayes coming?" I realize how rude it is after I've blurted it out, worse than not returning a smile— but Matthew's never wavers.

"She had an unexpected appointment."

I hope my disappointment isn't too apparent.

"Oh."

Matthew glances beyond us, directing his attention to Kel.

"Libations, Kel. You wouldn't mind."

Of course, Kel says, he wouldn't.

Matthew points to Tyler. "We have a new sour ale on the menu I'd love for you to sample and . . ." He brings his finger to his lips. "A cocktail for Georgia. Virgin, of course." My face warms as he studies me, thinking on it. "The DiMaggio. It's got a coffee base, very sweet. I think you'll like it."

Kel slips from the room, closing the door quietly behind him. Matthew sits on the bench seat that curves around the windows and gestures for us to join him, but Tyler stays where he is and I feel bound to that.

"It's good to see you both here today," Matthew says. "You especially, Georgia. Cleo was just sick about you. Not being able to find out how you were doing, after all that."

"George had—has—a concussion." Tyler steps forward. "The doctor told me not to overstimulate her, especially those first few days after. I'm sure we would have connected with Mrs. Hayes eventually." I can't look at him as he works his way effortlessly through the lie. "We appreciate what she did for George."

Matthew gives Tyler a bemused look before turning back to me. "I was in my twenties. Sixteenth hole, lining up for the putt and out of nowhere, this golf ball—" He makes a *whooshing* noise, taps his temple. "Next thing I know, I'm seeing stars. Couldn't finish the game—would've been the best of my life too, seeing as no one can prove otherwise."

I offer him a small smile.

"All this to say," he says, "I'm no stranger to concussions. How's your head?"

"Little better every day."

"And your arm?"

"I really can't complain about anything."

He leans forward, his arms resting on his knees, hands clasped between his legs. "Attagirl. That's the right attitude to have. Awful business. Awful. Cleo and I, we went to the funeral. Never witnessed anything more heartbreaking in my life."

"Right," Tyler says. "Good friends of yours."

Matthew stares up at him. "We encourage our local boys in blue to enjoy Aspera's golf course—it's just one way we like to give back—and Justin is no stranger here. But I wouldn't call us good friends."

"But he comes when you call," Tyler says.

"Isn't that what the police are supposed to do?" Something passes between Tyler and Matthew, but I don't know what. Matthew looks at me. "Anyway, it keeps me up at night, and if it keeps me up at night, I can't begin to guess what it's been like for you. You didn't see him, the man who did it, did you, Georgia?"

"No."

"Probably just as well."

"That's what Cleo—Mrs. Hayes said."

"Cleo," Matthew tells me.

I give him another small smile.

"That James girl . . ." I brace myself, not liking what always comes next and still liking him in spite of it. "You'd hear stories about her in places she shouldn't be, doing things she shouldn't be doing . . . drugs, alcohol . . . acting real adult—"

"She's a kid," Tyler says. "Was. She was just a kid."

"Of course. You're right."

Tyler moves to the window.

"See a bit of the road from here," he says, and Matthew nods. "They ever figure out how she ended up so close to Aspera?"

"Well." Matthew contemplates it. He shifts in my direction, concerned. "Does it upset you, Georgia, to talk about this?"

I shake my head.

He turns back to Tyler.

"If you're on that road, it's for one reason, and that's to come here—but not just anybody comes here. It doesn't see a lot of traffic between arrivals and departures, and I think that's what our killer was counting on. She'd been dead for some time before her body was dumped. We've been cleared as a place of interest, if that's what you're asking."

"If today goes how George wants it to, I'd like to be assured of her safety."

"Tyler," I say, mortified.

"I'm your guardian, George."

"I understand your concern. You almost lost her once."

Kel's return couldn't be better timed. He has our drinks carefully arranged on a wooden tray. He serves Tyler first,

Matthew second, and me last, bowing slightly, his eyes meeting mine over the thin-stemmed cocktail glass my DiMaggio's been poured in. It's a beautiful amber brown with a foamy top, a chocolate coffee bean in its center, and an orange peel curled over the rim. I thank him as I take it, then bring the glass to my mouth, suddenly aware of everyone's eyes on me. The smell of the orange hits me before that first sip and that first sip is incredibly sweet, like Matthew said, but it's also just a little bitter in a way that prevents it from being too much. I lick my lips. There's something else that I like about it, it's . . . I try to place it, and then I glance back at Kel, who's watching me extra close.

There's booze in it.

"It's good." I look at Tyler. "It's really good."

"Knew you'd like it," Matthew says.

Kel smiles to himself. Tyler takes a swig from his bottle, but he offers no opinion. Matthew's eyes stay on my brother, but he waits until Kel is out of the room before he speaks.

"Strange, isn't it?" he asks. "Never thought we'd be in the same room after everything that happened with your mother. You two didn't think much of me."

"No," Tyler agrees. "We didn't."

Matthew raises his bottle. "I respect that honesty, Tyler. I'd rather it than the alternative every time. So let me ask you—how do *you* want things to go today?"

"I'd just as soon turn around and walk her right out that door."

"Okay. Can I be honest with you now?"

"Might as well."

Matthew takes a pull from his bottle and then sets it beside him, rubbing the condensation off his hands onto his pants. "I like to say, 'Life is easy and the people make it hard.' When Cleo told me whose daughter it was she picked up off that road, I couldn't stop thinking about your mother. I consider everyone who works at Aspera family, no matter how big or small their roles here, and when I found out what she was doing to me . . . I felt that betrayal as you would in a family."

Tyler brings his bottle to his lips, his face impassive.

"I'm well aware of the dividing line in Ketchum. The rich and the poor," Matthew continues. "It's not a fair world, and while I make no apologies for what I've earned, I try to do my best by the people in this city. I give them work and I think there's dignity in the work I give them. I think I compensate them generously for it. But if your mother didn't feel that way, it means I failed her at some point. And that doesn't mean what she did was right, far from it . . . but I regret being too prideful to reach out and make peace with her before she passed, least of all because you're the only one left to carry it. You're a good son, Tyler. I thought it then, when we were going through that . . . mess. I think it now."

"I guess that's one thing we can agree on," Tyler says.

"So where do we go from here?"

I hold my breath while Tyler studies his bottle before turning his head back to the window, the road beyond. It feels like a fist is squeezing my heart. I want to tell him you can't betray the dead. That Mom is dead, and I'm alive and *I want this, Tyler, more than I've wanted anything else, ever.* After a moment, there's the slightest slouch to him, and I realize, with a small amount of sadness, I'm about to get what I want no matter how much he doesn't want to give it to me. And how much I wish he wanted, even a little, to give it to me.

He takes a drink without looking at either of us.

"You'll have to ask my sister."

"I understand you want to work here," Matthew says to me.

"I do," I say.

He picks up his beer.

"I remember our first meeting, Georgia. You remember that?"

I nod. I want to tell him if I closed my eyes, I'd be there again, next to him, in the passenger seat of his car. That I never forgot the way he looked at me when we pulled up to my house, and he told me I was beautiful enough to come to Aspera when I was a little older, if someone else hadn't discovered me first.

It's the way he's looking at me now.

thought you said you were gonna be an Aspera girl."

The gold letters above the gate recede in the sideview. I try to breathe around the awful sensation of something being ripped from your grasp just as soon as you have an idea of what it might really feel like to hold.

"What'd he call it again?" Tyler asks.

"Aspirant." I stare at my empty palms, the warmth of the cocktail not enough to blunt my anger, my embarrassment. My hands have never felt so empty. This wasn't how it was supposed to go, but this is how it's gone: at this point in the season, all of their staff positions are filled—and I'm not old or experienced enough for most of them—but Matthew and Cleo think I can fill some critical gaps because in the summer, Aspera's demands are greatest. The words *Aspera girl* never crossed anyone's lips, but when Matthew called me an *Aspirant*, I could see right through it: I'd be a glorified fetch.

"What?" Tyler asks at my silence. "What's wrong?"

I thought I was going to be an Aspera girl.

I thought I was going to be an Aspera girl, moving through the resort, turning heads like I was meant to, a final word on everything Mom said I couldn't be.

Made sure I wouldn't be.

"I'm not an Aspera girl because of Mom."

"What?"

My eyes well up. Who would I have met as an Aspera girl? What more could they have offered me? Because there's always more and I'll always want it, and just *once*, I want it to want me back. But it'll never happen as long as I'm Katy Avis's daughter.

"George, what are you talking about?"

"They can't have me running around the resort like that. They had to give me something where they could keep an eye on me. Make sure I don't steal from them too."

Tyler's quiet and when I look at him, I can see the fight that's happening inside. He says, "We're not doing this."

"Soon as I told her I was going to end up there, she tried to ruin it for me—"

"You think that's why she did it? Really?"

"She didn't want me to make something of myself because she couldn't—because she never did—and as soon as she realized *I* could, she did *everything* she could to keep me from it, and now look at where it's left me—"

"George, you got no idea—"

"You're supposed to want better for your kids than you had," I say over him. "You're not supposed to hate them for getting closer than you ever did to getting it—"

He slams his hands against the steering wheel and my heart stops and his seems to too. Tyler rarely loses control. He exhales, resecures his grip and gives his hands a warning look, like what just happened was entirely of their own accord.

"Look, I know I wasn't always there," he says, working hard to keep his tone even. "And I didn't always see how it was between the two of you. But I *was* there when that bull-shit with Aspera went down, and I'm telling you that you got no idea."

"Did she get caught stealing from members or didn't she?"

He reaches into his pocket for his Camels, tossing me the pack. I sigh and take out a cigarette and light it for him. He puts it in his mouth, inhaling so deep, I can almost feel the smoke inside my own lungs. Everything that happened with Aspera and Mom, all that ugliness, happened at Tyler's place. She'd take calls at his apartment, meet with Aspera's representatives there, and at times, the Hayeses themselves. She didn't want me to see it, and Tyler says that's what a mother's supposed to do, that she was protecting me, but she was really protecting herself because she was never supposed to be a casualty of her own pettiness, her spite—just me and all the things I ever dreamed.

"It's not that simple," he says.

"Explain it to me."

"No. I'm not . . . I'd like to keep at least one of my prom-ises to her." He takes another drag of his cigarette, a nicotine-calm washed over him now. "Just let her rest, George. You pretty much got what you wanted."

The next morning, I swipe my palm across the bathroom's shower-fogged mirror and see myself, my skin
flush pink from how hot I ran the water, my curls slicked
down, heavy and wet, their absence giving my face a rounder,
fuller appearance—younger, babyish. Closer to thirteen than
anything that's ahead. There's something about that that's
hard not to hate. The water drips off the ends of my hair
and onto my shoulders, trailing over my collarbone to the
floor. Tomorrow will be my first day at Aspera, and a prickly
sense of anticipation has been dogging me every second in
the lead-up; the knowledge that I have more to prove than
I should have ever had to prove. But I will. I'll make it so
Matthew and Cleo fall head over heels in love with me, and
by the end of the summer, I won't just be an "Aspirant," I'll
be an Aspera girl, and I won't just be *an* Aspera girl—I'll be
the Aspera girl.

Because it's always better to dream.

I peel off the tape keeping the garbage bag tight around
my cast, toss it all in the trash, then I reach for a towel and
wrap it around myself at the same time three short knocks
sound from the front of the house.

Knock-knock-knock.

I pause and listen.

Tyler's at work.

There's no one I'm expecting.

Thud.

I flinch. Like a fist against the door.

I leave the bathroom, peering down the hall into the kitchen, but I can't see the front door from here. I let the moment stretch out until I feel like I could say it's behind me, and then I creep across the hall, into my bedroom. My blood goes cold at the sight that greets me: a man retreating from my window, crossing the lawn.

He stops abruptly with his back to me, facing the street. I snatch my T-shirt and underwear off my bed, throwing them on fast, my eyes never leaving him, and maybe that's my mistake. Maybe he senses my disconcerted gaze and it's that feeling that compels him to begin a slow turn back around. I fumble out of my room before he can see me, pressing myself against the wall beside my door, trying to think past the alarm my body's become when the phone blares from the kitchen, sending a shock all through me.

Tyler, checking in.

It has to be.

I tiptoe quickly down the hall, and when I reach the kitchen, I realize how exposed I'll be because the window right over the sink lets as much of the room out as it lets the street in. I get down on my hands and knees and crawl across the floor, straining my good arm to grab the cordless from the wall. I curl up just under the sink and answer the phone, cutting it off mid-ring.

"About time—"

"Tyler, there's someone outside the house."

"*What?* Who?"

I hear construction in his background, the screams of power saws cutting into lumber, a sander against the floor, the discordant pounding of hammers. My T-shirt clings to my damp skin, and I wonder what would happen if I had to run like some girl in a horror movie, and then I realize it's always the girls in horror movies dressed like this, who look like me, that die. The faint sound of a car going past the house numbs me with the understanding the kitchen window is open. Sound in—sound out. If the man's close, he must have heard me pick up the phone.

"I don't know," I whisper.

"What? I can't hear you—"

"Tyler, I'm—"

An unexpected crash from Tyler's side of the line makes me yelp.

I press my lips together.

"George?"

I still, and after a long silence, there's the squeal of the screen door, the clatter of it as it hits the side of the house. I press even farther into the corner, but I can't make myself smaller than this. The doorknob moves slowly from side to side . . .

Locked.

"He's trying to get in."

"George, listen to me—" Tyler's voice is lost to the whine in my head, to my panting breaths in and out as I give into panic. I squeeze my eyes shut. *"Georgia."* He never calls me by my full name, and it sounds like it's not the first time he's said it. A tear slides down my cheek and drips off my chin. I don't know when I started crying. "Are you there?" I choke back a sob, and he hears it, takes it as his answer. "It's okay. It's going to be okay. I'm like, ten minutes out. Stay on the line. Don't open the door for anything. He still out there? . . . George, he still out there?"

I force my eyes open, my breath catching at the perfect silhouette of a man stretched across the floor from the window. He doesn't move.

Neither do I.

J esus *Christ*—" I nearly drop the phone, my face slick with tears. The familiar rattle of Tyler's truck reaches my ears and he says, "Stay in the house, George—" before he disconnects. A smattering of other noises soon fill the air: Tyler's truck door opening, then slammed shut, his footsteps up the walk, his rough greeting, and the stranger's gravelly, indistinct return. They speak back and forth. Tyler's heated.

I press my palm against my chest, feeling the still-frantic beat of my heart, and stand carefully, trembling. I face the window and see him now, who it is. Tyler notices me and it gives me away. Justin James turns slowly, and if the view in his picture window the day of Ashley's funeral was damning, this one is worse. He makes no case for living in a world that's done what this one did to his daughter. He's radiating grief, his skin gray with it, and he shuffles forward like his ankles are shackled to it. He breathes so heavily, I imagine his lungs full of it. The window's fine mesh turns his eyes and mouth into desperate hollows.

Tyler pulls his phone from his pocket.

"I'm calling Watt, get someone down there to take him home."

"I need to talk to you," Justin says to me, creeping closer. His voice is thick, drunk. Tyler grasps his shoulder to pull him back, but Justin shrugs him off. "I need to talk her, that's all, just let me—"

"George, get back—yeah, hello?" Tyler turns his head away, has a low and urgent exchange with whoever's on the other end of the line.

"Get closer," Justin mumbles. He presses his hand to the window, leaning hard against it. "Closer." I inch forward. As soon as I'm at the counter, he says, "Tell me who you saw."

"I didn't see anything."

His fingers curl against the mesh and that small tear in the screen gets wider.

"That's not what I asked," he says. "Tell me who you saw."

"I didn't—I didn't see anyone."

His face contorts with misery.

I want to look away, but I don't feel like I can.

"He was right *there*."

"All I saw was her."

He jerks forward, violently, and Tyler says, "Hey, *back off*—" in a voice I've never heard him use on anyone, let alone a cop, but it works—Justin lets go of the window.

"All you had to do was *look*," he slurs, and he stumbles away, knuckling his forehead, shaking his head, trying to shake all of this out of his head, muttering to himself. Tyler's eyes meet mine. Neither of us says anything.

After forever, a patrol car ghosts up to the curb.

He's gone, George," Tyler says through my bedroom door, but I already know. I watched the whole scene play out like a sad silent film through my bedroom window: Justin James escorted to the back of the patrol car with the kind of consideration the Ketchum Sheriff's Department would only reserve for one of their own.

I stare down at my shaking hands.

"I'm coming in." He opens my door. "You okay?"

"I thought I was gonna—" I clench my fingers. "I thought—"

"George."

"I mean, what was I supposed to do, Tyler? What could I have done—"

"Hey." He steps into the room. "Justin James isn't used to a world that doesn't bend to him . . . Ashley being dead probably makes him feel like God broke some kind of promise and not just because a thing like that shouldn't happen to any kid—because he doesn't give a fuck about any kid—but because he doesn't think a thing like that should've ever happened to *his*." He pauses. "I know it doesn't feel great wandering around scared all the time, but I'd rather you scared and alive a million times over because Matthew Hayes was right about one thing . . . I did almost lose you once."

My eyes fill with tears. He pulls me into a rough hug, and when he lets go, I see him struggling with what he's got to do next, his sense of duty torn between what I did to us and what just happened here. He's got to go back to work. He can't afford not to.

"You better get going."

"I can—"

"Just go, Tyler. I'm okay."

He sighs, stares at something beyond me.

"Anyone else like that comes to the door," he says, "don't you answer it."

But when Nora James comes to the door a few hours later, I do.

I stare at her through the screen and she stares back, crossing her arms, raising her chin like she's daring me to say it. I might as well. It's what's in my heart.

"I'm so tired of you," I tell her. "You and your whole fucking family."

"That makes two of us. But you should let me in anyway."

"And why would I want to do that?"

"Because I need something from you."

I stare at her incredulously, and she sighs, scratching at her forehead. She's wearing a black KHS volleyball team sweater it's too hot for and black mini-shorts with white edging and tiny slits up the side, boasting her muscly quads.

"Avis—" She shrugs. It's as conciliatory a gesture as I've

ever seen from her. "I didn't know he was going to do that, but it's not mine to be apologizing for."

"But Ashley's death is supposed to be mine?"

She opens her mouth, closing it just as quickly, whatever's going through her head something she's failing to find words for. She half-turns, about to make her way back down the walk, and I feel something in me I also can't quite name.

I push the screen door open.

She hesitates and then comes inside, rolling her shoulders, trying to work the knots out.

I ask her if she wants something to drink. She flushes at being met with anything akin to hospitality and accepts the glass of OJ I offer, sipping it while taking in my house. I wonder what she makes of it. Whatever idea I have of Nora's place is probably right—all the trappings of a middling class. No furniture older than say, five years, except for the recliner I imagine Justin sits in when he watches their smart TV. They probably call it "Dad's chair." And if the décor is a little bland and outdated, it's fine because it speaks to a different era, a happier one, when Ashley was alive and Mom was still around.

What Nora's looking at looks nothing like that. It's discolored floor tiles, peeling wallpaper, and threadbare carpets, the stucco ceilings and the stains that came before us, and the stains made since. She finishes the juice before handing the glass back to me. I set it in the sink and stare at that tear in the window's screen, fighting the impulse to tell her that her dad did it. That before he came here, there was one thing in this house in better shape than what she's looking at now.

"I went to the sheriff's department, like I told you about, and Watt had nothing for me. She was raped and torn apart, right"—I wince; there's a way Nora says the words that makes them feel less and less real each time they come out of her mouth, but maybe that's the point—"but the guy who did it left nothing of himself behind. You believe that?"

"I can believe anything lately."

"They're not doing shit because they think the guy's long gone. They're just giving up," she says, "but I'm not."

We stare at each other.

"So what's that got to do with me?" I finally ask.

She digs her hand into her pocket and produces a joint and a pink Bic lighter.

"Where's your bedroom?"

She sits on the floor, her back against my bed, amused when I tell her I don't want to smoke, but I don't care if she does. I don't like feeling away from myself, I say, and she says she gets it but the only thing she wants these days is to be away from herself. She inhales and holds the smoke for what feels like an impressively long time before blowing it out slow. The scent of weed tickles my nose, and I open the window. I stare out at the quiet, empty street. It's like nothing even happened.

"Brandon Oren was the first person to ever sell Ashley weed," Nora tells me. Brandon Oren was this year's salutatorian. "She'd just turned twelve. And he came to the funeral and shook his head about it all, so sad, like his hands were so fucking clean . . ."

"He sell you that weed?"

"God, no. The volleyball team looks after their own. This is courtesy everyone's favorite outside hitter, Chell Miller." Nora takes another drag. "She was happy to hook me up. Didn't have time to talk, though. They all treat me like I've got a disease."

"They probably don't know what to say to you."

"That's weak."

"You're right," I say. "It is."

Because when bad stuff happens to someone you know and care about, all you have to do is say you're sorry. All you have to do is be there.

"I wonder about you." The high takes that clipped edge out of Nora's voice, turning it a different kind of pleasant to listen to. I rest my arms against the sill and close my eyes to the breeze finding its way in through the screen.

"What's to wonder?"

"I don't know, like why you wouldn't even come to my birthday party? Your mom called my dad and said I best keep my distance or else. And I barely even talked to you before that. So I've been wondering what the hell I did to you ever since."

It's amazing, all the ways my mom can hurt me, even now. I knew she'd called Justin and said I wouldn't be coming, but I didn't know that she did it like that. And then it hits me—it's really something Nora *only* kept her distance afterward, because she could have made me miserable if she wanted to. Told everyone about my fully unhinged mother. She had all the social capital required to ruin me in the way only girls seem to know how to do.

But she didn't.

"I didn't know she called your dad until after. And I didn't know she said that until now." I pause. "My mom thought . . . she thought a lot of things about a lot of people. And they weren't usually true, but it doesn't matter."

"What did she think about me?"

"She said the only thing a girl like me was worth to people like you was how good I could make you feel about yourself."

"*What?* Wow. Okay. Jesus." She sounds equal parts appalled and impressed. "That's not why I invited you."

I half-turn, cheek to shoulder. "Then why did you?"

She takes another hit.

"So does that mean you always wanted to go?"

She's exhausting.

This whole day has been exhausting.

"What do you need from me, Nora?"

Because all this is starting to feel like a production, and I don't want to be in it if I don't know my part. When she exhales, the smoke plumes around her in a way that's almost pretty. She sniffs and puts the remainder of the joint out on the bottom of her lighter, tucking both back into her pocket before leaning forward, businesslike.

"Do you have a picture of your bike?"

"*That's* what you need from me? Why do you want a picture of my bike?"

"I want to put some 'if found' notices online about it," she says. "Maybe the guy who killed her will try to offload it and something will come up. I'll use my name and number. All you've got to do is give me a picture."

"Don't have any," I say. She gives me a look. "What? I don't take pictures of my bike."

"Make and model. I'll find it online."

"Vintage green Schwinn . . . it was my mom's. I scratched my initials into the paint."

She takes out her phone and after a minute, holds it up to me, shows me a picture. "Is this the one?" I tell her it is. "Okay. Good."

Satisfied, she leans her head against my bed. I can't help but wonder if a picture of my bike really necessitated all this . . . or if it's not the only reason she wanted to see me.

"I was at Aspera earlier this year," she says. "First time. It's a real nice place."

If she thinks Aspera's "nice," I wonder what passes for amazing in her eyes.

"With your dad? What for?"

She shakes her head, then changes her mind. "Well, yeah. He was there. Ashley was too. Mr. Hayes is sponsoring the girls' volleyball team next year, so we had an exhibition game on the grounds to celebrate. Then after, they gave us a limited tour of the property in the RTVs. You know they import birds for some of their game hunting? Special ones not native to the area? And if they get away, they just die because they can't survive out here."

"I didn't know that."

I wish I didn't. It's too sad.

She looks me up and down.

"Aspera girl, huh?"

"I—" But I stop, because there's something about the way she's looking at me. She still believes it. There's nothing that's happened between now and the last time I saw her that would ever make her stop believing it. Me being an Aspera girl is just Aspera seeing through the promise my body made for me. I'm too embarrassed to tell her otherwise, and I can't think of a reason she has to know the truth. So I nod, and I say, "Yeah. Officially. An Aspera girl."

She gives me a crooked smile.

"Congratulations."

"Now why don't I think you mean it when you say that?"

"I always thought it was kind of fucked up," she says. "All these girls getting a job depending on whether or not they meet Matthew Hayes's very particular qualifications."

"And what qualifications are those?"

It comes out a little more interested than it should, because maybe it's nothing to do with Mom, why I'm not an Aspera girl. Maybe there's something Nora knows about those girls that I don't, that's about more than being beautiful.

Something that's not too late for me to learn.

"Come on, Avis. I hear all Aspera girls lean white and blond, like you. The kind of beauty that's always leaving somebody behind." She holds up her hands, like she can see it in lights. "The patriarchy's dream!"

"Shut up," I say.

"And here you are upholding it."

She smiles a little, fucking with me, but she also means it.

"And how have you tried to dismantle it today?" I ask her.

Her eyebrow quirks. "Okay, let's say it's not that, even though we'd be very generous if we did. I've *also* heard Aspera girls look like variations of Hayes's wife. So maybe it's his dream."

I step forward, imagining how it looks—no, *knowing* it. I take my mind back to my photos, stolen from me now, and how undeniable I was in them. I raise my hands over my head in a stretch that has my T-shirt straining across my chest and give a soft kitten-sigh, moving my body toward Nora, biting my lower lip. She stares at me like everyone stares at me, and if I could, I'd hold up a mirror to her so she could see the look on her face. I crouch in front of her, gazing up at her from under my eyelashes, and in the weak light of my room, I'd swear she was blushing. I move a little closer and then I'm sure she is.

And then I want to ask her whose dream it is.

She swallows, hard, and looks away.

When Tyler drops me off at Aspera, he tells me to have a good first day, and the catch in his voice has me wondering if I'm doing something worse to him than I've already done. I'm about to let myself out of the truck when he says, "Hey, wait," and touches my arm. There's something in his eyes as he waves away the approaching valet. I let go of the door and settle back in the seat. He dips his hand into his pocket and holds out a phone, doesn't look at me when he says, "Should've given this to you right off the bat, but I wasn't even thinking . . ."

It takes me a minute. "That Mom's? You keep it up?"

He clears his throat, looking like he'd give anything to put this conversation in the rear view. "Yeah. Don't fuck around with it too much, okay? It's still got some of her stuff on it and uh . . ." His cheeks turn a little pink as he hands it over. "She's still on the voicemail."

I stare at it until he nudges me lightly on the shoulder, and then I fumble out of the truck, my world tilted slightly off its axis. I hear her voice as I stare up at the lodge, a diamond refracting the early morning light.

It's not shining for you.

. . .

"Now you work here," Kel tells me as he leads me through the lobby, "you should have your brother drop you off at the staff entrance around back."

He's immaculate in a sharp, slate blue suit with a beige tie, the tops of his dress shoes gleaming. Not a hair out of place. I'm dressed as neatly and sweetly as I can afford to be. I felt it wasn't enough when I put the peach romper on and slipped into my pair of creasy black flats, dusty now from the walk in, and I feel it even more with Kel telling me not to present myself in front of the guests. He glances at me, seems to realize how I'm taking it.

"You notice how quiet it is here?" he asks.

I nod, even as I'm considering it. Aspera is rich in atmosphere, so moneyed it's easy to overlook its silence; what little sound floats through the lodge is mainly the faint classical music from the lobby, the meditative trickle of various fountain sources, footsteps that always seem to be fading into the distance.

"Members don't come here to fraternize," Kel explains. "They come here to escape themselves and the world's prying eyes. Aspera isn't about socializing or networking, it's about retreat." I follow him around a corner, and we pass a gentleman who nods to Kel, avoiding my eyes. "They rely on our discretion. With few exceptions, it's most of the staff's job—it's your job now—to be invisible, to facilitate a level of space and privacy they can't get in the world beyond our gates. We keep members minimally exposed to the staff and to as few new faces as possible so they can feel safe here, and free."

"And you'd be one of those exceptions?"

"Of course. The dedicated, front-facing staff are Aspera's Polaris."

"Aspera girls too?"

He nods. "They're assigned the executive floor."

"The executive floor?"

He smiles and comes to a sudden stop, the lobby somewhere behind us, ahead of us, parts unknown, but immediately to our left . . . a surprisingly unadorned corridor whose only purpose, it appears, is to end at an elevator that's presently on its way down.

"The executive floor boasts some of the nation's most elite. The guiding principle of Aspera remains the same, but executive members enjoy staff who have been hand-selected and vetted to look after *only* them." I stare at that elevator, feeling the painful pull of the divide, feeling like I've never wanted anything more than a taste of what's beyond those doors, feeling like I should be there, beyond those doors. "Shall we . . . ?"

I linger long enough for the elevator to arrive, and watch its doors glide open. I hold back a gasp at what they reveal.

An Aspera girl.

She has long, silky brown hair that cascades over her shoulders, skin that's drunk up the sun and made her golden. The way she wears her makeup gives her face an air of mystery; the tilt of her head turning her into a thousand different girls—and all of them are stunning. She's wearing a white sundress I can tell costs money, and its thin, flowy material plays like a song against her body. She's incredibly tall, lacking my curves, but willowy, fairy light, a girl you'd see on a runway. She moves like it too. There's something about her beauty that makes me feel more and less sure of my own because it's not any more or less than my own. She runs a hand through her hair, then runs that same hand over her pink-painted mouth.

Our eyes meet.

I should be you.

The ferocity of the thought locks me in place. I can't look away.

She doesn't look away either.

"We should go," Kel says gently, breaking her spell, and I flush at the way he's looking at me, which reminds me of the way he looked at me when I first met him, that glint in his eyes as he served me the boozy cocktail. He knew then that I wanted to meet the moment and not be shoved aside of it. He has to know what I'm thinking right now. He brings his hand to my elbow, ushering me forward, and we continue on. I feel the Aspera girl's eyes on me, and I hope, for one brief moment, she thinks I'm one of them.

I know we've reached Matthew's office by the sun-bleached antlers mounted as handles to its doors. Kel watches me move to them, awed.

"A stag," he says, as I grasp one. "Mr. Hayes's kill."

Goose bumps prickle my arms at the cold, unnatural smoothness of it.

"He's in meetings all morning. He's not to be disturbed. But if you take the door to your left, you'll find your place at Aspera."

I lower my hand and turn.

There is no door to my left.

I give Kel a questioning look. He smirks and I look again.

After a moment, I see it—or at least the suggestion of it. A hidden door, built into the wall, almost seamless.

"Oh," I say softly.

Kel shows me its tell, the nearly invisible divot in the paneling just deep enough for fingers to grasp. He gives me a smile as he pulls it open and motions me inside.

Aspera has already conditioned me to expect a certain amount of splendor every time I step through a door, but the room that greets me when I step through this one is small and . . . uninspired by the rest of the lodge's standards, and not at all living up to the promise of its unique entry point. My heart sinks as two things become apparent:

This room is mine.

It isn't special.

I thought it would be special.

Kel moves past as I take what little in there is to take: the small desk with a computer and phone resting on it kitty-corner from the picture window overlooking the fairway. The relentlessly summer view has the effect of making this dull space feel duller. At room's end, a leather sofa rests against the wall next to a minibar, and on the wall opposite it, a fifty-inch television. I raise my eyes to the ceiling and find a single lightbulb that seems to hover, almost cradled, by the antler hanging beneath, smaller than the ones on Matthew's doors and not at all like the chandelier on display in the lobby. The simplicity of the fixture drives home its stark reality. I wonder if they're all his kills.

"Ready to work?" Kel asks.

I nod and sit at the desk in front of the computer, and he puts himself close to me. There's something comforting

in the fact his pine-scented cologne can't hide the cigarette smoke clinging to his expensive clothes. He smells just
like Tyler. He leans over my shoulder, commandeering the
mouse, while he explains what I'm here to do.

Earlier this year, Aspera implemented a digital comple-
ment to their concierge, Richard Lynn. The two of them—
Kel and Richard—have been sharing the burden ever since.
The Hayeses have brought me on to make it less of one.

"If members want to further minimize their direct in-
teractions with staff, they can make any and all requests
electronically from a tablet in their room. You'll receive the
request, confirm receipt, and direct it to the proper department . . ."

So a digital switchboard operator. It's bleak, impossible
to make more glamourous sounding than anything I thought
I'd come here to do. A chime fills the room, sharp and clear
as glass, and then it comes again. Two requests pop up onscreen, identified by room number only. One is for fresh
towels, another for a "couple's bath," scheduled to be drawn
at a specific time later tonight. When I ask Kel what that is, he
says it involves champagne and rose petals and scented oils
and two people who love each other very much, then laughs
at the way my mortification blazes a fire across my face. He
guides me through the process of fulfillment. A call to housekeeping, then room service, then confirmation of care sent to
the requesting room.

"Confirmation of care," he tells me very seriously,
"shouldn't take longer than five minutes and certainly no
more than ten. You're on the clock. Understand?"

I nod, and we wait for, and run through, a few more

requests until he's confident enough to leave me to it. He has to get back to executive.

"Wait—Kel," I say, and he pauses at the door, half-turning to me. "What if someone asks for something I can't make happen?"

"Like what?"

I shrug, unsure how to answer.

"Georgia." His voice dances that line between patient and patronizing. "You're going to learn very, very fast that money can make anything happen."

The requests that shape my morning at Aspera are so benign, they deny me even the cheap thrill of voyeurism. Rooms with an *E* in front of them are the executive floor. I try to find out who I might be serving—digging through the desktop to see if they left any identifying data—but I'm not tech savvy enough for that. Member names are kept from me because I'm not—what did Kel call it . . .

Polaris.

I have to search what that is on my phone. The North Star. The brightest star in its constellation. And then I feel embarrassed for not knowing, and then I wonder if he knew I wouldn't know it when he said it. That I'd end up here, alone, realizing belatedly that what he really told me is I'm not a star.

I can't smooth the raw edges of my injured pride, and when I reach a lull that lasts longer than ten minutes, I find myself fixating on the room and everything it's not, and everything I expected it to be, and whether I had a right to expect anything at all—but I can still see Matthew in the driver's seat, telling me I was beautiful, and not in a way that was untoward, but in a way you'd state any fact. And then: *Come to Aspera, when you're old enough.*

I wanted it. More than anything else, after that day, I wanted it.

But he had to want it first.

And he did.

He said it.

Come to Aspera.

He had to have more in mind for me than this.

I get up from my desk and move around the room, examining the picture window, the black curtains tied off to the side. I untie them, letting them fall in front of the view, and the room goes dark, leaving me to the eerie glow of the antlered light overhead. My eyes trace the curves of what remains of the buck, and then I open the curtains back up, blinking rapidly against the sunlight.

Inside the minibar, there's only booze, and on closer inspection, not all the bottles are full. I turn my face from it, to the leather couch, a little worn now I'm close enough to see. I lift the bottom cushions and there's a pull—a sleeper sofa. The back of my neck tingles, a thought occurring . . . I shut the light off and close the curtains again, turning slowly in the pitch dark until my eyes find it. The wall opposite my desk, a faint outline of light . . .

Another hidden door.

That crystal chime, another request. I ignore it and make my way to this new discovery, pressing my hands against the wall, looking for and then finding its secret handle. But this door is locked. I press my ear to it, listening hard, and after a moment, I can just barely hear the low timbre of Matthew's voice. I can't make out what he's saying, but he's there. This room adjoins his office. This room isn't just any room. This must be where he hides himself when his work at Aspera takes its toll, the place he sleeps when he's too tired to go home.

His secret.

And he's shared it with me.

I step into the hall, my eyes taking yet another moment to adjust to the light, and move to his closed office doors, feeling like I need to do something, but I don't know what.

I reach for the antlers.

"Georgia."

Cleo.

I face her, shamed to be so caught, but more than anything thrilled to finally be seeing her again. When our gazes find one another, there's something in hers that sparks the air between us, sending a current all through me. She's in a silky blue shirt, half-tucked into white pants, nude heels making her long legs impossibly longer. Everything holds to her so perfectly, I'd swear her outfit was made on her, no part of the material unaccounted for, all of it understanding her body almost in the way—

In the way a lover would.

"I think he's in meetings all day," I manage, and then I close my eyes because I can't have done that right. She's his wife. She doesn't need me to open those doors for her. She can see him any time she wants, no matter what.

"I know," she says, and the chime sounds once, twice, three

times from Matthew's—my—secret room. My room. I open my eyes. "But I'm not here to see him."

I trail a few steps behind, indulging in the no-nonsense sway of Cleo's hips, the way it leads her and the way she leads me. She takes me to the main dining room—spacious and bright, making use of creamy beiges and warm light—and through it, to the terrace outside. The air is pleasant, warm. We sit at a table facing the golf course. A pair of members in blinding white golf shirts tee off, caddie and cart nearby.

I try to settle my nerves, try to conjure a version of myself Cleo would be impressed with. She's quiet opposite me, her eyes closed and her face tilted toward the sky. I take a moment to admire it, the dusting of freckles across her cheeks I hadn't noticed before, the way the sun dances along her pale eyelashes, her lips that perfect cherry red. The way her lipstick looks on her makes me want to try it. I only use gloss, sticky and flavored, licking it off before ever successfully giving the world a perfect juicy pout, but I imagine myself in her red, and I know I would look devastating. I always thought you had to have a special reason for a red lip, but today could be any day.

Or maybe it is special.

"I like your lipstick," I say.

The corners of her mouth curl up, but she stays with her eyes closed until our server arrives, quickly and efficiently setting a delicious-looking lunch in front of us. As soon as he leaves, she straightens, reaching for a napkin to set across her lap. I hastily do the same.

"It's a house-made gemelli in garlic butter sauce," Cleo

says of the bowl of silky, twisted pasta accented by fresh peas and flakes of something I can't identify. She sees the question in my eyes before I can or would ask. "Shaved truffle." She points to the small plate of colorful tomatoes beside it. "Heirloom tomato salad with an aged balsamic."

I wait for her to start, to see what fork she uses first, and then I mirror her, embarrassed at what a cliché I am. I've seen those movies with the poor, uncultured girl who makes good enough for a fine dining experience when she suddenly realizes, in all her time alive, she hasn't actually learned how to eat or that she's never actually tasted real food before. Living the scene out is frustrating and confusing, like I've stepped through a door I don't understand the necessity of—unless it was always meant to keep people like me out.

Cleo watches my first few bites. I involuntarily close my eyes to the velvety sauce, the perfect chew of the pasta. I haven't tasted butter like this before; there's almost a hint of green in it. The peas have a pleasant snap to them. But it's the tomato salad that leaves me speechless; there's a depth of flavor there I can't quite articulate. Cleo notices my reaction and says it's the balsamic vinegar drizzled on top. She tells me it's been aged twenty years.

"So how was your morning, little Aspirant?" she asks.

I hesitate. She raises her eyebrow.

"That bad?"

I shake my head too quickly. "The work's straightforward. I can do it." I sip my sparkling water and keep my eyes on my food. "I'm doing it."

"But you thought you'd be doing something different."

I still, trying to untangle how to react, how she'd arrive at that conclusion if it wasn't something that was already on my face. I don't want to seem ungrateful. I don't want her to think that of me, or to tell it to Matthew and have him think it of me. The silence wraps itself around us, tightening its hold, becoming almost unbearable before finally, suddenly, loosening its grip. When I hear Cleo rest her fork against her plate, I feel it's safe to look up. She studies me, the stem of her wineglass between her index and middle fingers.

"I have something for you," she says.

"Lunch is more than enough."

"Don't put a ceiling on what you're meant to receive, Georgia. That's not how you ended up here. And it doesn't suit you."

I exhale softly, trying to reckon with being so seen, after waiting for so long to be so seen. As the girl I know I am. The girl one no one thinks I should—could—be.

But Cleo wants to see her.

Cleo wants me to be her.

I hold out my hand.

She laughs softly and slips a small, robin's-egg blue gift box from her pocket and into my waiting palm, a white ribbon wrapped around it. Her expression is expectant; there's only one thing I need to do. I clumsily push my plate aside with my casted hand and place the box in front of me. I pull the ribbon loose, then I lift the lid and cover my mouth, shocked at the sight inside: a blue teardrop necklace, half-gleaming in the light . . .

"Porcelain dipped in gold," Cleo says before I can ask. She points to the blue porcelain. "This is where you start."

And then she moves her finger down, toward the gold. "And that's where you're headed." She looks into my eyes. "It's special that you're here, Georgia. And you're special for being here. You should have something that declares it."

I lift it from the box and hold it up, letting the gold of it catch the sunlight, letting it sparkle just for me. She rises from her seat and rounds the table until she's standing behind me. She reaches over me—her perfume putting me in mind of figs and orange blossoms—and gently takes the gift from me. I swallow nervously when she asks me to hold my hair up before unclasping the necklace and bringing its chain around, her fingernails grazing my neck. I can't stop the shiver her touch inspires or the blush that follows because I know she felt it too. She clasps the necklace, then rests her hands on my shoulders as it rests against my throat.

I like how it feels. All of it.

"I thought I'd be doing something different," I finally admit.

"Matthew likes you very much, Georgia," she says. "He thinks you're wonderful. He thinks you have potential. Your mother left a scar. He trusted her. He thought he knew her." I stare at what remains of my beautiful lunch, my appetite gone. I knew it, and there's no satisfaction in knowing it: I'm not an Aspera girl because of Mom. "He needs to know he can trust you. He wants to know all this isn't only about what you can take from us. He wants to be sure of you."

"And once he's sure of me?"

"The sky's your limit."

"Where do I start?" I ask.

She leans forward and whispers in my ear before moving back to her seat, her hand raised but a moment before our server is upon us, asking her what she needs.

"Mr. Hayes's favorite," she says. "To go."

He returns swiftly with a small takeout box.

Inside, a slice of Matthew's favorite chocolate cake.

I knock on Matthew's office door. There's no answer. I wait just a moment, and then—with a deep breath—wrap my hand around one of the antlers and pull, inviting myself into the heart of Aspera.

Matthew's office is spare but imposing. Refined. The dark hardwood floors stretch toward his beautiful antique desk, a monitor atop of it, set before a massive window I know must offer the lodge's best view. It encompasses the unreal green of the course, the spectacular mountains beyond, the goes-on-forever blue sky overhead . . . which I suppose doesn't sound much different from every other view the lodge looks out on. But what separates this one is the way the window frames it, bordering it as though a painting—a painting that says all of this belongs to him. I imagine it through the shifting light of day, gleaming in the moonlight, through the changing seasons, how spectacular it must be to see all the leaves turning in the fall . . . If I owned this view, I'd never look away.

He's looking at it now, his back to me, as he talks on his cell. There's a chandelier above him; antlers, always. A smaller interpretation of the design in the lobby.

"We'll have Cleo pick you up at the airport next week." He pauses. "We'll take care of it. Hey, you're going through

a lot, and we don't want you to have to worry about anything, so you just let us know, man—"

My footfalls are silent as I cross the room, and I think I
see it, where the door to my office should be, a nearly im-
perceptible outline in the wood paneling, a space there for
fingers to grip. Matthew turns the moment I set the dessert
atop his desk. His eyes light, first at the sight of me, and
then, again, at what I've put in front of him.

"Hold on, Aidan."

He presses the phone to his chest, awaiting an explanation.

"I was having my lunch and I thought of you. I asked
them what you liked."

He reaches for the box, his long fingers pulling the lid
back for a peek inside.

"You angel," he says. "Thank you for thinking of me."

"I could think of you again tomorrow."

His eyes meet mine.

"I think I'd like that," he replies, then remembers himself, bringing the phone back to his ear, dismissing me with
a nod. "Yeah, Aidan, sorry. I'm back . . . what's that?"

I make my way out of Matthew's office, trembling with
pride, and when I reach the door, I hesitate, and glance
back. He's staring at the box, thoughtful. And I don't know
how much surer he is of me now, but I do know just before
I slip from the room—he smiles.

Gonna be late. Can you get a ride?

I stare at Tyler's text, trying to catch the breath this moment stole from me. When it came, the notification sound made my heart leap, my eyes darting left and right, because when she was alive, anyone texting Mom would immediately reward the surrounding area with Three Dog Night's "Shambala."

Mom.

I hate how hungrily I thought it, how desperately I sought her out, and I change the song to some generic tone before I can even think of responding to my brother.

I can't handle hearing it again.

I just—thought she was here.

And in that second, I think I wanted her to be.

He texts again.

You there? Can you get a ride? If you can't, it's gonna be a while. Don't know how long. You're not walking, though, so don't even think about it.

I can't just hang around Aspera, at least not in any place its members would see me. Hiding away in my little room for hours with nothing to do . . . if I *did* walk—but my brain refuses the thought before it can fully engage. It's hard enough driving that road in the relative safety of a moving vehicle. I imagine myself on it alone, exposed, space as wide open as it is suffocating. The air is staticky there, the sky weighty overhead, because you can't get a death like Ashley's out. The sun only sears it further in and the air just moves it around. But it's more than that. It's this constant feeling like I'm its unfinished business. The footprints around me. The missing photographs. What did Nora say again . . .

I heard killers sometimes go to the graves of their victims.

What about the scene of the crime?

Fear wins over shame or pride. I step back into the lobby and find Kel crossing the room. I wave him over, mindful not to raise my voice and give nearby members cause to believe I exist.

"What's up?" he asks. "Aren't you done for the day?"

"Yeah," I say. "But my brother's schedule got weird. Is there anyone headed into town I could get a ride with?"

Kel thinks on it, then he snaps his fingers. "You know what? I've got a break. I can take you. Meet me around the staff entrance."

I message Tyler back: I can get a ride.

Kel pulls up in a metallic blue BMW.

I see the look on my face reflected in the sedan's shiny exterior. My eyes wide, my mouth open. I try to figure out how much Kel must be making if this hot little number belongs to him.

"Wow," I say as I climb in, but what I'm thinking is *Jesus*. The cost of this thing could set Tyler and me up for . . . a while. I'm absurdly careful settling inside, worried I'm going to leave something of myself on any part of it. I wonder if rich people are this afraid of expensive things, if they think to attach a cost to any potential carelessness; a spill here, a tear there.

Kel knows where my mind's at. "Aspera has a handful of luxury sedans the staff makes use of if we're picking up members from the airport or representing the resort in any official capacity and, now, it would seem, when we're driving you home."

"I feel so special."

He puts the car in drive and we jerk forward.

"Sorry," he mutters. "She's temperamental."

"Beautiful, though."

"Aren't they all." His second attempt results in an easier departure. "If my Audi wasn't in the shop right now, I'd show you a *much* smoother ride."

"This feels pretty smooth to me," I say. And then, "God. How much does membership cost, anyway?"

Kel laughs. "You think that's where the money's coming from? Aspera might as well be Mr. Hayes's passion project." He glances at me. "He's a financier, Georgia." Grins at the blank look on my face. "He makes the rich even richer. That's why he's so connected. Turn on the TV, and the first famous face you see—whether they're in DC or LA—I bet you he knows 'em and they owe him something for the privilege."

I always thought I had an idea of Matthew's importance, and every day that idea seems smaller and smaller compared to its reality. We round the resort, and Kel turns down the pretty, tree-shaded path of Aspera's private drive.

"I really appreciate this," I tell him. "I didn't want to walk."

"It's a trek for you, isn't it?"

"Yeah. But it's not just that."

"You're not worried about . . . all that, are you?" *All that.* "You know the guy who did it, he didn't stick around."

"And you know that for sure, do you?"

"He's on to the next town, next girl."

It's off-putting, the way he says it—as if that, in itself, isn't horrible in its own right. On to the next town. The next girl.

"I didn't think I was worth the gamble."

"Georgia, you are absolutely right." His course correction is just a little too effortless. He has the decency to look somewhat chastened, but I can't help but wonder if he really feels it. "Let's talk about nicer things. How was your first day? Seemed to go well from where I was standing. I didn't get any complaints about the digital concierge."

"That's good to hear." I weigh my next question, and whether Kel likes me enough to answer it. I decide to ease in: "Can I ask you something about working at Aspera?"

"Shoot."

"What's it like assisting Mr. Hayes?"

"It's challenging. But make no mistake, that's less because of how he is and more *who* he is." Kel sounds like someone who has a bit of religion in him, reverent. "He's an extremely powerful man, like I said. Everyone wants a piece. It's my job to preserve the whole and keep him running."

"And you manage executive too? That's a lot."

"Don't make it seem that way, though, do I? I'm very good at what I do. I got promoted a few years ago. Once Mr. Hayes trusts you, the sky's your limit."

"That's what Cleo said!"

"Cleo?"

"Mrs. Hayes." But then I realize I don't want to relinquish this piece of Aspera that sets me apart from anyone else. "But she lets me call her Cleo. Insists on it."

He gives me a teasing look. "You're telling me you've only been here for five minutes and you're already looking for a promotion?"

"What's the executive floor like?"

"That's not something I can talk about with staff who don't work it."

Polaris only. I bite back the urge to beg him to tell me something anyway, even if it's just a crumb. I'm so bad at wanting things because I'm so terrible at not having them. Maybe that's one way me and Mom are alike.

"I want him to trust me," I say. "How did you get him to trust you?"

"You work. Hard. In my case, I showed up and I did the job that was asked of me, and then I did more than was asked. But you—you've got quite a hill to climb, don't you, Georgia?"

I lean back, the wind knocked out of me. Of course he'd know about my mother, the history there. But it's a shock to be so bound to something I didn't do. I rest my hands in my lap, flexing my fingers, anger in want of an outlet. If she were still alive, we'd be screaming at each other about this. *You're ruining everything,* I'd tell her. I told it to her so many times.

I turn my attention back to the road, dread branching from the center of my chest as the view gets painfully familiar and then—

Kel and I see it at the same time.

A big black SUV parked beside Ashley's memorial.

Someone kneeling at its cross.

The sight of it curdles my guts. It's a man, but what kind of man? Kel eases on the gas as the man rises to his feet and then faces us in a wide-legged cop stance, even though he's far from on duty. Justin James. I will him to let us go by, but he holds up his hand. Kel pulls over on the shoulder, next to the cross, and rolls my window down. The car becomes a cage, and my heart beats wildly against its sudden trap. At first, Justin doesn't approach. He circles the car in a way I don't quite understand, almost as though inspecting it. Whatever he does or doesn't find seems to perturb him; his brow furrows.

When he reaches me, I don't expect his eyes to be so clear. He's worn down, the old him mostly chipped away, but something has shifted in the time since I saw him last; some type of resolve that almost echoes Nora's. I like it less on him.

"Officer James," Kel says.

"Thought that was one of Aspera's cars." Justin nods at me. "What are you doing in it?"

"Nothing," I say instinctively.

"Nothing?"

"I'm driving her home," Kel says.

"From where?" Justin asks. I stare at Ashley's memorial. All that's left of it is the cross. Justin asks it again: "From where?"

I keep my mouth closed, shrinking in my seat.

"The lodge," Kel answers, giving me a look that wants to know why I'm being like this. But I want to know why he thinks he has to tell a cop something just because they ask. "Georgia works there now."

"Really?"

"Yes," I say.

"As what?"

"She's assisting the concierge," Kel answers when I don't.

"You're telling me Katy Avis's daughter is working Aspera?"

"Looks like," I mumble.

Get fucked, you worthless drunk.

"Anyway, we better be on our way," Kel says lightly after another long, awkward silence. "Unless there's something else you need. I'm using my break to get her home and—"

"You know what," Justin says over him, "let me relieve your burden, Kel. I'd like to talk to you, Georgia, about some things. I'll give you a ride back to town."

I look at Kel and he looks back at me, not seeing what I'm seeing, not feeling what I'm feeling. His eyes plainly say, *He's a cop*, like that makes him something to be less afraid of. I turn back to Justin, who lets out a slow breath through his teeth, like he's trying to grasp hold of a level of control just beyond him.

How could Kel not notice this?

"I—"

"I'll see that she gets safely home."

"If you're sure," Kel says, and Justin nods, all of this decided without me. I unbuckle my seat belt with shaky hands and get out of the car on equally shaky legs. Kel honks the horn once as he U-turns back to the lodge. Justin waves him off.

I watch the BMW get smaller and smaller.

When it disappears, I want to cry.

"My brother's waiting on me." I hear the fear in my voice, the feeble threat of it. *My brother's waiting on me.* People were expecting Ashley home too; that didn't save her.

Justin hears it.

"Why are you afraid?" he asks.

We look at each other.

"Because you scared me," I finally say.

He nods curtly. "That's what I wanted to talk to you about. I apologize for how I behaved the other day."

"Okay."

I don't think it's the reply he's expecting because it doesn't seem to make him hate me, or this, any less. His attention strays back to Ashley's cross. He contemplates it, a twitchy rise and fall to his Adam's apple, while I try to find one part of him I could trust enough to get in his car. His fingers tremor. He tries to hide it by clenching and unclenching them.

"Was she peaceful?"

"What?"

"My daughter." His eyes still on that cross. "Did she look peaceful?"

The question pulls me under, drags me back in those woods with her. Ashley, contorted like some psycho's doll, that film over her dead eyes. She might have been far past the point of any pain, but I wouldn't say there was any peace in her. She didn't look like she was sleeping, if that's what he means. He takes my silence as an answer, one he doesn't want.

"So you could see it on her," he says.

"Like I said . . . Tyler's waiting, so maybe we should—" I gesture to the SUV and step around him, but he grabs my arm and pulls me back, close. I gasp and try to jerk away, but his grip is ironclad. He smells faintly of booze, like he's sweating last night out, and the thought of Nora, alone in that house with him, like that—like this—makes me ache.

It makes me afraid for her too.

"Could you see it on her?" he asks again. "What he did?"

He's hurting me. Justin James out here, hurting me. His knuckles bulge against his hold. I whimper, and he drops his hand fast, running it through his hair, shaking his head slightly, like he didn't do that.

But he did.

I can still feel it.

"Just get in the car," he mutters.

I stay where I am.

"Go on."

"I—I'll walk home."

"You think that's safe? You? Out here alone? Get in the car, Georgia." I shake my head, stepping back. His eyes flash. "Oh, have I scared you again? Don't be ridiculous—"

"It's a beautiful night," I say, my voice cracking. "And I'd like to walk home."

His expression hardens. "Then do it."

I hurry past without looking back, but after a moment, I hear the SUV's door slam shut and the engine start, and I stop dead at the tires rolling over the gravel, knowing I can't outrun him now. I take a shuddering breath out and wait for him to meet me again.

But then his car gets—

Farther away.

I turn. The treads kick up dirt as he drives in the opposite direction.

There's only one place that road leads.

Aspera.

I let out a shallow breath, and then another, and then I wrap my arms around myself and push forward before this nightmare freezes me into place. My shoes crunch along the gravel and I try to let that sound steady me, but every so often, I hear the snap of twigs, not under my feet, and the soft rustle of leaves being disturbed on a path that's not my own. I keep my eyes off the woods next to me because I feel like if I looked, I would see her there, following alongside, her small hand with its stiff, clawed fingers outstretched.

ey, Avis."

I'm coming out of Mac's loaded down with a jug of milk and two bags of Flamin' Hot Cheetos (Tyler and I don't know how to share) when Nora pulls up to the curb in her blue Ford Fiesta. Her eyes travel over me, resulting in a slight downward turn at the corners of her mouth. Not quite a frown, but absolutely not a smile. Every time Nora sees me, it's because she's looking for me, but every time she finds me, it's like I'm not exactly what she hoped.

She's a vision of summer in a thin white tank and black sports bra underneath, her arm resting along the door, showing off the curve of her bicep. She's got her hair loose, and it seems like she's been driving with the window down a while; it's all swept to the side, some strands stuck almost sweetly to her flushed cheeks. It's sort of nice to think about, her driving around, carefree, though I know she's feeling anything but. I shift the bag up my arm, tightening my grip on the milk. She nods at my cast.

"When do you get that off?"

"Next Wednesday."

"Get in. I'll take you home."

I climb in the passenger's side, setting the milk and the bags between my feet. I give her a grateful smile. "Thanks."

Once the door's shut, I'm buckled in, and she's pulled back onto the road, she says, "So why the fuck didn't you tell me he has pictures of you?"

"What? What are you talking about?"

"Oh, just the guy who *raped* and *killed* my sister—"

I slam my fist against my thigh, and it stops her cold. I exhale shakily, uncurling my fingers. My leg throbs at the unexpected assault. I glance at Nora and she's staring, her shock mirroring my own. I rub at my skin, the comedown of it so brutal and fast. I don't know what to say. I just hate the way she talks about it.

"Okay," Nora says slowly. "So why didn't you tell me he has your picture?"

"Because I didn't want to."

"*Why?* I need to know everything, Avis, if I want get any-where with this—"

"Because you're not a detective? And because every time I've said or done anything, you find a way to give me shit and make me feel like it? I don't need to hear how a sick fuck stealing my photos was somehow my fault too!"

She sucks her teeth and after another block, pulls the car over and turns it off. She keeps her hands on the wheel, staring straight ahead, and I shift, my ankle resting against the milk jug, cool and damp against my skin.

"Look. I know it's not your fault. And I don't actually think it's your fault," she says without meeting my eyes. "It's just really fucking scary. This guy did what he did to Ashley, and then he hits you with his car and finds these pictures of you and takes them before fleeing the scene? Avis, he knows who you *are*. What if he wants to do something about that? You're part of this whether you want to be or not."

"He's got my bike too," I remind her, "and that didn't freak you out half as bad . . . anything turn up on it?"

"No."

"Watt said if nothing happened yet, it's probably not going to."

"Well, Watt's a fucking tool, trust me. I got the inside track on that."

"And how did you find out about the pictures, anyway?" I demand. "It's not like it's public knowledge, and I know Tyler sure as hell didn't tell anybody."

"My dad's spending more of his waking hours sober and the only good thing about it is he's been making calls, talking to his buddies, asking for details . . ." It takes a split second for me to decide not to share what happened with Justin on the road. "Not that he just hands his intel over, but I find it out. Today, that's what I learned." She leans back, then sneaks a look at me. "Who carries pictures of themselves around, anyway?"

"They were headshots."

"Headshots," she repeats.

"Yeah." I clear my throat, the lie forming as I tell it. "I wanted to start submitting my photo to some modeling agencies . . . I even got tapped by one, if you can believe it . . . so I saved up"—sorry, Tyler—"to have some headshots professionally taken, and I'd just picked them up that morning."

She smirks. "You want to be a model?"

"What's wrong with that?"

"You got big plans for yourself, Avis, that's all."

I hate the way she gets under my skin. How nothing I do seems to impress her.

I have this brief, awful thought it means Mom was right.

"So what, you don't think I'm good enough to have them? Is that it?"

"Jesus, I never said that."

"You don't have to."

Nora exhales, and then she rests her forehead against the wheel. Her shoulders start to shake. I stare at her and I think, this is it: the stress of Ashley's death and this constant friction between us has finally broken her. I reach forward tentatively, my hand almost to her arm, when she straightens and I realize she's not crying—she's *laughing*.

"It's not fucking funny!"

"No," she agrees, still laughing. "It's really not." She rubs her eyes. "Can we just like—I don't know. Have a normal conversation?"

I bite my tongue because any conversations we have, *she's* the one starting them and *she's* why they turn out like they do. She gets the car going again and pulls back onto the road. I turn to the window.

"So. First week at Aspera. Your day off, I guess?"

"Yeah," I say. I'm still mad at her.

"Well, come on." She pushes at my shoulder. "What's it like, Aspera girl?"

I turn back to her, waiting for that mocking smirk, but her eyes are encouraging. I jiggle my knee, wondering how many lies I'll have told her by the time I'm out of this car, but maybe my faith that I'll be an Aspera girl by the end of the summer makes it closer to the truth than it isn't. So I tell her about it, stealing Kel's words about how members come to the resort to "escape themselves and the world's prying eyes," so the staff has to be invisible, and that there are few exceptions, and that Aspera girls are one of them. That I'm one of them.

That I'm Polaris.

"That's the brightest star," I tell her, and she grins, amused.

I guess everyone knows it but me.

"You see anyone big time yet?"

"Can't say. It's against the rules . . . Remember how you and the other girls would sometimes bug me when my mom was working there? Wanting to know everything . . ."

"I can keep a secret," she says indignantly. Then, "I've heard some ex-presidents are members. Big tech bros too. A-list celebrities, of course. I used to ask my dad if he ever saw anyone famous when he'd come back from the course but . . ."

"I bet he had to sign an NDA before he took his first swing."

"Maybe," she says. My house is getting closer, and it might be my imagination but the car seems to slow down. A lot. "Sounds more fun than anything I'm doing now."

The guilt that puts in me makes me want to tell greater lies than I've already told, invent an ex-president sighting or some brush with a celebrity. I remember what Nora said about her friends, how they've shut her out, and I imagine her in the house all day with her dad, mired in his grief as she tries to claw her way out of her own, ear pressed against the wall until she hears something from him that gives her an excuse to come back to me . . .

God, what if I'm the only person she has?

My phone buzzes. A text from Tyler.

Caught some extra hours. Won't be here when you get back.

I sigh. This is going to be him all summer, scrambling for whatever hours he can take to make up what I stole from him, to get ahead of how much it costs for us to be alive. I heard him on the phone this morning, asking for an extension on some bill payment or other. It turned my stomach so bad, I couldn't eat breakfast after that. I check the time. If I'd gotten this at Aspera, it'd be just about my clocking out. I can't ask Kel to drive me home every day, can't pay for a pickup and piss away what I've earned so far. Can't walk that road alone.

I glance at Nora.

"Want to do me a favor?"

"Depends on what the favor is."

"I need a ride home from Aspera. Tyler's schedule is all messed up and he can't do it. He can get me there in the mornings, no problem, but in the afternoon, I'm fucked."

She stares straight ahead. "You must be, if you're asking me."

I look at her until she looks at me.

"Please don't make me walk that road."

She goes quiet, and I'm suddenly ashamed for begging her like that, when it's as much her road as mine and if it bothers me this much, there's no doubt it'll take something from her to go down it too. But maybe it would be easier for us both, if we did it together.

She doesn't seem to be arriving at the same conclusion.

"I shouldn't have asked," I mumble as she pulls up to my house. "Sorry."

She reaches across me for the glove compartment, where she grabs a pen.

"Give me your arm," she says. I hesitate. "Come on."

I hold out my arm. She scribbles her phone number down on my cast, and then her eyes meet mine, and there's something about the way she's looking at me that makes my insides flutter, makes my heart feel strange. It reminds me that Nora doesn't give anyone her time when she truly doesn't want to. It reminds me how good it feels when she does.

"You need that," she tells me. "Now I'm your ride."

The digital concierge has a break programmed into it after my first five hours of work; fifteen minutes when the chime goes silent and the in-room tablets flash a notice directing members to call the front desk for their needs. There's always a flood of requests when the green light goes on again, most marked "urgent," though none particularly strike me as such—but maybe when you're used to having everything the moment you want it, whether or not you need it, being forced to wait makes it feel that way.

I push back from my desk and stretch before leaving my little hideaway to freshen up. I'm halfway down the hall when I hear the doors to Matthew's office swing open, the loud, boisterous laughter of men preceding them. I turn to find Matthew and another man dressed for the course; Matthew in slate gray golf pants, matching golf cap, and a baby-blue shirt, his companion a starker contrast in white pants, a black shirt, and a gray cap. He's handsome in a way that's different from Matthew's handsome—much less rugged. Matthew notices me first, then the stranger, and I square my shoulders under their combined gaze. Today, I'm wearing my best: that same yellow dress I arrived at Aspera in. It's still not what it should be, but when I paired it with the necklace Cleo gave me—it's better. I bring my hand to it now, rubbing my finger over the shifting texture, which I find myself doing frequently throughout the day because I love it. I love how it feels. Porcelain and gold.

It's the nicest thing I've ever owned.

"Georgia Avis," Matthew calls, grinning, "it break time already?"

"I should be asking you the same," I return, and they both laugh. Cleo told me that about Matthew; he likes it when people hold their own with him, even at his expense, because most people find him intimidating.

I let the necklace go as they make their way over. Matthew's guest is shockingly tall, maybe six five or so. Close up, his white face seems like it was pieced together on the Ken Doll assembly line, chiseled and dimpled in all the right places, sparkling blue eyes. He takes his hat off and nods at me, revealing golden-brown hair that has the kind of swoop to it that makes me think, *Of course.* His looks interest me less than who he might be. I don't recognize him but my blood hums at the possibilities. If he's here, he's important—that much is certain.

"Who's this?" His voice is deep, smooth.

"Aidan, this is Georgia Avis," Matthew tells him. "She's our newest hire. Georgia, meet Aidan Archer." They wait on me to make something of him and when it doesn't happen, Matthew breaks into laughter, backhanding Aidan lightly in the chest. "She'd be my favorite new hire for that alone, if she wasn't already." I blush. Aidan's mouth quirks, but he no longer seems so amused. "Georgia, Aidan owns Archer Studios. If you haven't seen his movies, you've no doubt heard of them. He swept the Oscars last year for—"

"*Sadie*," I finish. It finally rings a bell. I nod a little too vigorously to compensate for my ignorance. "Yeah! Wow. Congratulations. It was an amazing movie. Really powerful." I haven't even seen it. "It's incredible to meet you."

"Well, now I feel like I can shake your hand," Aidan says, holding out his own. His grip is unsparing, almost painful, as our fingers close around each other. His hand is so large, mine disappears inside it. "I've never been so humbled before."

Matthew smiles wryly. "Georgia's very good at intuiting what people need."

Aidan turns to him. "Aspera girl?"

Matthew shakes his head, and I try to maintain the illusion it doesn't bother me.

"Computer stuff."

"So you're smart, then," Aidan says to me.

"I like to think so." It's not as certain as I want it to sound.

He nods slowly.

"What a waste," he says.

Matthew gives me a little wink. "I think we've monopolized enough of the lovely Georgia's time. Or maybe you're stalling? If you're too afraid to play me, man, just say so."

"It was nice to meet you," Aidan tells me, and Matthew ropes a rough arm around him, pulling him forward. On their way out, they both look back at me. Aidan's question echoes in my head: *Aspera girl?*

Big deal Hollywood studio head at Aspera today.

I stare at my phone's screen, awaiting Nora's reply. It took a few rides home with her before I felt like we'd fallen into a rhythm where I could send her a message that didn't have to be about anything important and she wouldn't mind. That she might even like it. That was the same day she came with two cherry slushies just because she "owed me one."

But the day after that was lime.

The computer chimes with a request. E8. Executive floor. Room 8.

Silk blindfolds & ties for intimate purposes left inside door at 5 p.m. NO CONTACT.

I freeze, cursor poised on the *request received* button, feeling my face crimson as I imagine soft skin, bound wrists, covered eyes, a mouth open in ecstasy. The part that makes me squirm the most is the knowledge that I'll be here, working, when it all begins taking place somewhere above me. I click the button, trying to let the ensuing race against the clock push me past my embarrassment, but it doesn't work because Kel's my line to executive requests, and I don't want to say these words to him.

I wait until I can't wait anymore.

"What've we got, Georgia?" he asks as soon as he picks up.

"Uh, room eight needs silk blindfolds and ties," I blurt out.

"Slow down. Sleeping masks and suit?"

"No, like for—bedroom stuff."

"Clarify? Not sure I copy."

"*Kel.*" I close my eyes. "You heard me."

"I'm just teasing. You're one of the team now, aren't you? It's what we do."

And then I'm embarrassed for a different reason, and I wonder if he'll tell that to Matthew, that I don't know how to play along. I send confirmation of care with less than a minute to spare and lean back, breathing like I just ran a marathon. I get a text; Nora. Her notification is a pretty shimmering sound throughout the room.

Who?

Can't tell.

Tease. You their AG?

No. Just met him bc he was with M.

HE, huh?

I've said too much. 😊😊

Just tell me.

What are you doing right now?

She sends a selfie. She's sitting in an old lawn chair on her front yard, the phone angled awkwardly enough I can see a bag of chips and a bottle of Coke nestled in her lap. She's got the beginnings of a sunburn on her face, her arms.

She's crinkling her nose, tongue out. If she meant to make me smile, it works.

Nice.

Your turn.

I take my selfie at the window, where the sunlight halos my face and hair, a hint of the green and the sky beyond. The tilt of the angle captures the nice curve of my breasts. The gold of my necklace is literally mid-sparkle. It feels excessive, maybe, but I want her to see it. Me.

Three agonizing minutes later, she replies:

You look like you could be a model.

I run my finger along my collarbone, alight with her compliment.

You look sunburned, I text back. Pack it in.

Can't. Avoiding my dad.

That sucks. Why?

He caught me listening in on a phone call to Watt. Now he's being an asshole.

Are you okay?

She doesn't respond. Two requests come in while I wait. One more before I realize she's not going to, that her silence, in itself, is an answer. The selfie she sent loses its sweetness, everything about it sad. I imagine her storming out of the house to escape her dad, getting as far as the yard and realizing she has no place to go, then grabbing some chips and the Coke to tide her over until, I guess, it's time to pick me up.

I'll tell you who it is. Promise not to tell.
Promise.
Aidan Archer. Archer Studios. I met him.

I lean forward, getting ready to soak up what I always dreamed would be one of the best parts of this job. I want to see the glamour of it through Nora's eyes. Aspera girl. Rubbing elbows with studio heads. And it's not even a lie. I did that.

But when she responds, she's got to be all Nora about it:

Pics or it didn't happen.

When Matthew and Aidan come back from the golf course, they shut themselves inside his office and, between requests, I stand at the door to my own, half-in, half-out, so when Aidan finally makes his exit, he finds me there, looking as though I've only just left or arrived and what perfect timing, that our paths should cross like this again. He closes the door quietly behind him, the satisfaction of the day's game in his red-rimmed eyes. He says, "So that's where they keep you."

"Mr. Archer—"

"Aidan."

"Aidan. I shouldn't be asking you this, but . . ." I clasp my hands, glancing at Matthew's office, just to make sure he can't somehow hear. It intrigues Aidan enough to move closer and the closer he is, the more overwhelming his presence. There's so . . . *much* of him and his height is so off-putting; I've never known anyone so tall. "Would it be okay—I mean, can I get a picture with you?"

He smiles. "Now that you know who I am?"

But the smile isn't quite reaching his eyes.

We both know the rules.

We both know I'm breaking them.

"I—I'm so sorry," I stutter, turning back. "I really shouldn't have—"

"No, Georgia—I'm just teasing." That's the second time I've heard that today from a man I'm not sure means it. He moves closer still, putting his hand on my shoulder. His touch has a real weight to it. "Of course you can. Why don't we . . . let's take it in here."

He pushes through the door to my office, finding the catch effortlessly, and leads me inside, his hand moving from my shoulder to the small of my back. I duck away, grabbing my phone from the desk. He says he'll take the picture; he's got longer arms. He squeezes me close, a hug, and he smells like the green, like cigar smoke, liquor. I only just manage to smile before he takes the shot, then shoves my phone into my hands, crossing the room to the minibar.

"You're very beautiful," he tells me without turning around, inspecting a bottle of dark amber booze. I smile, studying the picture of us. He was careless; the lighting, the slight blurriness of it makes it imperfect, but at the same time, it makes it look like more than it is—I could pretend it was taken at some party in LA. We look that cool. Nora's going to pick me up soon, and I'll get to show her how cool we look.

"Georgia."

My name sounds so sharp off his tongue, I glance up, startled.

"It matters," he says, eyes on me, intent. "What I just said to you."

"Thank you."

I try not to look like I already know it.

He's poured two shots of whatever he's found and holds one out to me. I step back, but he's undeterred. He crosses the room, his long strides quickly closing the gap between us and pushes a glass into my hand. The booze spills onto my fingers in the exchange.

"What, we can take a picture together, but we can't share a drink?" He cocks his head. There's a cleft in his chin. I fight the urge to press my finger into it. He seems less real the longer I look at him. "If you break one rule, why not break them all?" He must see the panic in my eyes because he chuckles. "Don't worry. I won't tell them about any of this."

"You're just teasing." I'm catching on.

A flick of the wrist. He knocks the shot back and nods at mine before pouring himself another and finishing it in one swift motion. I bring my glass to my lips for a sip. I nearly choke. It's—I don't know what it is. It's strong. Awful. I take another sip and it doesn't lessen the vileness of it, so I end up doing as he did, forcing it down in one swallow just to put it behind me. It burns. He pours us both another. My stomach churns at the prospect.

"Why do you think it matters?" he asks. "That I called you beautiful?"

"Because . . . you see beautiful people all the time?"

"That's right." He runs his tongue along his teeth. "So you must be something special."

My eyes light up and I nod eagerly.

"I've always thought—I mean . . ."

"What have you always thought?"

"I have big plans for myself."

"Well, let's drink to that," he says.

How could I not? It's still terrible, but I bear it a little bit better than I did before. Aidan smiles, and it's the first time it seems like he means it. Some of the tension leaves me now he and I are on equal footing. He moves back to the bar. I'm flush from the shots, but not only that, something else—pride. Real pride. I think of my mother, of all the promise she denied me, and how futile she made it seem, believing in myself. But she didn't kill it out of me, did she, and I'm reaping the rewards of it now. You hear that, Mom? The head of Archer Studios thinks I'm *very* beautiful. You see this? The head of Archer Studios is raising his glass to *me*.

Aidan tells me about the last film festival he was at. Sundance? It was important. He won distribution rights to the festival favorite after a frenzied auction; only cost him fourteen million dollars. *Took it right out from under those bastards at A24.* I don't know what that means. Fourteen million. How many times over could that pay Tyler back? *You can't imagine.* At first, I think Aidan's read my mind, but it's just that he's moved on; what I can't imagine is the pressure inherent in following a seminal work like *Sadie.* It's destroying his liver. He came to Aspera to drink less, but it's not quite working out that way. At least here, he tells me, with a conspiratorial look, he's doing it for better reasons. I tell him I'm sorry it's so hard, but it's good he's drinking for the right reasons. Now we're on the sofa, his legs crossed, his knee touching mine, and I'm giving him my full attention, leaning close with my eyes wide, listening, rapt, like I imagine an Aspera girl would do. I'm good at this. Someone should tell Matthew I'm so good at this.

"So let me guess your big plans—you want to be an actress," Aidan says. "And that's why you're so desperate for my attention."

An actress.

Is that what I want?

. . . Desperate?

When he gets up to refill our glasses, I break pose, the one I made for him, and rub my eyes. Men are exhausting. I check my phone. Nora's coming soon. Nora. *That's why I wanted your attention,* I almost tell Aidan. *I wanted to impress a girl.*

The computer chimes, and I have the sense that maybe it's not the first time it's done that. Shit. I press my hand against the couch, but Aidan sits down before I can stand, jostling me into place. My head falls back until I'm staring up at the antler, a halation of light around it. I blink slowly, surprised at how easy it is to keep my eyes closed.

"I'm tired," I say.

He brings the glass to my lips. I raise my hand weakly, trying to push it away. A shadow crosses his face. I force a thin smile. *Just teasing,* I want to say, but he says, "What, we can't share a drink together?"

"I—" I shake my head. "Haven't we?"

He presses the glass into my hand. "Would you drink with me, Georgia?"

"Okay." I bring the shot to my mouth, not wanting to insult him, but I can only get half of it down. He finishes it for me. The aftertaste is awful and familiar. Wait. "I *have* been drinking with you . . ."

"You didn't answer my question."

"You think I could be?" I finally ask, once I remember what it was. "An actress?" The word melts out of my mouth. I never thought about it before, but when I go home tonight, it's all I'm going to think about. Me, beautiful Georgia Avis, on the big screen. Maybe they'd pay me fourteen million dollars just to say things I didn't even have to think up myself.

He smiles at his empty shot glass.

"Can you act?"

"Never tried," I admit.

"I'm sure you can." He takes a noisy sip of his drink. When did he get another? "Girls like you act all the time . . ." I open my eyes. When were they closed? I don't know how to respond to that. I don't like how he said it. He nods at my arm. "What happened?"

"Got hit by a car."

He laughs like I said something funny. Maybe I did, but something about it makes me uneasy. He notices Nora's number scribbled on my cast. He reaches over and traces it with his finger. I don't think I like that either.

"Boyfriend?"

"Nora."

"Who's Nora?"

"The girl I want to impress," I tell him without thinking. I blush. The computer chimes. How many times is that? I say, "Fuck," and I just about manage to get up, but he grabs me by the arm and pulls me back down. The sudden shift in altitude is disorienting. He leans forward, closer to me, and I use his face as a fixed point to try to stop the room's spinning.

"You're very beautiful," he tells me.

"I think you said that before."

"It means something every time I do."

And then he presses his mouth against mine, the weight

of him forcing me farther back into the couch and my first thought isn't *he's kissing me*—if that's what you call mashing the inside of my lips against my teeth hard enough to make my eyes water—my first thought is: *I'm drowning.* I'm drowning in a sea of him, nothing I can grab hold of, no surface here defined. I push at his shoulder but he doesn't understand; he takes it as invitation to leverage himself more against me. Two things are happening: he's drunk and he doesn't understand that I want up.

"Help me up," I mumble.

And then I realize only one thing is happening.

And then I'm only thinking *help me.*

I make a small, surprised noise as his hard-on presses against me. Finally, he leans back, and I feel like I've crashed against a shore, panting in a way he isn't, my heart racing in a different way than his must be. His eyes search my face before trailing down my throat, my heaving chest.

"Oh," he says.

He reaches forward and I flinch, but his fingers only find my necklace. He studies it, running his thumb over it.

Porcelain. Gold.

He glances behind him, in the direction of Matthew's office, like he knows that door is there. But this is a secret room. He says softly, to himself, "You break one rule . . ." He reaches behind me, unclasping it, taking it off. I grab for it clumsily, but he sets it aside and then slowly begins to unbutton my dress.

One button.

Two buttons.

"Mr. Archer," I slur.

Three.

"Aidan," he corrects me.

"Aidan, I can't do this with you. I gotta . . . I gotta go home."

I manage to get my feet anchored to the floor enough to finally stand, but he pulls me back again and I overbalance into him, and he thinks that means something it doesn't. His hands paw at my chest, his grip on my breast, bruising. I'm so small under him. I've never felt so small. The computer chimes. Nora's shimmering ringtone fills the room. Nora. He moves his mouth to my neck, his tongue tracing the path my necklace used to be.

"I wanna go home," I say, the room fading out. Maybe . . . maybe, if I close my eyes and open them, I'll fade in where I'm meant to be. Just like a movie. I close my eyes.

"Georgia, what the hell's going on? Front desk is getting complaint after complaint about the digital concierge—we have several outstanding requests—"

And then: Aidan's weight, finally off of me.

I force my eyes open.

Kel stands at the door, staring at us both.

've spent nearly my whole life running to Aspera, but I don't remember running from it. The reality of it is too painful for my mind to hold, or maybe my mind is holding too many other painful realities to accept one more. A girl in the woods. The most intimate part of her, a bruise. Foot- prints all around me. It must happen, though—pushing, stumbling my way out of that room, away from Aidan, past Kel, out of the lodge, the sound of my name behind me. *Georgia.* Because then I'm outside. I'm past the gate. The air tastes clean in my dirty mouth. When I see Nora's car parked at the side of the road, I stop, the blood rushing to my head like I've been pitched upside down. She doesn't notice me. I bring my hand to my necklace but it's not there. *Don't cry,* I think. All the booze is crawling up my insides, searing the back of my throat. Nora turns her head and finds me in the sideview. I don't cry.

I bend at the waist and throw up.

She has a Coke slushie waiting for me in the car. Tries to make me drink it. It's too sweet.

"How did you get this fucked up?" She takes the giant

cup back and pushes my hair from my eyes to get a better look at them. I slap her hand away. She reaches for me again, and I slap her hand away again. We do this one more time before she exclaims, "Christ, Avis, I'm trying to buckle you in."

I let her do it, and the careful, thoughtful way she navigates my body upsets me in a way I don't know how to explain. The restraint of the seat belt becomes a welcome relief when I realize it means I don't have to do the work of holding myself up. I slump forward.

"This is . . . You are so wasted."

"I'm fine."

"Yeah, I don't think so," she says. "They let Aspera girls drink like this? Did Hayes miss the memo where that's not fucking legal?"

"I broke the rules. With Aidan Archer."

"*What?* You were drinking with Aidan Archer?"

I take out my phone and I show her the selfie. My chest hurts where he grabbed me, I realize. When my eyes find hers, I realize something else: all of it was for nothing.

She doesn't even seem impressed.

"Avis."

Nora sounds uncertain. I've never heard her sound like that before. She always knows exactly what she wants to say, especially if you don't want to hear it. The world passes by my window, Ketchum still somewhere ahead of us, the scenery a wild smear, at the mercy of my wavering focus.

"Avis, you still there?"

"Yeah," I breathe.

"What happened?"

"I broke the rules."

"No, I mean . . . did something else happen? With him? Did he—" She pauses. "Did he . . . hurt you?"

"No."

"Then why are you crying?"

I bring my hand to my face, the tacky feeling of tears against my fingers. I'm so overwhelmed, my mind doesn't know which broken pieces of the last hour to start putting together, but this is the next—which maybe should have been the first: Kel's shocked face, his mouth opening and closing like a fish. Matthew must know what happened by now. So I think I know what's going to happen tomorrow.

"Because I broke the rules," I say, "and I got caught."

Nora asks me if Tyler's home, and it's only when I say he's not, that he'll be at work a while, that she drives me to my place. She tells me to wait while she rounds the car, like I'm some kind of flight risk, but by then, I just want to sleep. I'm almost too tired to move.

"God, this is going to be . . . fun," she says. She pulls me up and then slings my arm around her shoulder, bringing her own firmly around my waist. My fingertips graze her collarbone, my face close to the curve of her neck. I breathe her in. She smells chemical, coconut sunscreen, summer-sweet. She smells good. We shuffle up the walk, and she slips her hand into my pocket for my key, and she says, "Avis, it's okay," and I realize I've been mumbling *I fucked up* over and over and over.

Once we're inside, she helps me to my room, sits me on my bed.

"I fucked up," I tell her. "I'm gonna get fired."

"He gave you the drinks?" she asks. I nod. "And you were alone with him? Were you? Avis." I nod. "It doesn't even matter. It's not your fuckup. It's his."

But I asked for his picture, I think I say. The words sound mushy to my own ears. She stares at me a minute, then reaches down and pulls my flats off.

I bring my hand to my forehead. "I feel bad."

"Shocker. I'm gonna get you some water, and then you're going to drink it before you pass out." She's as good as her word, leaving and returning with a glass full, staying crouched in front of me as I force it all down. She won't let me leave a single drop behind. When that's done, she eases me back onto the bed slow enough to keep the room right side up.

"You're good at this," I mumble.

"Yeah, well, Ashley gave me a lot of practice. I snuck her in so many times after some fucking party or other . . ."

"I'm sorry."

I rub my hand across my chest, and I realize how open my dress is. I fumble one-handedly to button it back up, but I can't get my fingers to cooperate. Finally, Nora says, "Avis, can I—" and I nod hazily and she buttons those buttons back up, one by one, while I fight to keep my eyes open. When she's done, I reach for her hand and hold it. After a minute, she asks, "What? What is it?"

"I just want to hold your hand."

She pauses. "Okay."

". . . I wonder about you too."

"What do you wonder?" she asks. I don't answer. I feel like I said too much, but also like I don't know what I just said. She pushes a strand of hair from my face, her hand staying briefly on my forehead, then sits on the floor at my bed.

"I'll stay here a while," she tells me. "To be sure you're okay."

From here, I could reach out and touch the back of her neck, and there's a part of me that wants to so badly, but my arms are so heavy.

"He said I could be an actress," I tell her, because I want her to know. I want her to know something happened in that room with Aidan Archer that was amazing, something to hold onto when I lose everything else. I was good enough.

"What?" she asks.

I can't manage to repeat it.

"So you were alone with him, he got you like this, and said you could be an actress?"

I'm afraid, somehow, she knows every part of my body his hands were, his lips were. She turns around, leans over the bed, and shows me her phone. Onscreen, there's a picture of Aidan at some movie premiere or other, his arms wrapped around a leggy brunette, curls waterfalling over her shoulders. The words headlining the photo are beyond me, and Nora reads them aloud, her voice flat: "'Aidan Archer and Bella Olsen split after fifteen years of marriage amid growing rumors of Archer's gross professional misconduct . . .'"

"What's that mean?" I ask.

Nora lowers her phone. "That he gets women alone, gets

them drunk, and tells them they could be actresses." My eyelids flutter shut. I'm so close to the edge. Nora reaches out and grasps my shoulder, trying, futilely, to keep me from going over.

"Avis," she says.

There's a memory of my mom hovering in that thin space between asleep and awake, and it folds me into itself, keeping me from either. When I was sick, she would care for me. When circumstance reduced us to the least complicated parts of our whole, I was hers and she was mine. The sweet simplicity of it was inescapable; when your daughter is sick, you care for her. You press the cold, damp cloth against her skin. You give her medicine that brings the fever down. She would grasp my hand, that soft space between my thumb and index finger, and press there gently with her own thumb, tracing circles. *It makes headaches go away,* she'd tell me, and I don't know if that was true, but it was the kind of tender flourish that made me realize she didn't hate me all the time and might not hate me at all, even if I wasn't and would never be what she wanted.

When I wake up, I can almost feel the impression of her fingers on my skin and then it disappears. I'm sick, but it's not the kind of sick that deserves any kind of tenderness. My mouth is cotton-dry, my skin sticky, my pulse pounding behind my eyes. I squeeze that space on my hand, and if anything, my headache gets worse. My alarm clock goes off with a skull-shattering buzz. Time to get up. Time to get up so Tyler can drive me to the job I can't still expect to have. I swing my legs over my bed and lean forward, my mouth flooding with saliva, a precursor to throwing up. I breathe through it, swallowing back bile.

I hear the faint sounds of Tyler in the kitchen. There's a fresh glass of water on my nightstand, two aspirin, my phone. The notification light blinks. I reach for it, afraid of what I'll find, but there's nothing from Aspera. Only Nora.

Tyler knows you were wasted but he thinks it happened with me at my place.
I only told him because I didn't want to leave you like that.
I wanted to make sure someone was looking after you.
Anyway, see you after work.

I raise my head to the ceiling, trying not to be angrier with her than I am with myself, but I still end up sending her a text telling her Tyler wants to pick me up, because I know she'll want to talk about it and I don't want to talk about it before I know what it is.

Then I'll see you tomorrow, she texts back.

I get to my feet and cross the hall to the bathroom. I have a hard time looking in the mirror, at my sallow skin and swollen lips, yesterday's sundress. I unbutton it, letting it fall open in front of me, and if I didn't feel fool enough, there it is written in my skin: bruises the shape of fingertips above my left breast. I get into the shower and make the water hot, scrubbing my skin hard, and when I'm finished, everything is still the way I don't want it to be.

. . .

Tyler's washing out his coffee cup when I step into the kitchen, cigarette dangling from his lips. I move past him to the half-full coffee pot, get a mug from the cupboard, and fill it, staring at my rippling reflection inside, thinking of the money I won't be making him anymore. We still need that money. I close my eyes.

"I was fourteen, I think, first time I got drunk," Tyler says. "Party at . . . shit, doesn't really matter. Threw up all over the yard, then I sat on the step for an hour, I was so afraid to come in. And Mom's right inside the door, and she knows what's going on because she saw me staggering up the walk, so it's not like I could pull one over on her. I just felt so fucking stupid, you know? Anyway, she finally opens the door and she says, 'It's not the end of the world, so stop looking like it.'" He claps me on the back, and I open my eyes. "It's not the end of the world, George, so stop looking like it." He pauses. "It happens again, though, it might be."

"It won't," I manage.

"Finish your coffee, whatever. We're running behind." He starts putting his work boots on. I sip the coffee and manage to get it down. What will happen when we reach Aspera's gate? Will they turn me away or let us in? Maybe Tyler would be proud of me for being fired; I'll never be more my mother's daughter, and what more could I say about her, if we have that in common? Tyler looks up from his laces. "You know, I never thought I'd see the day a James gave a fuck about an Avis, but Nora James sure seems to give a fuck about you."

I turn my face to the window in time to see a sleek black

car pull up to the curb outside our house. I frown, peering at it through the screen.

"What?" Tyler asks. He heads to the window to see what I'm seeing. If any car this nice has ever been on our street before, it could only be passing through, stopping maybe, because they took a wrong turn and need to figure out how to get the somewhere better they're supposed to be. But then the driver's door opens and a man in a black suit steps out, pulling his phone from his jacket's inside pocket. He makes a call.

A moment later, the phone in our kitchen rings.

sit in the back seat of the sleek black car, listening to the faint, fast sound of my own breathing, the morning sun shining bright and on me like a spotlight. I open my phone's gallery and find the selfie of Aidan and me, some blurry LA party, another life. I delete it and watch the crumbling houses of my street blur past until I can't stand to look at them anymore. I close my eyes. I keep my eyes closed as we leave the city, keep my eyes closed as we drive down Ashley's road, keep them closed until we're past Aspera's gate. When I finally open them, it's in time to see the lodge disappearing behind us.

"Where," I start to ask, and the driver tells me we're going to the Hayes cabin, just a few more minutes away. Before today, there'd be nothing I'd want more than the privilege of seeing where Matthew and Cleo live, but I want to earn my way into their lives by my specialness, not by my mistakes. It's tucked into the trees, not far from the fairway, a two-story cabin with a wraparound deck. The wood is stained so dark and the windows reflect so much of the trees and sky, it almost disappears into its surroundings.

The driver tells me I have clearance, that I can let myself in. He watches my tentative journey up the walk and doesn't pull away until I've opened the front door and stepped inside, where I realize I didn't ask him his name, as if it matters, as if I'd need to know it after today.

I stand at the threshold, the door closing gently behind me as I take in the Hayeses' spacious home, which is comprised of all Aspera's gleam—its gorgeous wood and stone, its windows reaching heavenward—but it's the details that separate it, these intimate glimpses into their lives: the photos on the wall, books scattered on all available surfaces, notes written on the whiteboard mounted to the fridge. They're the kind of things I want to investigate further but am forced to accept at a distance while I wait to be met.

To my immediate right, there's a small kitchen and dining area, the hum of the fridge so loud against the surrounding quiet. A balcony overlooks the main floor, its short and winding staircase descending to the living room to my left, which extends to a hallway leading places I'll never know. A distressed leather sectional sits before a massive flatscreen on the wall that's cycling slowly through artwork. A landscape fades into a painting so unexpected, I step back—and then forward, for a closer look.

It's an old painting. My limited knowledge of fine art allows me to arrive at only this conclusion with any amount of certainty. One of those pale, fleshy women lay on her back on an emerald chaise, her eyes seeing something beyond the canvas's edge. She's nude but for the white sheet spread across her midriff, concealing nothing, her pillowy breasts on full display, her legs spread, one languidly outstretched with its toes angled toward the floor. At the end of the chaise is a swan, its wings open, its neck gently curved between the woman's legs, its beak pointed toward the soft painted line of her vagina. The subtle way the light plays off her porcelain skin and the swan's white feathers, the muted colors and velvety brushstrokes, put me in mind of a dream. But it doesn't feel like one, doesn't have that sweet sheen that all good dreams do. There's something dangerous and unsettling about it—like how I imagine standing at the edge of a cliff would feel . . . a choice you never considered suddenly in front of you, and it's not that you want to die, it's that you've never felt the real possibility of it before. Like a razor dancing along your skin before that first cut. My gaze drifts back to the woman's face, and I wonder if that's the look in her eyes. If this is her dream. I step toward it, mesmerized, when the sharp and sudden crack of gunfire sounds outside.

I gasp and whirl around.

"Game hunting," Cleo says, behind me, above me. "It's not that close."

I exhale shakily, trading my shock for sheer dread of what's to come, but I can't bring myself to face her. I just listen to her footsteps making their way slowly down the stairs, closer to me.

"Georgia," she says, and then she says it again, near enough for me to feel the breath of my name from her lips—or to imagine that I do.

I turn, my eyes finding her pristine white sneakers before traveling slowly to her face. Her black leggings. The fine curve of her hips. The white tunic draped over her slim frame. Her pale throat, the swallow of it. Then, finally, her beautiful blue eyes. A desperate panic rises inside me. This will be the last time I see her, has to be. She reaches for me, pressing her palm against the side of my face, and she sighs, disappointed, and I feel that more than her touch. It demands explanation, and when I open my mouth to give her one, what happens instead is a secret comes out, my heart speaking before my head can get in its way.

"There was a man at the mall," I tell her.

The story comes slow and halting, not always in the right order.

There was man at the mall, but before that, there was Matthew, me, and the road.

I tell Cleo the man at the mall told me I could be a model and I'd never heard anything so promising since I was thirteen, when Matthew told me if I didn't end up at Aspera, it would only be because someone else discovered me first.

How after Mom betrayed him, all I had was hope of someone else.

So there I was with the man at the mall—discovered.

I tell her about the money I paid him, and the house it took me to. About the photographer there, and the beautiful photos he took, how I saw the truth of my beauty in them, but how, after, when the camera's flash finally faded away, I realized what I'd done to my brother. I tell her about being on my knees in the mall's dingy storeroom, and what I almost did to undo it, and that the only thing that stopped me was remembering what Matthew said: *Come to Aspera*.

"I feel an affinity with you," Cleo says softly when I'm done. "Do you know what that means, Georgia?" I shake my head. "It means I know you."

She turns from me, for the fridge, and pours us each a

glass of water. I need it. I sip, trying to settle myself, but I can't. Something important is happening here.

"I knew you the day I came to your house," she says. "It was like looking in a mirror. But I was older than you when I started to see the world for what it was . . . and how to bend it to me, and you . . . you're still so young. There's so much you don't know. What happened yesterday shows me you need guidance. Protection."

"I want that," I manage.

She sets her glass on the counter, and then she notices mine trembling in my hand. She takes it from me and sets it down.

"Tell me how your mother made you feel," she says.

"My mom?"

"She was so afraid to dream."

"She made me feel like . . . like . . . she told me over and over . . . she told me I wasn't good enough for everything I wanted . . . for this."

"And that's how you end up on your knees." My skin tingles at the way she says it, the way she lays my life so bare. "You get lost between what your mother made you feel and what you know is true. And you knew, deep down, what Matthew told you is true. That you deserved more. And it saved you."

"Yes." My voice cracks. "It did."

Aspera came to me on my knees—but it wouldn't let me stay there.

"But your mother also wasn't wrong, and that's something else you need to know." And her voice stays gentle, almost tender, the way she lays my mother's life so bare. "Some holes, you can't crawl out of. Some circumstances can't be changed. She knew what her life was, and she couldn't reconcile with the fact it didn't have to be yours. That you have something she didn't. You can't blame her for being so broken, she couldn't see it. For being so broken, she didn't want to."

"See what?"

"Come here."

Cleo holds out her hand and I waver, not because I don't want to take it, but because more than anything, I do. I want to know the feel of her hand in mine, her fingers wrapped around my own, and it's so visceral, I'm afraid of it. But then I remember what she said to me before, sitting across from me when we dined together. *Don't put a ceiling on what you're meant to receive, Georgia. That's not how you ended up here.*

And it doesn't suit me.

I take her hand.

It's . . . everything.

She leads me down the hall where there's a plain full-length mirror hanging on its wall. She positions me in front of it, and I'm made breathless by the pair of us, by how beautiful we look together. Like we belong. She slips her hand into her pocket and pulls out my necklace.

"You won't lose this again," she tells me.

I go weak with relief at the promise of it, what this moment guarantees. She holds it up and brings it around the front of me, clasping it, a second time, around my neck.

She's right.

I won't lose this again.

"Beauty like ours always has a cost, Georgia," she murmurs, our eyes meeting in the mirror. "But you don't have to be the one who pays it."

lean against Matthew's door, staring down the sun-bleached antlers before I finally knock.

"Come in."

And even still, I wait.

He's at the window when I gather the courage to step into the room, a silhouette whose features slowly take form the closer I get. My courage wanes as he rounds his desk and leans against it. I set the small takeout box beside him. He glances at it, and then me, and says nothing. There's no hint of yesterday in his eyes, but it hangs between us, cheapening the ritual. But I thought it would be worse not to bring it. He needs to know whatever he makes of me now—I'm still thinking of him. He needs to know something else.

"I wanted to talk to you," I say.

"Oh?"

"I want you to know that—" I raise my chin. "I'm not my mother. You can trust me."

"And what if I told you that's what your mother said?" He pushes off the desk and makes his way slowly to the window. "What if I told you I hold that expectation of everyone I hire? That it's not something I should be reassured of after the fact?"

Behind him, a magnificent cloud shelf that looks like it was painted by Michelangelo himself moves slowly across the brilliantly blue sky. Even the clouds and the sky don't look the same over the city as they do out here.

"Aspera reveals everyone who steps through its doors," Matthew says. "People believe they're prepared to work here and find out they're not."

"I don't know what you mean."

"Maybe they're like your mother. They covet it, and their jealousy consumes them. What they don't have, they end up trying to ruin."

It's a special kind of agony, I want to tell him, to always be answering for her crimes, to have all of my actions and intentions filtered through them.

It's not fair either.

It's not fair he's doing that to me.

"Or maybe they get so caught up in the idea of this place, it's like having a fever, and they slip. Even with the best intentions, they share something they shouldn't or wander places they ought not to wander or find themselves in situations they should never be in . . . This isn't a Cinderella story, Georgia. A lot of the girls who work here, that's what they think. So tell me: Is that what you thought?"

"That's not what I think."

"Cleo told me you didn't. And I trust Cleo. But I still don't understand."

"I just want to be part of this," I say, trying to keep the desperation out of my voice, trying to make him see it for how it is. "Ever since you picked me up on that road, all I've ever wanted was to be part of this. I would never use you like that."

"Then what happened yesterday?"

"Do you think . . . do you think members ever get caught up in this?" I ask. Matthew's eyes flicker, the slightest confusion. I step closer. "Aspera? They're finally free in a way they never get to be, and it goes straight to their heads? Because that's what I think happened with Aidan. That was *his* moment in this place, and I was just there—but it wasn't mine. I wasn't looking for that . . . I couldn't have been because I—"

My face is hot, my eyes suddenly everywhere but him, feeling his only on me. There's a chasm between knowing something and saying it out loud, and I've lived in the silence of myself for so long. Not because I'm ashamed—that part is over—but because that piece of me felt like it was for the future, like only the best of me could be ahead of me.

But if I'm finally at Aspera . . .

"Because I like girls."

It's the first time I've ever said it out loud. Matthew absorbs it slowly, his face softening. He runs his palm across his chin, his expression a little distant, and I'm light-headed at the admission, half-giddy.

"So you can trust me."

After a moment, he says, gruffly, "I want you to know I hold members to the same standard I hold staff. No one is above the rules I set here. Including Aidan."

"I know that. Because I trust you."

It's those words that seem to take him most by surprise.

Those words he asks me to give him time to sit with.

"You impress me, Georgia," he says at my back as I leave. I stop, bringing my hand to my necklace. "And I meet a lot of impressive people."

He must really like you," Kel tells me. "Anyone else do what you did . . ."

I readjust my seat belt. The bite of Aidan's bruises in response to that pressure steals me back to my office, to the sensation of him on top of me as we sank into the couch. I suck in a breath.

"Okay?" Kel asks.

I press against the bruises harder and the sense of Aidan's hands is fainter this time, but I'm still in that room and I can still hear his voice. *You break one rule* . . . I press down hard enough to wince, and finally, the only touch I feel is my own. I'm back in the car, and Kel is beside me. I smooth my dress over my knees. I thank him for the ride.

"Keep asking me to do this for you," he says, "and I'm gonna think you've got a crush." I force a smile. He grins back at me, seeing it. "Still teasing."

My stomach clenches as Ashley's cross comes into view. The sun glints off it—

Off something attached to it.

"Hey, pull over."

"What?"

"Pull over—"

"You carsick or something?"

"Just stop, please?"

He pulls over, and I get out of the car fast, half-jogging to the cross, ten feet behind us now. I crouch in front of it. There's a picture taped to its center; the sunlight must've caught its gloss. All I see is the pink of it first.

That pink.

Then, more memories my mind refuses to let go of; things I feel more than see. The stiffness of her body becomes the stiffness of my body. The cold of it becomes my cold. The air takes on the tang of her rot.

"Georgia."

"Just a second," I say faintly.

I peel the photo off. It's of Ashley in that pink shirt, her blond hair a tornado around her head, skinny in a way that seems frail to me now. She's standing next to a small Black girl her age, whose hair is in braids flying above her, a mischievous glint in her eyes. They're dancing. There's music in this photo I can't hear, a hot summer night I can't feel, sugar on their tongues I can't taste. They're both smiling at the camera and I find myself smiling back at them. It's in a bedroom, but I'm not sure whose. The ink of them comes off on my hand. This was printed at home and cut sloppily to size. I turn the photo over and scrawled on its back, in messy teen girl writing: *fuck hulick!!! at least you got away. LOVE YOU FOREVER.*

"Georgia."

I move to put it back, but there's something unbearable to me about something so beautiful and vital discarded, left

to the elements like she was. And *fuck hulick!!!* . . . maybe
that's something Nora needs to see. I fold it carefully in half
and tuck it into my wallet, and then I stare into her woods,
those sweet, all-caps words hovering, lonely, in the air.

LOVE YOU FOREVER.

Tyler's body doesn't know anything but work. On his day off, the memory of his alarm wakes him, and once his morning routine starts, he's almost helpless to stop it. He dresses, knots his hair, has his smoke, and then calls upon everything inside him to fight the urge to get in his truck, drive to the latest site, and clock in. He anchors himself to the couch, his legs stretched out and his boots unlaced, his eyes closed, his hand against his chest like it's helping to keep him down. If he's lucky, he'll fall back asleep, but he rarely does. I almost hurt with love at the sight of him. He moved back home when Mom got cancer. Didn't complain when the diagnosis went terminal and he knew I'd be stealing the next few years of his life. He'd had a girlfriend before it was settled, and then, when it was settled, he didn't have her anymore. I don't think it was his choice. I remember my brother when he was younger and on his own. I didn't see him so much. The only responsibilities he had were to himself, and I'm haunted by what that looked like on him. It wasn't exactly weightless, but it wasn't so bound. I hate what I've done to him, and I hate that I wouldn't change it for anything.

I toss an envelope on his chest.

He snorts, jolting upright, rubbing his eyes with the heel of his palm, then picks up the envelope, turning it over.

"What's this?"

"An advance on my first paycheck."

Kel gave it to me before he dropped me off yesterday. *And something extra for a job well done.* It's so worth seeing Tyler's eyes widen at the money inside. He counts the bills, and then shakes his head in wonder, and this is the moment all his choices pay off. I would have never made this much in the same amount of time at Mac's, and I'm prouder of it than I should be, given everything that led us to it, but it feels so good to make good.

"It won't always be that stacked," I warn. "I got a little bonus."

"Jesus. Well, good for you, kid. You should keep a little bit of it for yourself." I shake my head. He gives me a tired smile and nods at my cast. "Need me to drive you?"

"Nora's giving me a ride."

And when I step outside, she's there, twirling her keys around her finger. Her hair is slicked back from her face, wet from a shower, the morning light shining on her in a way that makes the line of her jaw look sharp enough to cut glass. She's wearing a cropped gray workout hoodie, hinting at her abs, her matching joggers slung low off her hips. The full force of her attention and the sudden humiliation I feel at the way she saw me last keeps me frozen in place. I wonder what it would be like to have one without the other, and that stills me further.

"Morning, Avis," she says.

"Morning," I say.

"I found something out." No preamble. So very her.

"What's that?"

"Right after they found Ashley, the cops set up check-points every way out of the city for forty-eight hours. They were looking at the tires of everyone headed in or out."

"Why?"

"Because the car that hit you had one tire with a different tread pattern," she explains. "It's like . . . a vehicular finger-print. Three were block, one was symmetrical. I'm going to tell you what to look for, and you're going to look for it at Aspera."

"But Aspera had nothing to do with Ashley. They cleared it."

"Yeah, they cleared *Aspera*, but you know how many people in town work that place? You know how many deliveries they got going in and out? Something might turn up. And I'm kind of thinking it might, because my dad's getting real hung up on that road and it only goes one way."

And then I remember—Justin, rounding the BMW with Kel and me inside, inspecting it . . . he must have been look-ing at the treads.

"I'll see what I can see, but no promises." I pull my wallet from my pocket. "I found something too."

I take out the photo and unfold it. It's in even worse shape now, the gray morning light leeching the color from Ashley and the other girl's image, the ink more smudged than before. Nora's face falls as she takes it, a resigned sort of heartache. She asks where I got it.

"It was taped to the cross on the road. There's something

on the back, but I don't know if it means anything. That's why I thought you should see it."

She nods, but she doesn't look at me. "That's Livvy—Liv Adamson. Ashley's best friend. She was so inconsolable, she couldn't even make it to the funeral." Nora flips the photo over and frowns. "Hulick . . ."

"You never heard that name before?"

She shakes her head. "Person, place, or thing?" Her frown deepens. She takes her phone from her pocket, firing off a quick text. "Watt questioned Liv, but she never said anything about whatever this is. Might be an inside joke or a new dealer she didn't want to narc on."

"What did you say?"

"I told her we need to talk ASAP." She shoves her phone back in her pocket, then, after one last look, the photo too. "Liv's a good kid, but she really liked being bad with Ashley. If she doesn't want her parents to find out the highlight reel, I'll hear from her soon. Thanks." She pauses. "About the other day—"

"Forget it," I say. "I mean. Thank you, for everything. But forget it. Please."

"Why?"

"Because—" I fumble for an answer. Even knowing Nora's determination to do exactly the opposite of whatever anyone wants her to do, I was hoping she'd at least have the grace to give me this. "Because I'm embarrassed, that's why."

"Why are you embarrassed?"

"Just—you seeing me like that."

"Avis," she says slowly. "What do you think I saw?"

"Look, can we just get going?"

She gives me a long look, but we get in the car.

"So did you get in trouble or what?" she asks.

"No."

"Did he?"

I don't answer. She shakes her head. I turn my face from her, and there's a memory there: her fingers carefully buttoning my dress back up. I realize there's how Nora thinks it was with Aidan, and how it actually was, because she didn't see the way he looked at me—but I didn't either, not then. That was before Cleo told me how to recognize when you bring a man to his knees. Before she told me how when a man looks at you the way Aidan looked at me, and you know it, there's nothing he can do to you or force you to do.

oc Abrams cuts straight through Nora's phone number and then splits my cast apart, revealing a more
diminished part of myself, the skin of my arm scaly
and dry. I marvel at how light I feel without it, relieved to
be finally rid of it. I glance at Nora, and she glances quickly
away, her lips pressed together and her eyes bright. I'm hit
with the guilty realization that the sight of my cast might
have comforted her, the knowledge there was someone other
than her carrying that day on the road long after everyone
else moved on.

Another piece of Ashley, disappearing.

After it's done, we head back to her car. She leans against
it, and I settle beside her, our arms brushing, neither of us
in a hurry to head out.

She stares at the street, silent.

"Thanks for taking me," I say.

She shrugs. "What are you doing the rest of the day?"

"Staying out of Tyler's way. Think he deserves a break
from me."

"My dad's not home. Wanna come over?"

". . . Okay."

We get in the car, slamming our doors shut at the same

time. She pulls out of the parking lot while I run my hand over my arm, reacquainting myself with it. It's as weak as it looks, aches in a way I'm not expecting. On the way to Nora's house, I grit my teeth and flex my fingers, willing it to feel as strong as it did before.

"Squeeze my hand," Nora says suddenly, holding hers out, palm-side up. I reach over and wrap my fingers around hers, squeezing, like she told me to, but my grip is shy of where I want it to be. She laces her fingers between mine, telling me to squeeze again. I watch her as I do, but her eyes stay on the road. I decide to keep my hand in hers until she decides to let go, but she doesn't let go and, after a while, I forget to squeeze.

Her house is exactly what I imagined it would be. Cookie cutter, paint-by-the-numbers, tasteful beige stability. It's so much bigger than it needs to be now, down half its family, and as Nora and I move through the entryway into the kitchen, I hear the echoes of us. We're not enough to fill all its empty spaces. There are hints of a life unmaintained, dishes left in the sink a little too long, the scent of stale laundry from some far-off room, dust accumulating over surfaces where mail's not piled up.

I stand in front of the fridge, staring at the school photos pinned there. Nora and Ashley through the years. Ashley's are hard to look at, so I focus on Nora instead. She's familiar to me at every stage, and I realize how closely I've watched her in all the time we've been in each other's lives, remembering my longing stares at her in the halls at school, the half turn I'd make just to see what she looked like when she walked away. She *swaggered*. She was always so strong to me, always so together. Her graduation photo's pomp and circumstance is lost to her strained smile, to the dullness of her eyes, and I really see her now: a girl abandoned by her mother, navigating Ashley's drama in that abandonment's wake.

"What are you doing this fall?" I ask. "College, right?"

"Deferring," she says. "Graduated early . . . and for what?"

"Be nice having you around, though." I grimace at how it sounds.

I study the last school photo of Ashley ever taken. She's wearing a lot of makeup, her waterline coated with smudgy black liner, her concealer just a smidge too light for her skin, calling attention to the breakout she was trying to hide. She's duck-facing, her lips stained wine purple. There was no makeup on her face when I found her, but she looks young, either way. She was around eleven when whatever switch it was went off inside her, what I think of now as a countdown. Eleven when she started living faster than the speed of life, becoming a whisper through Ketchum. A girl called Trouble. I always thought of Nora as just handling it; making the grades, leading the volleyball team to win after win after win. Her problems would always be surmountable, especially compared to my own, given her every advantage over me.

But it couldn't have been that easy.

"What?" she asks.

"Did you know when I found out my mom pulled that shit with your birthday," I say, turning to her, "I was so mad, I ran away from home?"

A smile breaks over Nora's face, goes all the way to her eyes, and it feels like the first time I've ever seen that. It changes her. It doesn't make her prettier—it just reveals another aspect of her prettiness, a more complete picture of what had always drawn me to her in the first place. She laughs a little and it's a nice sound. It makes me smile back.

"Seriously?"

"Seriously. I got so far out of town too . . . and then I got tired of walking and I had no idea how I was gonna get back and . . . Matthew Hayes picked me up. My mom was totally furious, but I didn't care."

She grins even wider. "All because you missed my birthday."

"Yeah. But it wasn't just your birthday . . . it was going to school after that and seeing you and . . . I don't know. I felt like I got cheated out of knowing you, being around you." Her smile slowly vanishes. "I would've liked it. You never even looked at me after that."

"Avis," she says quietly. "I was looking at you all the time."

"Oh." My voice is small.

And then, because I can't help myself: "Why?"

She regards me in a way that reminds me of that time in my bedroom when I was teasing her, teasing something out of her . . . a tentative and knowing look, the kind that puts you on a fever's edge . . . but unlike then, the blush is off her and onto me. It tingles across my skin in a way that tells me this moment belongs to her. Except I don't see the point in fighting it. I surrender to it quickly with a shaky exhalation. She moves closer, a strand of hair falling across her eyes as she ducks her head to look into mine. A want bears down on me, and I'm scared suddenly, of her answer being so far from what I think it should be—

But how do you get to a moment like this with someone if it's not?

"You really want to know?" she murmurs.

I tilt my face up to hers.

And then the rough, unwelcome sound of someone clearing their throat. Nora jerks back, running her hand through her hair. I stay where I am, too far into what just happened—didn't happen—to move. This ugly new presence turns Nora rigid; she goes in on herself, and that makes me ache in a different way than I'm already aching.

She says tersely, "I thought you were out."

"I was." Justin stands in the doorway, eyeing us. "And now I'm back. Hello, Georgia."

"Mr. James."

He crosses the room to the fridge, and Nora looks on as he pulls out a bottle of beer. It's early in the day to start drinking. He pops the cap off and takes a swig. "I never see Chell around anymore. You two break up?"

Nora's cheeks turn pink, but she raises her chin.

"My life got too complicated for her."

"That's too bad. I liked Chell." He takes another pull from his bottle and sets it on the counter. "How's your brother, Georgia? He working that place down on Wheatley Street?"

"Yeah. It's a big job."

"Hear he does good work. Not that you'd know it, looking at your house. He ever thought about going independent?"

I ignore the dig, but I only do it for Nora's sake.

"Takes money to make money."

"And how's Aspera? You there every day?"

"How do you know about Aspera?" Nora asks him.

"Crossed paths a little while ago," Justin tells her. Nora's eyes flit between us, displeased, and I explain that it was before she started picking me up. At this, Justin turns to her and says, "You're doing what now?"

"She's been picking me up from work," I tell him. "And I really appreciate it."

"And how long you been doing that?" he asks Nora.

She gives him a bewildered look. "Why does it matter?"

"Who told you that you could?"

"Didn't know I needed permission."

"I don't want you on that road."

The sudden tension between them reminds me of what it was like when Mom was alive, the two of us fixing for a fight, that split second before one of us would decide to strike, because one of us always would, both of us too stubborn to back down. I step back. Nora notices, says, "Go wait for me in my room, Avis. Upstairs. The very end of the hall. I'll be there soon." What's in her eyes is something I haven't seen since that day she was asking me to lie down in the woods and show her the last way the world knew Ashley.

Please.

I nod and leave the room to Justin hissing: "It's not *safe* out there—" And I haven't even reached the top of the landing when their voices begin to overlap, low and furious.

Nora's bedroom door is open, sunlight streaming across its cushy white carpet. I can see her desk from here, her team sweater draped over the back of its chair. I make my way there, and then I stop suddenly, feeling a pull in the opposite direction. I turn and find myself in front of another door. It's shut tight, a handwritten sign taped to it. The uncontrolled scrawl of an angry girl who should have nothing left to hide.

STAY OUT!!!!

A shley: clothes still on the floor, a pair of lilac underwear half-hidden under the bed.

Ashley: red plaid bedsheets clashing wonderfully
with her dainty, flower-wire bedframe.

Ashley: books half-organized by cover color before she
gave up.

Ashley: a teddy bear stuffed between her bed and the
wall, like she didn't want anyone to see it, but couldn't bring
herself to throw it away.

This is the first of her things that I touch. I pick it up,
its fur matted and well loved, the printing on the tag worn
away. I run my thumb over its scratched eye—years of rough
and unprotected tumbles in the washer and dryer, maybe—
and a flash of movement startles me, sends the bear tum-
bling back to the floor and under the bed.

I let out a breath, bringing my hand to my chest as my
reflection in the mirror on her closet door does the same.
It's partway open, and what other way to take that but as an
invitation? I cross the room and use my foot to nudge it wide
enough to slip inside. It's small and overstuffed, smells clean
and bright like lemon detergent.

The door continues its slow swing open behind me as

I run my fingers over her clothes, all monochrome, moody blacks and grays. The absence of that bright, painful pink is what I notice first. It makes me think it's not her favorite color—but it's the one she died in. That terrible revelation unfurls inside me. What if I've gotten it wrong? What if Ashley wasn't a girl courting her end, prescient enough to know one day soon, she would meet it? What if she was a girl who thought she was invincible, thought she would live for-fucking-ever, and that's why, on the last day of her life, she reached into her closet for nothing special to wear?

"Hey."

Nora tiptoes in, closing the door carefully behind her. I can only assume we're doing something we shouldn't be doing, but it feels safer, breaking the rules with her. I pretend not to notice the tearstains on her cheeks, the vestiges of her fight with her father in her red eyes as she tracks my tour of what remains of Ashley's life.

The heart-shaped mirror above Ashley's desk has been turned into a beautiful collage, pictures of her and her friends—Liv in most of them—torn and glued over the glass, a love letter to the glittering parts of the mess of her life, and I'm relieved that as young as she was, as angry and lost as she was, she could still see the glitter.

On closer inspection, almost small enough to miss—but placed very intentionally at the heart's center—is a picture of Mrs. James.

"Why did your mom leave?"

"She thought my dad was cheating."

I turn to her. "Was he?"

"I think so. Signs were there. Out late. Not where he said he'd be. I think she might've found something in his texts. Once I heard her say, when he came home, that he—he 'stank of sex.'" She clenches her jaw. "Anyway, that's why she left him. I don't know why she left us."

"Hate that for you," I say.

"Think it'd be easier if she was dead like yours?"

I shrug. "Comes with its own baggage."

"I miss her," Nora says.

I miss mine too, I think suddenly, in spite of myself.

"She was gone longer than—"

Nora stops. She runs her hands down her face. There's the tiniest sway to her, her shoulders slumped, and in the stark light of Ashley's room, the circles under her eyes are so pronounced, I don't know how I didn't see them before. I remember asking her what feels like a lifetime ago, *Who's looking after you?*

No one, still.

"What?"

"Ashley. She was missing longer than people know."

"What do you mean?"

"Before she died, she was so off the rails . . . it felt like it was all building to something bad, and I was the only one who could see it. I kept trying to get her to talk to me, and she wouldn't. That whole last month, she kept telling me— she kept telling me I was 'the untouchable one.' But she didn't get that every time she tore something apart, I was the one who had to put it back together." She wipes furiously at her eyes, but the tears come anyway. "So she'd go sometimes, disappear for a night with her friends, usually Livvy, and she'd turn up the next morning but it was never—*never*—more than a night. This time, she was gone for two days."

"That's what Tyler said," I say. "She'd been missing a couple days."

"That was two days from when Dad called it in, which was two days *after* she left. Four altogether." She stares at me. "He fucked up, Avis. He waited too long. He kept telling me it was her usual bullshit, but I knew it wasn't, and I was the only one looking for her the first two days. She was dead for forty-eight hours, but those first two days, she was alive and it was only me out there looking. She was alive then and—"

Alive then and what?

What happened in those two days?

The bruise.

That bruise.

"What you saw downstairs—how he's been? It's because he's so goddamn guilty. You heard him. 'It's not safe out there.' Like he knows anything. He doesn't know shit. The only reason he's been sobering up enough to look into this is because he wants to prove it's not his fault. And I feel like I'm doing it just to prove it is."

She's trembling, I can see it, and everything I want to do in response is touching her, stilling her enough to give her some kind of peace. I move cautiously toward her, and I get close enough that I can see her grief, map it, the unhealed, ragged borders of it.

"I'm so tired, Avis—and I'm so—"

"Hey," I say.

"And I'm so *sad.*"

"Come here," I tell her.

She shakes her head. I say it again, but she doesn't want to hear me, burying her face in her hands, and I don't know what to do about a girl who has made her pain a fortress. I reach out and put my hands over hers, feeling the flinch of her, her resistance, as I slowly pull them away.

Nora: her eyes wild, Ashley in them, and there's nothing I can do.

Nora: her mouth opening, closing, no words inside her, and there's nothing I can do.

I bring my hands to her cheeks.

"It's gonna be okay," I tell her.

She feels the lie of it as much as I do, and it pushes us nearer to each other, dares us to stand against it, but Nora can't do it anymore. She half-collapses into me, pressing her face against my shoulder, and she is so tired, and she is so sad.

"Nora," I whisper because it's the only thing I can think to say that isn't a promise the world will break. *Nora.* I wrap my arms around her, cupping her head with my hand while she clings onto me and cries, her sobs filling the room, and beyond them, the heavy sound of her father's footsteps in the hall.

idan Archer leaves Aspera in the early hours of a gray, overcast morning.

It's not information I'm supposed to know, but I find it out when I pass the executive corridor on the way to my office. The elevator doors open, and I stop to look because when those doors open, there's always something to see.

The sight of him brings the afterburn of booze to the back of my throat, and I force myself to breathe through it until the honeyed scent of the lodge reclaims me. He wears a charcoal-gray suit, paired with a black T-shirt and shoes. His dark sunglasses give his face an uncanny valley quality, more carved from plastic than ever, and his eyes are locked on his phone, minuscule in his large hands, and I remember the feel of them on me, the way he made so much of me fit into his palms. I fight the impulse to run, remembering what Cleo told me: *I* had *him*.

I just didn't know it yet.

The day you do, a whole world is going to open up for you.

I steady myself so that what Aidan Archer sees when he finally notices me is the girl who noticed him first. He smiles and puts his phone away, taking off his glasses.

And the way he looks at me . . .

"LA calling," he says, smiling, his teeth a dazzling white. "I'm sorry I'm leaving before we could finish what we started—but this won't be the last you see of me. I'll be back."

I give him an almost bored look. "But who knows where I'll be by then?"

He raises his eyebrow, no indication he heard my voice falter.

"Well okay," he says, still smiling. "Okay then." He dips his hand into his jacket's inside pocket and holds out a business card, a number on it. "My personal line. Direct. You have a lot of promise, Georgia. Let's not lose touch. Maybe there's something I can do for you."

As soon as it's in my grasp, he uses it to tug me closer, bending down to give me a swift, if not sloppy, kiss on the cheek. It happens so fast panic has only just begun to seize me by the time he's already halfway gone. I watch after him, running my thumb over the pebbled texture of the business card. When he's out of sight, I press it to my lips, closing my eyes to a feeling that's like nothing I've ever felt before and all I can think is *I have to tell her.*

I had him.

Now I know.

The sky is clearing when I reach the cabin, the miserable-looking clouds retreating, a diamond in the light. And it *is* shining for me.

I knock on the front door.

No one comes.

I knock again and still, no one comes.

But I know she's here because when Cleo's close, it's like that crackle in the air, that sizzle of electricity against your skin before the first strike of lightning, and then—release. It's a moment that demands something of all of your senses and pulls you so deeply inside it, you can't remember a time there was never a storm.

I grip the door handle.

. . . Locked or unlocked?

I turn it slowly.

It opens for me.

The cabin is silent.

"Cleo?" My eyes follow the winding staircase to the second floor, imagining their bedroom there. I wonder if that's where she is, if I have the nerve to find her in it. Upstairs feels sacred. I hear movement down the hall off the living room. "Cleo?"

And then another sign of life, from that same place.

I tiptoe toward it, past several closed doors until I reach the one at the very end of the hall. It's open, sunlight streaming from it. I peer inside. Two Eames lounge chairs in front of a glass wall face the deck. There's a hot tub there, pointed toward the woods, what looks to be a gentle slope down to a small ravine. Cleo's presence reveals itself to me in pieces around the room: her heels scattered just past the threshold, kicked off. Black silk joggers and a black silk shirt like an ink stain on the floor. A black-and-red—at this, my heart skips a beat—lace thong and matching balconette bra. I bring my hand to my chest, tracing the outline of my plain white push-up. From the clothes, my eyes travel back to the window, and as if she simply materialized from thin air, Cleo is there.

Naked.

I take an apologetic, almost shamed step back, hovering at the room's entrance, and it reminds me of a long time ago, when I thought the sight of a beautiful woman should never be for me . . . before I realized the sight of a beautiful woman could be more for me than anyone.

I know I should leave her to this moment I was never invited into, but I'm afraid it will give me away, so I squeeze my eyes shut instead.

Except I want to see.

When I open my eyes again, she's there, as she was.

The stillness of her makes me wonder if she knows she's not alone.

That she's here, with me.

Her skin glows in the morning light, the sun loving her

up. I'm so overwhelmed by her, how anyone so perfect could be made so real in front of me, that I can only take her in little by little, starting with her red-polished toes, and then, as my eyes wander the path of her legs, I feel a warmth between my own.

A wiry tuft of hair.

Here, she's beautiful too.

The curve of her hips.

The way my palms tingle, imagining the curve of her hips.

Her breasts are exquisite, everything about the way they look a suggestion of how they might feel, and I can't help but imagine that: the gentle rise and fall of them as she breathes, the soft promise of them pressed against someone else.

Me.

My breath catches as she raises her hands to push her hair from her face before stepping into the hot tub, allowing me an unobstructed view of her incredible ass. She moves so gracefully and the way she does reveals new secrets about her: the announcement of muscles in her back and arms as she eases herself into the bubbling water . . .

She raises her face to the sky, and I feel so—

"Georgia," a voice says softly behind me, and my stomach drops. I turn slowly. Matthew's at the opposite end of the hall, his hands in his pockets, studying me. He knows what I've seen. He'd know it from the blush of my cheeks and the way I'm wearing my heartbeat right outside of my body. He knows how I feel about it.

He extends his hand, gesturing me to him.

"Let's go back to the lodge."

I can't look at him, not even when we're outside and the

chill summer air bites away my blush. The pace he sets for
us is more leisurely than the break I took allows, more leisurely than I'd like because I'm so mortified. I feel like I
should explain myself, but I don't know how.

I say, "Matthew, I—" and he interrupts me, kindly.

"Don't worry your head about it."

"How did you two meet?" I finally dare to look at him.
There's an easy expression on his face, and my question has
elicited a small smile.

"Her daddy was a member a long time. He died a few
years back." He looks skyward. "So she came to Aspera one
day—it was his birthday—and I came down for the well
wishes and our eyes met over the cake and Cleo's got a way,
hasn't she? And a will, and a strength. It was unlike anything I'd ever known before. And the life she's had, Georgia, the way she's been passed around, it's not my story to
tell, but . . ."

He trails off, his memories taking him to places that can
only lie between what Cleo has told me and all she hasn't.
And then I frown slightly, remembering the way she stood in
my house, the way she looked when she saw it . . .

Members don't live in places like the one she said she
grew up in.

"I thought she was—I mean, that she wasn't . . . well off.
That she was . . ."

Like me.

"She tell you that?" I nod. He gives a low, impressed
whistle. "I'll be damned. She *does* trust you." It turns my
insides fizzy, like champagne. "It's all a little less straightforward than that. Cleo was the result of what polite company

calls a . . . dalliance. And her mother wasn't—well. Again, it's not mine to tell. When that situation became untenable, she tracked down her father. And he was something entirely different." He clears his throat. "Anyway, long story short: she came here, we fell in love, she uncomplicated my life, and I swore I'd spend it looking out for her. I've been looking out for her ever since. It all seems to happen for a reason, doesn't it?"

We round the bend, the lodge looming gloriously ahead. I'll never tire of that sight.

"Just like you finding me on the road," I say. "And her finding me after."

He looks at me fondly.

"I'll look out for you too, Georgia. We both will."

He guides us around the front—not the back—and God, it's something entering Aspera with him, the staff rising to answer to him even if there's no question he's asked. And it's not just *Mr. Hayes,* they move to—it's me. With Matthew, like this, I'm suddenly *Ms. Avis.* More than staff. And the cadence with which they greet me, the importance they infuse into my name . . . that's a sound I can see myself chasing for the rest of my life, no matter what I turn out to be. We step into the lobby, and I'm so heady from our talk, it takes me a moment to register the ugly interruption marring the landscape. Justin James stands near the concierge, and it feels like every day he spends on this earth ages him a decade. The busted capillaries across his face, his bloodshot eyes.

"Mr. James," Matthew calls when we reach him. He holds his hand out and Justin stares at it before he remembers what he's supposed to do. "How are you doing? You here for a round?"

"No," Justin says. "I wanted to talk to you. Ask you some questions about—" He pauses when he realizes I'm standing next to Matthew. "Georgia."

"Mr. James."

Matthew touches my arm.

"Why don't you head on back to your office, Georgia."

I nod, flustered, and wait until I'm out of sight before I text Nora.

Your dad's here, I tell her.

She tells me to find out why.

"Come in."

Matthew's voice sounds frayed, enough to give me pause, a marked difference from this morning. When I open his office doors, the room is dark, windows shuttered, the light overhead adjusted to a point slightly past twilight. I peer into the dim. He's hunched over his desk, his hands at his forehead. He straightens when he sees me, manages a smile, but can't maintain the charade. He grimaces, closing his eyes, and, with his eyes closed, asks what he can do for me. The question agitates him, the sound of himself a further assault on his senses. Maybe I should ask about Justin another time. I wonder if this is the result of his visit.

"Headache?" I ask quietly.

"Garden variety. It'll pass."

When I reach his desk, he's still as anything, breathing shallowly out through his mouth and inhaling deeply through his nose. He winces suddenly, the lines of his forehead drawn together. He needs more than deep breathing and the dark.

"Want me to get you something for it?"

"That—" He exhales. "Would be wonderful. Ask Kel. He'll know what I need."

But I know something he needs that Kel couldn't possibly. I move closer and grasp his hand, turning it slowly over, palm side up. His eyebrows jump a little, startled.

"Georgia—"

His hands are softer than I imagined they'd be. I press my thumb and index finger into that space between his own and try to remember how it was she did this. Mom. Held a gentle pressure there, made small, deliberate circles in my skin. I draw one slowly with my thumb, then another.

"Georgia, what are you doing?" Matthew asks.

I explain I'm doing for him what my mother did for me when I had bad headaches. That it's all about pressure points, or it's supposed to be, and that hopefully the circles I'm tracing in his skin will pull tension from those overcrowded spaces inside his mind and give him room to think again. He opens his eyes and looks at me, astonishment in them where pain used to be.

"We'll look out for each other," I tell him.

Nora waits at Aspera's gate, her eyes on the sideview, seeking me out. I see my arrival on her face, and there's something about being anticipated by a girl like her. It's so satisfying, it could be the entire point of my day.

As soon as I get in the car, she asks if I found out what her dad was doing. I pause and in that second before I answer, witness the subtle way she steels herself, constantly on guard against a world that's already hurt her too much.

"That exhibition game you played after Matthew started sponsoring the volleyball team?" Nora frowns, not following, but she nods. "Aspera hires a photographer for resort events and it all goes into their archives. He just wanted to know if they had any pictures."

"You think he was looking for someone in the photos?" She mulls it over, then makes a frustrated noise. "But *who*? God, who does he think he's looking for?"

"I got to look at the photos, Nora . . . I think he just wanted to see her again."

Matthew showed them to me, stepped away from the glare of his computer screen while he waited for the pills to kick in, and I studied them, hoping to find some kind of clue to bring back to Nora. Ashley and Justin, sitting on the sidelines beside each other, Cleo and Matthew behind the two of them, all of them captured through the frenzied blur of the girls' volleyball team doing their best against one another. Ashley was sullen, her arms crossed, her eyes on what must have been Nora, an impatient pucker to her mouth— but still so incredibly alive.

It was the physical space between her and Justin that gave me pause. The way she held herself from him. I couldn't believe how much she seemed to hate him, and wondered if he'd known it then, or saw it for the first time today. I think he must have known. I think he must have been willing to risk seeing it laid so plain, because I have a feeling those were the last photographs taken of the two of them together.

"Oh," Nora says quietly, and at first, I think the sadness of it will bury her, but she squeezes her eyes shut, and buries it. "Have you checked out the treads?"

"Not yet," I tell her, and then, before she can get on me about it, "I did some digging, and I found out Aspera has one big delivery day a month and that's next Monday. And it turns out when Ashley—when her body was found, that was a delivery day. I'm going to check then."

"Good thinking." The way she says it makes my chest swell because there it is—the first time I've ever impressed her. She starts the car. Pauses. "I got ahold of Liv. I'm meeting her at Devore Park after I drop you off unless—"

"I'm going with you."

She smiles to herself. Or maybe for me.

. . .

Devore Park is bustling, parents and kids making the most of what's left of the summer. They'll be tearing down and replacing the decrepit playground equipment in the fall— old metal slides and rusted swings with cracked plastic seats—for something safer. Adults complained when it was announced, as though it was a bad thing to rob their children of the same sharp edges that made them who they are because just look at them: they turned out fine.

Liv hasn't shown yet. Nora and I wait for her at one of the picnic tables, our backs against it. I close my eyes and let the summer sounds soak in: kids laughing, shrieking to the low murmured warnings of their parents. *Don't hit your sister. Stay where I can see you.* Water slaps against the concrete at the splash pad not too far away. I open my eyes. There's a cluster of girls by a food truck, all of them about Ashley's age, sharing one small container of fries. Ashley should be there in the thick of it all, and so I imagine it: her in her pink shirt, holding court. Happy and alive. *Stay where I can see you.*

"Hey, Avis," Nora says suddenly. She's staring at her running shoes, gripping the bench. "Whenever I think of you, it feels nostalgic, like this . . . vintage movie in my head. Like everything we're doing now is worth remembering." She looks at me, squinting against the sun, gives me a crooked smile. "I just don't want it to be all sad things, you know?"

I give her a small smile back. Her hazel eyes are more green in this light than I've ever seen them. They're beautiful. I lean forward and press my lips gently against hers, a kiss as soft and sweet as I can make it. It's fleeting, but right. A kiss to claim, a kiss you feel after it happens in the hum of your blood and the beat of your heart, in a world you can no longer sense above or below you and all that's left to anchor you to it might be cupping her face in your hands and kissing her again and again and again—or maybe you'll both just drift away together, and that's how it's supposed to be.

She presses her fingers to her mouth, like she can't quite believe it.

Now kiss me back, I think.

And she does.

She leans forward and the return is just as soft, and just as sweet, but she stays there, brings her hand to my cheek to keep herself there, and her mouth opens against mine, inviting me to her. There's something so sure about the way she kisses, a girl who has known other girls, who has understood more than just the shape and desire of her own body. She moves even closer, letting me feel the warmth of her, stopping just long enough for me to understand how untenable it is to be kissing her one moment and then not the next. She rests her forehead against mine and says, absurdly shy, "You were my first crush."

You were my first kiss, I think—

But then I realize it's not true.

I close my eyes and while they're closed, I feel Nora's attention shift from me to something else. I open my eyes and the girl I recognize as Liv stands about five feet from us. She regards us, embarrassed, hands clasped in front of her. She's in a pair of denim overall shorts, a white cropped tee underneath, her braids pulled back into a ponytail. I think of her in the picture with Ashley, all motion blur and joy, and how robbed she is of it now.

I think maybe when a girl dies the way Ashley did, we all do a little.

"Liv." Nora rises to greet her. They hug. Liv falls into it and I remember what Nora said about her. A good kid who liked being bad with Ashley. I get to my feet, hovering outside the two of them. Liv apologizes for not coming to the funeral. Nora says, "It's okay, it's okay, it was no place for anyone. Not even her."

Liv glances at me a half second after they part.

"I thought you were with Chell."

Nora shakes her head, waving me closer.

"This is Georgia Avis."

"Hi," Liv says.

"Hi," I say back.

"I can't stay long," she tells Nora, but it sounds more like she doesn't want to.

"Right," Nora says, nodding. "Of course."

She goes into her pocket and pulls out the picture, handing it over. Liv isn't expecting it, and the surprise of it seems cruel for what happens next: her hands start to shake, pulling the paper. She presses it to her chest, to either get the shaking to stop or protect her precious cargo. Her eyes fill with tears.

"Ashley," she whispers.

"Liv, what's Hulick?" Nora asks her.

Liv starts to cry.

Y ou have to—" Liv stops.

She sits opposite us at the picnic table, methodically picking at her baby-blue nail polish. It flakes off, carried away by the breeze. I sense Nora's patience waning, but she doesn't push. Maybe she's scared of the thing she needs to know. Maybe this excruciating in-between space is the better one to occupy because whatever information Liv has, it can't be good.

Nothing so achingly unsaid could ever be good.

Liv finally draws a breath and gathers herself. "Promise I won't get in trouble and you won't tell my parents and that after you know this, it's not mine anymore."

Nora presses her hands flat on the table.

"I promise, Livvy."

"It's Hulick Ranch."

As soon as it's out of her mouth, a fury flashes across her face, so pure and so intense, I swear I feel it running through my veins. She tamps it down with an expertise that disturbs me. I imagine her anger resurfacing at various points in her life, and in the cold aftermath of whatever it produces, she'll remember its source: when she was thirteen years old, her best friend was raped and killed.

She makes finger quotes. "'Ranch.'"

"What is that?" I ask.

"Look it up."

Nora unlocks her phone, fingers flying across its screen. I know when she finds it before she says it. It's her eyes—no dawning realization, but a dimming one. Something terrible.

She hands her phone to me.

Hulick Ranch: A Residential Treatment Facility for Teens

"Ashley found the emails on your dad's laptop. It was all arranged and paid for. He was sending her there this summer . . . if you can call a kidnapping that," Liv says, while I skim Hulick's "About" page, a bright design with playful fonts. It could almost sell itself as a glorified summer camp for teens *who have lost their way and need a helping hand to get back on track,* and *require firm boundaries and innovative disciplinary strategies . . .*

Liv tells us she and Ashley researched it. Found horror stories on subreddits. Watched hysterical YouTube videos of kids talking about being kidnapped in the night, yelling for their parents, who, conveniently, found someplace else to be while their children were forcibly ripped from their homes and taken to this fucked-up boot camp. There's a TikTok community of #HulickSurvivors who share videos about their time in, about being denied basic human rights for minor infractions. Of being screamed at by counselors. The closer I look at the website's gallery, the more I can see it. It doesn't look like a ranch, but a facility, concrete and gray. There are no pictures of the rooms. It's in the middle of the Virginian wilderness, no easy way in or out, boasting limited outside influence by virtue of no internet and no cell phones allowed . . .

Nora buries her head in her hands, twisting strands of her hair tightly around her fingers.

"She wasn't going no matter what," Liv says. "She was going to get away. She just needed someone to help her . . . and then she found someone who would."

Nora looks up sharply. *"Who?"*

"I don't know." Liv crosses her arms. "She said the less I knew the better, in case you and your dad tried to find her and drag her back. She was really clear she—she was never coming back. I thought it was a man, before I knew for sure. She was like . . . floating on it, like how she got when she had a crush—" Nora winces. "Anyway, she said this guy was going to take care of her—not just help her get out, but look after her, and for as long as she needed. Ashley said he told her . . ." Liv takes a deep breath. "That she wasn't going to have to hurt anymore . . . that she wasn't going to have to struggle. The two of them came up with a plan."

"Disappear together," Nora guesses, her voice flat.

"Yeah, pretty much."

"Why didn't you tell anyone this?"

"Seriously, Nora? You know what they say about Ashley . . . you hear how they talk about her, even now—how what happened was all her fault . . . you know what would happen to *me* if everyone could blame me for it?" She stares at Nora. "You know." Nora flushes, chastened, because Liv is right. "And besides . . ." Liv shrugs, tearing up again. "It ended up being the last promise I could keep for her."

It reminds me of Tyler. Mom.

"You're going to tell me everything now. Everything you know. *Everything.*"

"It's not a lot. She kept it real tight. Every so often, I'd ask. The closer we'd get, I'd ask. She'd tell me not to worry because she wasn't worried. And then there was a party." Liv closes her eyes and takes herself there. "Ashley really wanted to go to this party. It was the night Hulick was supposed to come for her."

"Wait." Nora raises her hand. "What day? What day were they supposed to grab her and go? You know which one exactly?"

Liv's answer is another blow, no matter how much Nora expects it, and looking at her, I wonder how much more she can take.

"That's why my dad didn't report her missing right away," she whispers to me. "He thought she was at Hulick. That they'd come in the night and taken her to Hulick." She smashes her fist against the table. "Fuck." Again. Liv flinches. *"Fuck!"*

"What about the party, Liv?" I ask. "What happened there?"

"I pregamed hard. It's kinda blurry." Liv doesn't meet our eyes. "Anyway, we got to this house and it was nice enough, but the people there were kinda . . . older? Like . . if I hadn't been so wasted, I might have been scared."

"Jesus Christ, Liv," Nora says.

"We were there a few hours . . . the last time I saw Ashley, she was getting into a car."

"What kind of car?"

"I'm not sure. It was dark. It could have been black or blue. There was this . . . it was like a cross? But it had a star in it . . . it's hard to describe. It was hanging from the mirror . . . it was gold . . . like an ornament? And there was this man inside. He had dark hair. I think he was in his twenties. I didn't get a good look. But maybe I don't remember him right . . . that cross or whatever it was, it was so weird to me, though. It stuck."

"You talk to her before she drove away?"

"No. I saw all that as they were leaving. I ran . . . I was calling her name because I knew—I knew it was happening right then and I wanted to . . . and she just . . . she just went." Liv looks stricken at the memory. "I wanted to say goodbye."

"Do you remember a cross?" Nora asks me. "The car that hit you?"

"I don't think so. But I think I remember less than Liv."

"Where was this party?" Nora asks her.

"I . . . don't know," Liv says, and Nora makes another exasperated sound. "I was so fucked up, Nora. Ashley literally had to walk me there." The polish on her index finger and thumb is gone now. "The house had these planters mounted on the side of it . . . three of them. Little upside-down metal umbrellas. They had purple flowers inside." I draw a sharp breath in and open my mouth. A voice inside me says, *Wait*, and I close it again. Neither of them notice, Nora's eyes are on Liv, and Liv shrinks under their intensity. "That's everything. Then she was gone. And then she was dead."

"It's not everything," Nora says. "How did you get home?"

The question catches Liv off guard.

"I don't remember," she admits, and Nora shakes her head, disgusted, and I don't think it's at Liv but Liv takes on the shame of that reaction regardless, and I wish, so desperately, I could take it from her. "But I was fine. I'm here, right? I'm fine."

"No," Nora says. "You're not."

Liv's eyes fill with fresh tears that spill down her cheeks. "Well, I don't care, because I wouldn't change it. We went to that party and we danced and we danced and she was *so* happy, Nora. I never saw her that happy since before your mom left." Liv swipes a hand across her face and that flash of anger returns, lightning in her eyes, and this time it doesn't go away. "Ashley called it our last summer. She said it was gonna be the best of our lives."

"Was it?" I ask.

Liv looks away from us and nods.

on't say anything," Nora tells me as we cross the park. "I need to—"

She never finishes. I bring my hand to my throat. Somehow, my necklace got turned around. I pull the teardrop to the front as I glance behind me. Liv is still at the picnic table, watching a pair of little girls sprint past. The sight of it puts her palm against her heart.

She's still crying.

When we get to Nora's car, we sit silently inside of it. Minutes go by, and then she slaps the wheel over and over and over again. When she's done, she's breathless, panting, her face splotched red. I reach for her and she holds her hand up.

"Please," she whispers. "Don't."

I lower my hand.

She's shaking, keys jangling in her fist as she jams them in the ignition. Her lower lip trembles. She bites down on it so hard. We leave the park, and she takes the streets faster than she should, and at first, I think she'll drop me off at my house, but she pulls up to her own, parking crookedly in her driveway, and before I can say anything, she says, "Stay here," and undoes her seat belt and gets out. She storms across the lawn, into her house.

She leaves the front door open.

By the time I get out of the car, I hear the screaming.

Nora, screaming.

"You killed her! This is your fault!"

I don't need to see it. I'm not supposed to see it. But I can imagine it: Nora, on her knees, and Justin, above her, tears streaming down his face, the sight of his daughter's anguish finally forcing him into the shape of fatherhood—

But it's too late.

It's always going to be too late.

The violets are dying, their petals curled from the sun. If not for their planters, nothing about the house they belong to would distinguish itself from the two next to it; three bungalows with gray vinyl siding all in a row. They're just like Liv said. Three small decorative umbrellas, made from metal, mounted on the wall next to the front door. I knock and wait, and I think of Nora, think about how this is something I'm doing for her, not something I'm hiding from her. If there's anything about Ashley here, I'll tell her, talking around the parts I'm entitled to keep to myself.

When the door finally opens, I don't expect the middle-aged Asian woman who answers—but there's something about her tired eyes that seems to expect me. She's pretty, her hair cut into a lob. She wears a white, oversized work shirt like a dress, pairing it with fire-engine red sandals. Maybe his wife? He didn't mention a wife.

"God," she says softly. "I thought I'd seen the last of you girls."

I blink. "I'm sorry. Is Ryan here? I just need to talk to him."

"There's no Ryan living here."

I step back and take another look at the house, just to be sure I haven't gotten it wrong, somehow. But those are the planters. This is the place.

"I don't understand," I say.

She tells me to come in.

Her name is Allison—Ali.

She sits me down at her kitchen table and asks if I want anything to drink. I don't, but I accept a small glass of water anyway. It's a relief to be inside, because I remember this too. The vintage green and chrome dinette set. The pale yellow curtains. Past the kitchen, a hallway that opens up into a large living room that leads down another hall, a small room at the end of it.

That room, I know best of all.

"I'm not here to make any trouble for him," I say. "I promise. I'm not looking for the money. I know he was just hired to take the photos. I know he didn't have anything to do with the upsell. I want to ask him about something—"

"Look." Ali sits across from me. "Georgia?" I nod, belatedly wishing I had given her any other name. "That was all a scam—"

"I know, but I need to talk to Ryan."

"He's not here."

"Do you know where he is?"

She sighs, staring at her own glass of water, a wedge of lemon on the rim, and takes the kind of sip that makes me think she wishes it were booze.

"I just want to be sure of some things," she says. "Okay?"

I swallow. "Okay."

"You got 'discovered' at the mall by a modeling agency, right? By a man who claimed to be an agent?" My grip tightens around my glass. I nod. "And this agent told you to pay them for the pictures they needed to represent you, is that right?"

"Yes."

"And you came here and you got your pictures taken?"

"Yeah." It's a relief to hear her say that, at least. This *is* the place. "Ryan took them, but he wasn't part of it. He was a professional freelancer . . ."

That's why the man at the mall said the pictures cost so much.

It wasn't until I looked online I realized they shouldn't have cost *that* much.

"No," she says, "he wasn't."

"He was."

He met me at the door with the camera around his neck and a smile on his face. He said I was more beautiful than he'd been told. He led me to that room at the end of the hall, and it was a muslin-covered dream, a real live set just for me, and there were lights and light boxes at all corners. Professional.

But Ali shakes her head.

"Yes, he was," I insist.

She stands and crosses the kitchen. She takes a pad of paper stuck to the fridge and grabs a pen, writes something on it. "This is the number you need to call. Ketchum Sheriff's Department. Ask for Detective Resnick." She tears it off and hands it to me.

I stare up at her. "But this isn't why I'm here."

She sighs and leans against the table, flexing her fingers across its shiny surface. There's something about the look on her face that scares me.

". . . Why do I need to call them?"

Her gaze drifts to the window.

"I wish I didn't have to be the one to tell you this," she says.

Those men, she says.

The "agent" and the "photographer."

"They work as a team."

Moving from town to town, luring—

She says this word, "luring," and it turns my insides acid . . . lured, *lured* like I'm some stupid fish on a line, but I wasn't *lured.*

—young girls with false promises of fame, fortune.

"It's a two-part operation . . ."

The hook. The photo session.

"And at the first signs of trouble, they skip town and they take—"

They take it all with them.

I bring my hand to my forehead.

"You let them use your house?"

"*Let* them?" She laughs mirthlessly. "I was out of state for over a month for a family emergency. They found out the house would be empty. They used it to help legitimize the grift. The detective told me they usually stick to motels."

"How did they know it was empty?"

"I'm a professor at KU. I assume one of my students tipped them off."

"Okay, but—" I take a deep breath. "That's not what I'm here for. I'm here to find out about a party. One of my friends got in trouble at a party here and I need to know if Ryan saw anything, heard anything—"

"I can't help you with that. They had several parties." She taps the paper she gave me, the phone number. The detective. "You should really call. They're trying to get as much information and to hear from as many victims as they can. They'll want to hear from you."

Victims?

"Look, I know I'm not getting the money back, so I don't think—"

"It's more than the money, Georgia."

"What do you mean?"

"The pictures they were taking." Ali's expression is encouraging, wants me to connect the dots, and when I only stare, she says, "Georgia, you're a minor . . ." I shake my head. She closes her eyes a long, long time. "I've said this too many times this summer." Her voice breaks. "The detective will want to talk to you and your parents about the pictures. Please call them."

"But they were just normal pictures."

"Are you sure about that?"

"They were professional," I insist.

They were special.

Beautiful.

They were me.

But there's something like pity on her face.

"You know what, I'm really sorry you got tangled up in all of this, but it's not why I'm here. I just wanted to know if he saw someone at this party—" I stand quickly, my hip glancing the table, toppling my glass to the floor. I flinch as it hits the floor and shatters, water spilling everywhere.

"Georgia—" She reaches out.

I jerk away.

"I said that's not why I'm here."

And I leave her there, staring at the pieces of broken glass, her eyes filled with tears.

set the phone on my desk, its selfie cam facing me.

I take three steps back until I'm fully in its view.

I test the voice command.

"Take my picture," I say.

The countdown begins.

The shutter releases.

I see my image, captured, before it's filed away.

We did headshots first. I remember how it felt, sitting stiffly on the small stool in front of a white backdrop, lights blinding, tilting my head this way and that, not used to being scrutinized so intently by a man for a purpose that didn't serve only himself. Because I know what it's like to be looked at too long, to be leered at, for nothing in return. This wasn't that. It wasn't. He pulled those photos up on his Mac right after, and they looked amazing compared to what they felt like to take. I could *see* it, what the man at the mall saw in me. And when you can see it, why shouldn't you believe people are who they say they are?

We took a break.

We sat at that green chrome kitchen table, and he gave me a glass of water. He told me about what it takes to be a model. He knew that no one ever told me I could be one before. He asked if I was sure it was what I wanted. The question was jarring. I didn't know what to say. I couldn't tell him I hadn't really thought about it, not even then, that the point was taking from the world whatever I could, and as far as I could take it—all it needed was to be more than what my mother told me I was worth, and that could be anything, because to her, I was nothing. But maybe it could turn out to be my calling? Or maybe: if I'd stolen four thousand dollars from my brother for this, I should be sure.

We decided to take more pictures.

Different kinds of pictures.

To be sure.

I lift my shirt slowly over my head and leave it on the floor. I pull the straps of my bra down, crossing my arms, holding myself. The straps tickle my fingertips.

"Take my picture," I say.

The phone takes my picture.

The straps, we thought, were ultimately too distracting. I pull down one of the cups and cover my breast with my palm, my nipple hardening against my hand.

"Take my picture."

Again.

I turn from the camera and slip out of my bra and then I face the lens, the pose cleaner this time, my arms holding myself, my chest still covered. I remember how mesmerized I was by the way he established this shot, how comfortable and uninhibited I felt as he did.

He talked about my body the way an artist would.

"Take my picture," I say.

I turn slowly for the side view. The profile of my breast

against my arm is perfect, the undercurve of it. People pay for breasts like these. I tilt my head back, smiling a little at the thought, letting my hair tickle the nape of my neck. I tell the phone to take my picture again. Then I try to remember how else it was. I close my eyes and part my lips.

"Take my picture."

I wriggle out of my shorts, and I sit on the bed, opening my legs wide, leaning forward, my pale peach underwear almost reading as part of my skin.

It did then too.

My right arm reaches for my left shoulder, and I see more of myself here than I showed there, my breasts bared for the camera, but I don't know how to work with light, is the thing. I don't know what a photographer knows. And I don't know how Ryan could have known if he wasn't really a photographer.

I lie across my bed, one leg up, the other outstretched. I keep one arm crossed over my chest and the other between my legs, not doing anything, just resting there, and I arch my back, and *oh* my mouth, replicating the pose in the photograph I was most sorry to lose.

"Take my picture," I whisper.

When I'm done, I pick up my phone and swipe through the photos and even these lesser, grainy approximations of what we captured at the house that day are still special. They're still me. Still the most beautiful girl I've ever seen in my life. They're not bad. Not wrong. Not some dead little girl decomposing in the woods.

Monday, at break, I slip out of my office, taking a circuitous route through the lobby, trying to stay out of members'—and Kel's—line of sight as I make my way down to Aspera's parking garage, like I promised Nora I would. It's under the lodge, and all drop-offs happen here, preventing any transport from suggesting the outside world to members and shattering the illusion. Today is delivery day, and I'm looking for a gold cross or something like it. I'm looking for a unique tread pattern: three block, one symmetrical. I need a new lead for Nora before she finds the house for herself because it would only be a waste of time—because it wasn't them. Neither of them looked like the guy Liv described. The man at the mall, bald and squat. The photographer, a lean, pretentious blond. Both of them middle-aged, their twenties long past.

That party was a pick-up point, a grim coincidence. Nothing more.

I start my investigation with the line of delivery vehicles waiting their turn at the loading doors, and it's a tricky thing to do with any amount of subtlety, but I catalogue them all and nothing turns up. I decide to double-check staff and member cars because I imagine Nora asking it of me, making sure everything is accounted for. She's been quiet since the weekend, not answering my texts. Upset about her dad.

I make my way deeper into the garage. Here, it's all concrete and metal beams, white lines painted on pavement. It smells damp, musty. The harsh lighting doesn't reach all of the garage's corners, leaving more of it to shadows than I'd like. This is the most lackluster of Aspera's offerings, but it still asserts its luxury in the cars of its members, in the gleam of their Teslas and Porsches and Ferraris and Mercedes. I run my hand along their shiny exteriors, just to know what they feel like, a little horrified at the fingerprints I leave behind.

My footsteps echo as I investigate each section, scanning rearview mirrors, mostly unadorned, and those that aren't don't have the ornament I'm looking for. I check tread after tread, my knees cracking and groaning with the repeated up-and-down of it all. I wait for that moment my heart claws up my throat, a signal that what we're meant to find has been here all along, but it never comes. It wouldn't. Staff and members were cleared.

And all this is assuming Ashley's killer is still around.

And hasn't changed out their tires by now.

I clench my jaw, trying to quell the rage rising inside me that every strange, fated moment of this summer hasn't brought us closer to justice; that the purpose of all of this has only driven home what we've lost.

And then: a noise from some far-off corner.

I whirl around.

"Hello?"

I wait a few minutes and there's nothing.

I know I heard something.

I move in that direction, and end up in the darkest part of the garage. Staff parking. The rusted-out makes and models are the majority here, more what I'm used to. Toward the end of the row though, in an almost-vulgar contrast, sits a series of incredibly fancy sedans. I spot the blue BMW Kel drove me home in.

And then, at the farthest end of the farthest row, I see a light.

"Hello?" I call again.

Still no answer.

I follow the light until I'm standing in front of a gorgeous black Audi—is this the Audi Kel talks about?—its passenger side left open, the source. How recently it was left this way, I can't tell. I bend down and peer inside, and it reveals nothing. The treads have nothing for me either. The roar of an engine and the whine of a delivery truck as it slowly eases up to the loading doors reaches my ears. I check my phone. I'm out of time.

I close the Audi's door and head back up to the lodge.

N ora, waiting for me. Even in her silence, I knew I could count on that. She leans against her car with her arms crossed. I wave, but she doesn't wave back. Her eyes are pointed firmly upward. I bring my fingers to my lips, feeling the absence of her kiss as much as the memory of it. I want to kiss her again. I want her to kiss me again.

"Hey," I say.

She lowers her gaze and I'm stunned by the sight of her. The state of her calls to something deep inside me: the want to fix, the need to hold. Her eyes are dull and I'm desperate to spark light in them. I reach for her. She recoils and I realize—something else has happened. Or something that's already happened has gotten worse.

"I found the house," she says.

"What?"

"The one Liv was talking about. The party. The umbrella planters outside."

I step back. "You did?"

"Yeah. It's on Pavao Avenue. Let's go."

"I—"

"Or maybe you've already been," she says, and the look she gives me hollows me out. She laughs, running a hand through her hair, tangly and unkempt, reminding me of the first time she showed on my doorstep. "I drove around the city all weekend. All day and night, just looking until I found it. And you knew. You'd already been. And you didn't tell me."

"Because it turned out to be nothing."

"Oh, really?" She pushes herself off the car and moves closer to me, but not the kind of close I want her to be. My mouth goes dry. "That's what you call two guys who set up shop in Ketchum to take sick fuck pictures of kids? Nothing?"

"Nora—"

"That's what you call two sick fucks who pack it all in and leave town *right after* my sister's murdered? Nothing?" She shakes her head in disbelief. "They have someone on this at the sheriff's department. I asked about it. You know one of those guys is wanted for sexual assault?"

"No," I say, barely audible.

"So is it still nothing?" Closer still. "You know Ashley was so fucking desperate to get out of here, there's nothing that says she didn't go to the mall and—"

"Did you see their pictures?" I ask. "Have you seen what those guys look like? Because I saw them both, and they don't look anything like Liv said. It was a dead end. If they'd matched, I would've told you—"

"Liv was wasted! She could barely remember! And who knows what else those fuckers got up to while they were here? Why were they even having those parties? Who's to say they didn't have a third guy on this, huh?" She pushes past me, knocking hard against my shoulder. I turn to her at the same time she turns back to me. "So I get to the house, and the woman was like, 'I just did this.' And I said, 'What do you mean?' And she said another girl just came by a few days ago." Nora takes a breath. "And I got this feeling and I asked her if it was you. Showed her your picture and—surprise! You knew and you didn't tell me. And *then* I kept thinking, why the fuck wouldn't Avis tell me she had a lead?"

"Because it *wasn't* one! They didn't—"

"That's not why and you know it," she says. "You didn't tell me because you fell for it. That's what Ali said. And I was thinking how before that, you'd been talking about how you got tapped by some modeling agency? And the photos you had on you when the car hit you." She taps her forehead. "Hello? They took them because they were taking them *back,* Avis! They didn't want anything that tied them to the scene! Pictures like that—what about this is not connecting, huh? Where the fuck is your head? God, what the fuck is wrong with you?"

"Nothing's wrong with me—"

"Are you really so fucking stupid—"

"I'm not—"

"What were you *thinking*?"

"He told me I was beautiful!" I explode, my voice breaking, echoing. Nora's mouth drops open. I raise my arms helplessly. "What was I supposed to think?"

"Oh my God. You really *are* that fucking stupid—"

"I'm not—"

"You kept this from me. It's the most important thing, and you kept it from me because you were too—"

"*I'm not stupid!* I'm telling you they didn't match the description! Either of them! If they had, I would have told you, Nora. I *swear*. But they didn't, so I didn't—"

I bring my palms against my eyes, trying not to cry.

"I just don't believe you," she says.

When I lower them, Nora's heading back to her car.

"Nora. Wait—"

"Nope."

"Don't make me walk that road."

She pauses, just briefly, but then she opens the door and gets in.

"Nora, please, *please* don't make me walk that road alone—"

"Bye, Avis," she says.

I turn because I don't want to see her leave without me. I haven't cleared the gate by the time she's gone. I'm crying when I reach Matthew and Cleo's cabin. A gunshot sounds in the distance. It feels close. I test the door.

Locked.

Did you leave the door open?

In the waning light, the flaking blue siding of our house takes on a grayish pall, and the half-rotted roof looks diseased. But it's the inside door flung wide open that unnerves me the most. Through the screen, I can make out the hall, half in shadows like it wouldn't be if someone were home. If someone were home, that door would be open and the light would be on. But the front door is open and the light is off. "Shambala" cuts through the air and I recoil, the song playing in my hand, sounding my brother's response.

I changed that sound.

I know I did.

No. It's open?

Yes.

Wait for me, Tyler texts back, but by then, I'm already halfway up the walk because I don't want to let him turn this into something it's not, because I had to walk Ashley's road home, alone, and I can still feel the death of it on me and now I want to bury myself. I did something terrible: when I got to the cross, I tried to take it down. It was stuck too far into the dirt, so I started kicking it, and when I heard the first *crack,* my blood turned to ice.

I thought I could feel her eyes on me.

I left it there, splintered.

I pull the screen door open, and as soon as I step into the house, I know I'm not alone, and my heart leaps, hopeful, because if it's not Tyler's mistake, it could only be Nora's apology. She found the door open and she's waiting for me. It takes a long time to walk from Aspera to Ketchum; time enough for her to realize she was wrong.

I'd forgive her.

"Nora," I say, stepping into the kitchen.

But it's not Nora.

The sound of ragged breathing fills the air. He sits, hunched over the table, his back to me. The sight of him is less surprising than it should be. A horrible thought occurs: Nora told him everything and now he's come to tell me what he really thinks of me, and more.

"Mr. James?"

His shoulders rise and fall as he attempts a deep, steadying breath in.

"Mr. James?" He doesn't respond. I step forward tentatively. His shirtsleeve is torn, a slash of red on his arm. My eyes follow the red to the drops it leaves on the floor. Blood. "Mr. James, I—"

"I'm tired."

He sounds like he's at the end of himself.

"I'm going to call Nora," I tell him.

"No," he says. "I have to tell you something."

I can't decide if he's been drinking. I round the table slowly and stop at his profile. His face is gray, tinged with green, his clothes rumpled, dirty. He looks like the kind of hell that has nothing to do with booze.

"I didn't—" He rubs a hand down his sweaty face. I reach into my pocket for my phone. His head snaps up, his eyes startlingly clear. Angry. "Don't."

I freeze. "I think I should call someone to help you."

"There's no one who can help me . . . I can't—I can't protect myself anymore." He takes another breath, and it's so shallow, a struggle. "I ran and now there's nowhere left to run. I'm not here for help, Georgia."

"Then what are you here for?"

"I never taught her fear. Never taught her where not to go. I didn't think—I thought—we look out for each other . . . and then I couldn't do it anymore, I had to . . ." He shakes his head.

"You didn't think what?"

"It's all above you."

He's out of his fucking mind.

"Okay."

"Your mother." His eyes lock on mine, and those two words—*your mother*—send me reeling, so impossibly wrong coming out of his mouth it makes me more afraid than anything else has. "Your mother wasn't better than me."

I swallow. "She didn't think she was." She never thought that.

"Oh, but she did. She said . . ."

I edge forward, carefully trying to clear the table, because after the table is the hall, and maybe I could get to my room and lock myself in until help comes.

But part of me wants to hear this.

What did my mother say?

Why was she saying it to him?

"She said, 'One day the world's going to stop turning for you.'" He stares at me, his face eerily blank. "And maybe she's right . . . and maybe that time's come. But it doesn't stop turning, does it?" I don't say anything. "Does it, Georgia?" He slaps his hand on the table. I flinch. "Does it?"

"No."

"And she can't stop it now."

"I don't know what you mean."

"She can't save you now."

"What?"

She can't save you now.

My heart pounds.

Get out, a voice inside me whispers.

Go.

I keep moving toward the hall as Justin calmly tracks my progress.

When he comes into full view, my eyes travel to his hands.

His hands.

One of them holding—

Holding—

"Oh my God."

I make a break for it, and then he's on top of me, crashing into my back, saying, "Wait, wait, wait, wait, *wait!*" The pure force of him sends us both lurching forward, and my head connects with the doorframe, turning the world red, unfathomable. I scream. I scream, and then we're both on the ground. *She can't save you now.* I struggle underneath him, screaming still, and he covers my mouth. I yell under his palm, choking on my voice. He says, "Listen to me, no, listen—"

I moan, tears hot on the side of my face. I can smell him, us. Blood. He's bleeding. I'm bleeding.

I think of Ashley.

Ashley.

"George? *George!*"

Tyler, red and blurry, and here, oh God, he's here. Justin scrambles off me, and I curl onto my side, clutching my stomach, coughing, and I can hear them, the fight, and it occurs to me that this might not be one Tyler can win, and then what will happen to us both? I have to help. I claw my way back to the nightmare, fumbling to my feet, only to end up on my knees. I dig my hands into the floor, nails catching on the tile.

There's blood on the tile.

"George," Tyler says, and he's frantically putting his hands on my shoulders, my face, making me look at him, pulling me to him, pulling me close to him, one arm around me while the other goes for his phone. I try to focus on the warmth of my brother. The safety of my brother. The familiar scent of cigarette smoke. The kitchen slowly takes form.

Justin, gone.

My eyes drift to the glossy photograph at my feet, the one he had with him. The girl stretched across the length of it. I take in her long, perfect legs, reaching for the smooth plane of her perfect stomach, extending toward the soft swell of her perfect breasts. Her perfect blond curls spill over her shoulders, haloing the peaches-and-cream complexion of her perfect face.

Her pretty little lips form a perfect pink—

Oh.

PART TWO

They find him forty-eight hours later.
A motel outside the city.
My bike in his trunk.
A note: *I'm sorry.*
A bullet in his head.

t's quiet now.

I sit on the step and stare out at the street.

First, it was chaos, media everywhere. News crews camped out in front of the Jameses' house, the sheriff's department, and the road, shaping explosive headlines and status updates around us: *Ketchum police officer rapes and murders youngest daughter. Ketchum Sheriff's Department devastated; sheriff's deputy was an upstanding officer with an impeccable record.* They kept lookout for shell-shocked faces, swarming anyone they thought they could get a quote from. Burned us away in their spotlights, burned Ashley away in their spotlights before deciding it was a story too straightforward to sustain itself; one man's depravity so much less captivating when its mystery is solved. But it's no less an aftermath because the world's passed the moment by.

The rest of us are still here, trapped inside it.

The door opens behind me.

"We have to go back to the sheriff's office," Tyler says.

"What?"

But he's already stepped back inside. I get to my feet and pull the door open. He's at the sink, putting a Camel between his lips and lighting it, cupping his palm around the flame until the cherry sparks, taking a deep drag. He closes his eyes briefly, that moment he holds the smoke belonging to him and him alone, then stares out the window, bringing his hand up, tracing his finger along the tear Justin made worse.

We have to go back to the sheriff's office.

That's what he said.

But I already told Watt everything.

"Something else happen?"

"No," he says. "No, it's not . . . that."

"Then what?"

"You're going to talk to a detective about those photos you took."

"No, I'm not."

"Yes," Tyler says, turning to me, "you are."

"I'm not fucking doing it, Tyler."

"George." He rips the cigarette from his mouth, lets it burn between his fingers, ash flaking onto the floor. "You *need* to talk to them about it."

"Why?"

"So they can find these fuckers! So they can pay for what they did to you and who knows how many other girls like you—"

"What does that mean?"

"George—"

"Girls like *what*?"

"Look. I would've never—*never*—agreed to give those photos back if I knew what they were and if I'd seen them.

I would've gone to the cops myself. You told me they weren't—" His voice catches. "No kid should ever be in pictures like that."

"Pictures like what?"

He stubs his cigarette out in the sink, goes immediately to his pocket for another, and then changes his mind, rubbing the back of his neck. He wants to be doing anything but having this conversation, like he doesn't realize he can stop it at any time.

So stop it, Tyler.

"This Detective Resnick I spoke with—she's nice. I don't have to be in the room when you talk. You can tell her anything."

"Like *what*, Tyler?"

"*Enough*, George. You know." He brings his hand to his forehead. "God—Mom always said you scared the shit out of her—"

"What's that supposed to mean?"

"It means you get so caught up in these *ideas* of yourself." He lowers his hand. "You've got to start thinking about the situation and who you are for one fucking second, instead of who you think you're meant to be!"

Tyler's spent his life walking a tightrope between me and Mom, the distance between those two points as wide as an ocean, the fall, impossibly high.

I've never heard her words out of his mouth before.

"And who am I?"

"You're sixteen years old! You're a *kid*. You're not a model. You're not—" *Good enough.* Just say it like she said it, Tyler. "You scare the shit out of *me!* The kind of trouble you're borrowing just because you can't let these fucking *ideas* go—because you're so desperate to—" Desperate. "This isn't what Mom wanted for you—"

"She didn't want *anything* for me!" I pound my hand against the wall, feeling the sting of it against my palm, the recoil of the impact up my arm.

"That's not true—"

"*Yes,* it is!" And he starts shaking his head. *George, it's not.* But he's wrong. He wasn't always there. He said it himself. Didn't always see how it was between us. I dig into my pocket for my wallet. "If I believed Mom, I wouldn't be at Aspera! If I believed Mom, I wouldn't've—" I pull Aidan's card from my wallet and cross the kitchen, shoving it hard against Tyler's chest. He stumbles back into the counter. "You see that? You see that, Tyler? That's Aidan Archer's number. *Archer Studios.* He makes fucking movies, and he gave that to me because he thinks I could be—" I choke on it. "Anyone. So tell me again who I'm *meant* to be."

Tyler swallows hard, staring at it.

"Good for you, George."

He says it so quietly, and then he hands the card, half-crumpled, back to me. I bite the inside of my cheek until the taste of copper is on my tongue, and I ask, again:

"Girls like what?"

He swipes his hand across his eyes and clears his throat, phlegm rattling around his chest.

"We're going to the sheriff's office."

"No, we're not—"

"George—"

I cross the kitchen, wrench the inside door open, and

push against the screen door, its whine breaking Ketchum's miserable quiet. It hits the side of the house with a crash. I hurry down the walk, and when Tyler pushes out after me—"George! *George!* Come on!"—I run. What's left of summer has made itself vicious with heat, the air thick, blanketing me. I keep moving in spite of it, and with every furious step forward, a memory there, a story unfolding in reverse:

Justin's hands on me.

Red.

It's all above you.

Nora.

I thought I'd seen the last of you girls.

Liv.

Nora.

Her mouth against mine.

Nora.

LOVE YOU FOREVER.

Could you see it on her?

Was she peaceful?

Georgia.

PRIVATE. NO ADMITTANCE. MEMBERS ONLY.

A body in the woods.

Ashley James.

A bruise.

Hey, kid. You all right?

Footprints around me.

The car, coming back.

Stupid little cunt.

I'm at the mall.

I'm on my knees.

Aspera.

I don't know how far I've walked when the car pulls up beside me.

At the Hayes cabin, Cleo sits so close. I focus on the sweet scent of her perfume, letting it steady me, while Matthew talks on his phone, pacing the kitchen. The fight with Tyler has worn me away. It's never been like that between us before, not even when he found out about the money. I hated him, I think, and it scares me, how deep that feeling went. I haven't felt anything like that since—

Since Mom was alive.

I breathe in. Figs and orange blossoms.

When Matthew's done talking to Tyler, a heaviness has made itself at home in him, one that wasn't there before. Nothing easy about any of us now.

"He's going to pick you up tomorrow, Georgia. Of course you can stay here tonight."

"I'm sorry to ask . . ."

"It's all right," Cleo says. "It must have been quite a fight."

My eyes prickle. "I don't really want to talk about it."

"You don't have to. We're just glad you're here."

The push and pull beyond Aspera is too much, I want to tell her. When I'm safe inside its gates, I feel like I'm where I'm supposed to be, and I don't understand why no one believes this world could be meant for me, when it's always just so glad I'm here.

"I'd been waiting for things to settle before I went into town again, and I felt like today was that day, but I couldn't pinpoint why. And there you were." Matthew studies me. "It's always you, me, and that road, isn't it?"

I nod.

He takes his jacket from the hook next to the door and shrugs his arms through its sleeves. "Anyway, I have to get back to work. I'll have them send down a nice lunch and dinner for you both and join you for the latter, I'm not too tangled up."

"That would be nice," Cleo says.

"Life goes on, doesn't it?"

A sadness to his voice, like *how could it?*

And how could it.

"How has it been without me?" I ask him.

"Nothing I hope to get used to." And it's such a nice thing for him to say, it makes me feel worse. He claps his hands together lightly. "All right. Ladies." He's almost at the door when he stops, then returns to give Cleo a kiss on the cheek. She raises her face to it, closing her eyes to his mouth against her skin, a small smile on her lips, beatific. "I'll see you later."

He goes, and then it's quiet, and I realize something horrible: it was better to live in the question of Ashley's murder, than it is living in its answer. I think of Justin, Justin at the kitchen table, holding my picture, pushing me into the wall. My head against the doorframe.

The world felt like it was ending, and it did.

"What are you thinking?" Cleo asks.

"I was so scared." I stare at the space Matthew was. "I came here and I knocked on the door and no one answered. I didn't know where any of you were. So I walked home and Justin was there." I force my eyes open even wider because if I even blink, I know I'll see it again, and I see it enough. "And I thought . . ."

"What?" Cleo asks.

"I thought I was going to die."

Cleo regards me, then gently tucks an errant strand of hair behind my ear. She does it again, moving it carefully back, her fingers lingering on the damage hidden in my hair. When the stitches came out, I asked the nurse if it would scar. She took her time thinking about it before finally saying, *Could,* with a glint in her eye, as though it was a vain question that deserved a cruel response. She couldn't know what it felt like to have this on me, that thick little line, an ugly pink road going nowhere.

"I'm sorry I wasn't here," Cleo says.

"It's okay."

She brings her hand to my cheek. I lean into her touch, her tenderness, the first I've experienced in the nearly two weeks since everything came apart. I know it hasn't been long enough to feel this starved of it, but maybe it's not how much time passes—it's what it takes from you when it does.

My face crumples.

She pulls me to her.

Y ou're exhausted," she tells me.

As soon as she says it, my body gives into the idea, my bones weary from the effort of carrying so many terrible things, and for so long. Cleo touches my arm as my eyelids flutter, and I struggle to keep them open enough to see myself through what remains of this moment. I follow her up the small winding staircase to the second floor. She leaves me in the guest room immediately before the landing, shutting the door behind her with a soft *click*. A king-sized bed is parallel a picture window. A glass door leads to the balcony beyond. I sit on the bed. Outside, the trees sway back and forth, the sky a murky gray, threatening rain. I take my phone from my pocket, the bright screen harsh against my scratchy eyes, and swipe to a string of text messages— over fourteen in all, all begging some sign of life—but Nora hasn't answered any of them.

When I think of her, there are two memories there.

First, her lips, soft and sweet.

I can't tell if I'm remembering that kiss better than it was, if it was as good as the ache it's inspired. I'd need to kiss her again to be sure.

Then, at the gate to Aspera.

Bye, Avis.

I hate her for it. For what she said to me, for being wrong, for leaving me there, for letting me walk that road alone, for her father in my house, for my picture in his hands.

The police took that photo.

Justin James.

All that time, he had them.

All that time, the footsteps circling my body were his.

Tyler said the police didn't recover the rest of my photographs. Not from the motel, not from his car, not from the Jameses' house. I think they just didn't look closely enough. A man with as many secrets as Justin turned out to have would have no end of places to hide them. I set my phone on the nightstand, and then I cross the room and step into the bathroom. It adjoins another room. The question of that wakes me up a little, and I glance behind me.

I shouldn't do this . . .

But I want to know their lives.

And every want inside me, I can't help but answer.

I lock the bathroom door, so I'm not caught, and open the other.

A bedroom.

It's Matthew's. I realize quickly that it's his alone. The absence of Cleo is a quantifiable thing, and I don't know if it's strange there's no trace of her here. Not every couple shares a room. It's impersonal, even compared to his hideaway at the lodge. Maybe that's why they don't share? He's always working. Maybe he doesn't want to disturb her when he comes in late, if at all . . .

The bed is on a raised platform, the sheets a silky black. I make my way to the closet and the lights inside turn on automatically as soon as I open the door. It's as big as my room at home, all soft suits and perfectly pressed slacks and golfing outfits and shiny dress shoes and silky ties and on and on, and every label has a name and every name is worth more money than I want to think about. I step back and the light goes off. I close the door. On his nightstand, a wake-up light and yesterday's Rolex. I sit on his bed and open the nightstand's solitary drawer and a half-cut blister pack of blue pills catches my eyes. I turn it over, the name semi-intact.

SILDENA.

I set it down.

Next to it, a flipped Polaroid.

I turn it over and I'm confronted with the image of a younger Cleo, one that leaves me breathless. She sits in front of a mirrored sliding door, the camera between her long legs, resting in front of her crotch. She's in a white tank top, no bra, cutoffs. Her nipples prominent through the thin material. The cutoffs are so painfully short, its strings glance the very tops of her thighs. Her hair is longer than I've ever seen it, past her shoulders. Her jaw tilted stubbornly upward. There's someone just at the doorway reflected behind her. The flash casts that person in shadow and blows out Cleo's features, turning her pupils a glowing red. I hold it up. The room is familiar to me in the way the rooms in all shitty houses are, the way mine was to her: their crumbling walls, fractured ceilings, dirty floors. Cleo's baleful eyes stare into mine, both of us seeing each other at these different, similar points in time.

This is the Cleo she told me about.

The one who knows me.

"Georgia."

Her arrival a silent, sudden thing.

Or maybe it wasn't.

Maybe it's just that I was somewhere else, in a different room with her, years ago.

She stands in the doorway with an appraising look, then crosses the room. She extends her hand for the Polaroid, and I give it to her, watching the careful way she holds it, her expression growing distant as she falls into it the same way I did. I should apologize to her for this but I don't get the sense it's what she wants from me, and if I'm being honest, no part of me is sorry.

She sits next to me, but she doesn't speak.

I do.

"Those photos I took," I say. "The man at the mall. That's what Tyler and I fought about."

And then I finish the story I started the first time I was here.

It wasn't something I was keeping from her, I say.

This part of it just ended up written by someone else.

She stares at her Polaroid while I tell it to her, and when I'm done, she says, "When I was a girl, I lived with my mother." She points to the picture. "Here."

"Matthew told me."

"Did he also tell you how my mother's boyfriend raped me?" The words turn my guts inside out. I shake my head, queasy, as her finger glides to the shadow at the corner of the frame. "For years. She let him."

"I didn't know," I manage.

She nods slowly, eyes still on herself.

"For years, I was a function of his need. His perversion. His violence."

"I'm so sorry, Cleo."

"Don't be sorry." She looks at me. "It's the way the world is, Georgia. Do you accept it?"

I can't imagine accepting a world that would hurt her.

I shake my head.

"Not even now?"

"I . . ."

"Not even after what it did to Ashley?"

I frown. I don't know what she wants my answer to be.

"I don't think I should."

"But you should. Because this world is made by men. Beauty is decided by them. And power is held only by them. And there's nothing you can do about any of it." I dig my fingers into Matthew's silk sheets, my mind swimming, trying to understand why she's saying all this. "So if the question isn't what you can do about it, what is the question?"

I feel like I'm failing some kind of test.

"I don't know, Cleo."

"Even a man like this," she says, pointing to the monster in the Polaroid, "has more power than you and more power than me. But if the peak of a man's power is *only* the power he has over you, you know what happens then?"

"No . . ."

"You gain nothing from it. You get nothing for it," she says. "I knew that." She lowers the photo. "So I found Aspera. I found Matthew, a man who is untouchable, a man with no limits to his power, and the way he looked at me . . . what did I tell you before? When a man looks at you that way, you have him . . ." She stares at me expectantly, until I murmur the words along with her: "There's nothing he can do to you or force you to do."

"Like with Aidan."

"Like Aidan."

"You said a whole world would open up for me."

"And it will, but you have to remember it's still their world."

I find the crumpled business card in my wallet. I show it to her. It might be Aidan's world, but I had him and now I have this.

"Exactly, Georgia," Cleo says. "You understand. It's not what you can do about it, but what you can attain *within* it. Once you realize that, there are no limits for you either, on what you'll gain from it, what it will give to you."

I stare down at the card.

"You don't have to talk to anyone. Whatever anyone else . . . those men, your brother, the detective . . . whatever they think those photos were, whatever they think they are, it doesn't matter. It's what they are to you. So what are they to you?"

I think of the photos, what it felt like to see them for the first time. It was Matthew, all those years ago, who introduced me to the idea of my beauty . . . but when I saw myself gleaming in those eight-by-tens, I became my own proof of it. And that's what Cleo means, isn't it? They took my photos, but they never wanted me to *see* myself.

But I did.

And now look at me.

I'm here, at Aspera.

A revelation.

"It's an ugly world, Georgia. Don't concede to it. Don't let it make you its victim."

She tells me to get some rest.

I return to the bathroom and splash cold water on my face. In the guest room, I lie on the bed, staring at the ceiling, slowly surrendering to the soft give of the mattress, the feather pillows beneath my head. I'm on the brink of sleep when I pull myself from it, fumbling for my phone.

I swipe back to my texts messages with Nora, suddenly angry.

I want the rest of my pictures. I know they're at your place, I thumb out.

But something keeps me from hitting send.

I open up a search instead: sildena

Did you mean sildenafil?

Sildenafil, sold under the brand name Viagra.

The bedroom door opens, pulling me from a light slumber. Footsteps quietly cross the room. The mattress sinks as she sits down on it, near me. I feel the heat of her. I keep my eyes closed until she draws me out with my name because I want to hear her say it—

"Georgia."

Because no one says it like she does.

I open my eyes slowly. Sunlight floods through the window, all of it seeming to concentrate on her. If I were the sun, I'd want to shine on Cleo too.

"Good morning," she says. "It's still very early. You can go back to sleep after this. I just wanted to say goodbye."

"Goodbye?" I sit up quickly, and she smiles a little at the sight of me. I can feel my hair, a wild mess around my head. I always get pillow creases in my cheeks.

She tells me she's going to Miami for a little while, but she'll be back.

"What's in Miami?" I ask.

"I'm looking into properties for Matthew."

"What like—" I'm fully awake now, seized by a terrible thought. "Are you two moving? Are you leaving?"

"No. We're *expanding*. Isn't that exciting? Think of Aspera, but with palm trees. We want it to be the perfect place and when we find it . . . have you ever been to Miami, Georgia?"

"I've never been out of Ketchum." I try to imagine myself there. Miami. Its gleaming buildings surrounded by every shade of blue . . . me, there.

With them.

The hug she gives me feels like a promise. I wrap my arms around her, memorizing the shape of her, the softness of her skin as I press my fingertips into her back.

"Look after things while I'm away," she says. "Look after Matthew."

Tyler has to get up earlier than usual to drop me back off at home before he heads in to work. He waits for me outside the gate, leaning against his truck, no cigarette, though I know he's got to be dying for it. It breaks my heart. My brother, forever steady, forever there for me, and me, forever pushing back at him because I want different things and I can't seem to stop wanting them. Seeing him like this almost makes me wish I could.

Almost.

When he notices me, he looks—sad. It hurts to see the damage I did, hurts that it's bad enough he can't even hide it, and he usually tries.

"You good?" he asks.

"No," I say. "I'm really sorry."

I hug him, my fingers clutching his shirt. I blink, trying

not to make a tearstained mess of it. He doesn't hesitate in the return. He rubs my back, says roughly, "You've been through a lot, George."

"I still don't want to talk to the detective."

"I think you should. But I'm not going to force you."

When we're in the truck, I tell him I'll be back to work at Aspera on Monday. He frowns. "Maybe you should relax. Take off and do nothing with what little's left of the summer. I meant what I said. You've been through a lot. You should go easy."

"That's not gonna get you paid back," I say, and he makes a disbelieving sound, and it is hard to believe somehow—everything that's happened, and I still owe him money.

I stare out at the road, watching as That Part of it draws nearer. Ashley's splintered cross is gone now, and I wonder if that's only because I ruined it. I shouldn't have. It made no difference. There's no escaping it. Some part of me will always be finding her here. Some part of her will always be here, waiting to be found.

R oom three wants a massage table sent up," I say into the phone, staring at the all-caps request from the executive floor. I hesitate. "And a certain Aspirant needs a ride home tonight . . . and tomorrow."

"Is that right?"

"Maybe indefinitely, if you can swing it."

"Lucky for you, all of this can be arranged," Kel says, and I exhale, relieved. I push the confirmation of care button. "My Audi's been back from the shop a while now. Looking forward to finally introducing you."

"Yours, huh?" I don't tell him I'm pretty sure I've already seen it.

"Oh, wait." I hear the snap of his fingers. "Won't be able to drive you home until about a half hour after you clock out. That okay?"

"Yeah. How come?"

"Top secret stuff."

That probably means the executive floor.

"Like what?" If it means the executive floor, I want to know. I want to be important enough to be told. My computer chimes.

"Did I just hear another request come in?"

"If you want me to answer it, you should answer me," I say. "Because I'm not the one who has to answer to irate members . . ."

"Dirty pool, Georgia," he replies. "But . . . since you'll probably be hearing about it soon, I have some travel arrangements I need to sort out for Mr. Hayes's end-of-summer summit the week after next—"

"What's a summit?"

He laughs, my ignorance an unending source of his amusement. "Think of it as a very, *very* important meeting. Mr. Hayes will be connecting some of his most esteemed associates with mutual interests in hopes of mutual gain."

"And that happens on the executive floor?"

"If it was going to happen anywhere, it'd be there, don't you think?"

I feel a pang, suddenly sorry I asked the question but not sorry enough to keep from asking the next so I can sharpen my envy into a lethal point to use as a weapon against myself. "So the Aspera girls will be there?"

"Let's put it this way: when you're wining and dining some of the most powerful men in the country . . . you don't keep the good silverware in the drawer."

I'm glad he can't see my face.

The computer chimes.

"Back to work," he says and hangs up.

I stare up at the light, at the antler, that gleam of bone, and then I check my texts, a force of habit. Nora hasn't replied to any, but my latest is still there, unsent—I want the rest of my pictures. I know they're at your place.

The phone on my desk rings, startling me. When I pick it up, it's Matthew, telling me to come into his office.

"It just occurred to me," he says, gesturing, "you've never tried it."

A slice of chocolate cake sits on his desk, presumably the one I've been bringing him every day since I started. I've never once peeked inside the box or imagined anything more complicated than a cut from the black forest birthday cakes I see at the grocery store, but of course it would be a thousand times more special than that. Everything here is.

I sit in the chair Matthew's placed in front of his desk, and he takes his seat across from me as I inspect the dessert. It's a beautiful slice, if cake can be beautiful. The outside a rich, matte brown ganache, covered in shaved chocolate, the inside made up of a three-layer chocolate gradient. It's a spiced cake, he tells me, with buttercream, and the shaved chocolate is coffee-infused. I pick up the fork. He smiles at my hesitation.

"I don't want to ruin it," I admit.

"You can't. Besides, this is what it's meant for. Fulfill its purpose, Georgia."

I draw the fork down the cake. It falls effortlessly against the tines, and I put the piece on my tongue, my eyes closing to the perfect balance of chocolate and coffee and spice. Cinnamon, I think. Nutmeg. And I've never tasted chocolate like this before, so deep and earthy, and when I say so to Matthew, he says, "That's because you've probably only ever had cheap chocolate. And cheap chocolate is mostly sugar."

"It's so good," I say, and I take another luxurious bite,

slowly licking the crumbs off my lips. When I look up, Matthew's fidgeting. "You'll have to tell Cleo I tried it."

"Of course. There's nothing I do Cleo doesn't know about."

"Can I ask you something?"

"I wish you would."

"The antlers," I say, and he chuckles. "Why do you have them . . . everywhere?"

"Ah." He laces his fingers behind his head. "It would be worse if I didn't, don't you think? To go out there, make the kill, and not make use of every part."

"You like to hunt."

"I *love* to hunt. Your brother hunt? Ever take you out?" he asks. I shake my head. "You feel strongly about it, either way?"

"I never really thought about it," I say. "What do you like about it?"

"There's nothing else in the world that compares," he says. "Most people, they spend their days asleep. You have to find the thing that wakes you up. Hunting demands all of your senses. It asks you to access every part of your virility, forces you to be present in your body on an almost . . . molecular level to fully understand what it is you're really doing when you pull that trigger. You feel yourself. That's powerful."

I set the fork down. The cake isn't even half-gone. I give him an apologetic look.

"It's so rich. I'm not used to it."

"Well, we'll do this more often and get you used to it." He studies me. "How are you doing, Georgia?"

"I don't know," I say before I can think of a better answer. But I don't know. It's a constant reckoning of Justin James's atrocities, a road I could walk, if I wanted to, and not be afraid, and all of Nora's silence. If all this means what we've been through is over, my heart doesn't know it yet. I wake up in the morning feeling like my chest has been split wide open, like I can't breathe.

"I keep running it over in my mind." His brow furrows. "I spent some time thinking about what I would say to you . . . I wanted to make you feel better. But I'm at a loss. It makes me so goddamn sick. Am I right, you're friends with his eldest? Nora?" I exhale softly at her name, then nod. "How's she doing?"

"I tried to reach out. She's not talking."

"I'm sure she just needs more time. Where is she now, do you know?"

"Tyler heard she's staying at the Millers'. That's a . . . friend of hers."

"And let's not pretend that you're all right," he adds, and the simple, unfussed way he says it forces me to blink back tears. He reaches his hand across the desk. "What do you need, Georgia? Will you tell us?"

"What's going to happen to me after the summer?"

"What do you want to happen?"

"I want to keep working at Aspera as long as I can. In the summer, during the holidays, whatever you'll give me while I'm in school." My stomach gives a nervous twist at what I dare to put to words next: "But not hidden away in that office, at that desk. That's not what I need."

"Okay," he says slowly, leaning forward. "And what is it you want to do here?"

How is it even a question?

I close my eyes and there's a memory there.

Come to Aspera.

He was the one who said it.

Aspera girl.

That's what I was always supposed to be, wasn't it?

And the way he looked at me—

When a man looks at you like that—

Did I have Matthew?

I open my eyes.

. . . Do I?

"What did you want me to do?" I ask.

"What do you mean?"

"You picked me up on the road that day, and you told me I was beautiful. You said to come here. I know what happened with Mom changed things . . . but the day you said it to me, they hadn't happened yet so . . . why did you want me here, Matthew?"

"Georgia . . ."

"It's still true, isn't it?"

"What's still true?"

That you think I'm beautiful.

I bite my lip, pulling gently at my pout.

I stand at my heart's insistence.

I have to know.

Matthew stares up at me.

I think of Nora and me in my bedroom, of Nora's awed expression as she took in every inch of my body. *Maybe it's his dream.* I touch my necklace, then let it go, letting my fingers graze that dip of cleavage before my hand comes to rest at my side, and then I cross my arms in front of me, pushing my breasts close, the buttons of my dress holding tight, but tenuously. A soft kitten-sigh.

Matthew's expression, awed.

Matthew's phone buzzes, and he startles back to himself, rising hastily to his feet.

"Ah, hell—I'm running late—"

He stops abruptly, glancing down, and I follow his gaze to the undeniable bulge in his pants. The shock of the sight hits me first, a strange thrill quick to follow.

That's where I made his blood go.

And I didn't need any pills to help.

Our eyes meet.

"I've got a meeting," he manages. "You'll have to excuse me."

I nod and go back to my office where I sit at my desk, my hands pressed against it, my heart beating fast, all of me . . . awake . . . and how did he put it?

You feel yourself.

I can feel myself.

Powerful.

The lights are off at Nora's place. Deserted because—the thought bitter inside me—she's at the Millers'. I glance up and down the street. It's late. After midnight. Clouds cover the moon. I take a deep breath and shove my hands in my pockets.

I've never broken into a house before.

The front door is locked. The windows of the first floor shut tight. I test each of them until a dog barks in the distance and it sends me fumbling back, my pulse pounding. It feels like a warning. Not enough of one to put me off, but enough of one to get me to hurry up, so I quickly investigate my other options, the other two entrances into Nora's: the back door and the door to the garage.

I try the garage's door first and gasp as it opens, quickly slipping inside and squinting into the dark. Justin's SUV takes up most of the space and I shiver, fighting the urge to touch it, to make real the vehicle that hit me. The treads . . . God. Even if he got stopped by the cops, they never would've checked them. He was one of their own.

He was her *father*.

I search out a light switch then realize I shouldn't, instead using the flashlight on my phone to guide me to the door leading inside. I don't know Nora's well enough, and I scare myself more times than I can count. Every shadow has become an alive thing, has me scrambling backward into a work bench, or hitting the garbage cans—loud—with my side. I wield the light like a weapon, but the threat is gone, long gone now.

Dead and decaying now.

I find the door and it's locked. I press my head against it, and then I jiggle the handle, angry, and then rear back, angrier, and kick it.

I want my pictures.

I push my hair from my face, my fingers glancing the scar he gave me. Think. What if I lived like the Jameses lived. What if I was a dad of two girls, and no wife to speak of anymore. What if I wasn't always there to pick them up after school. What if I worried they might not always remember their keys. I slip back outside, my eyes on the ground. I lift an empty planter next to the door. Nothing. I turn back to the door, and then I reach up, running my hands along its frame. My fingers close around a key, and I try not to smile. Easy. And then I wonder if it's not that the pictures are hidden too well. Maybe they're in such an obvious place, they're impossible to see . . .

I go back into the garage, but the key doesn't unlock the door there.

It unlocks the back door.

I let myself in. At the threshold, I hold my breath

and listen. It's not entirely silent—the electronics hum, a clock ticks on the wall—but it's absent all human sounds. I turn my phone's light on and try to orient myself. I'm standing in a hall. At the far end of it, the kitchen. Front of the house. That's where I came in with Nora that day.

The stairs up are between here and there.

I slip out of my shoes so I don't track anything in and move forward, my hand against the wall, the carpet soft under my sock feet. I head upstairs, unnerved by the creaking steps. At the landing, I face Ashley's room, the sight of it nearly unbearable now.

Directly opposite it, Nora's room.

I never saw her room.

Its door is wide open, cloud cover gone, letting moonlight in from the window. It casts a glow over what little of it I can see, and it takes everything to keep myself from going to it, to pick through what she left behind, to breathe in whatever of her might still be there.

The bedroom between hers and Ashley's must be Justin's.

I step inside.

Justin: filthy.

Justin: a dresser covered in empties.

Justin: the dresser's mirror smudged with fingerprints.

Justin: his bed eerily tidy, made with military precision.

Justin: dead, but it's not enough that he's dead.

There should be something worse than dead.

I inhale and gag at the acrid taste of the air, my stomach revolting at the idea of any lingering part of him in me. I reach out, leaning against the wall to steady myself, sweat beading on my forehead. I don't want to be here.

But I want my pictures back.

"Where—"

I don't even want the sound of my voice in here.

But where?

I get to work, shining my phone's light in the room's darkest corners, the closet, under the bed. Under the mattress. I rifle through his nightstand. A belt, some receipts, a small sewing kit. Two rings that look like they could be wedding bands. I hold them up. They're heavier than they look. I test their weight in my palm, and decide I hate Nora's mother too because why wouldn't she take her daughters with her? Why wouldn't she spare them all this? I drop the rings back into the drawer with a clatter, and then I cross the room to the dresser, and I'm not careful about the way I dig through his clothes, throwing to the ground what I can't shove aside. I'm in the middle drawer, nightshirts and shorts and socks, when my fingers close around something at the back, cool and metal. I hold it up to the light and peer at it.

A gold compass.

A car ornament.

The hands of the compass, its center, reminiscent of both a cross and a star, depending on how far away you were seeing it from . . . I run my fingers over it.

There's something on the back, an engraving.

I turn it over, holding my light to it, and feel the blood drain from my face.

Justin's not the answer to every question, but his death has made every remaining question feel less urgent, enough to be left unexplored.

But there's still this—Ashley, plotting her escape.

She was going to meet someone. A man with dark hair.

Who?

He picked her up at the party.

There was this . . . it was like a cross? But it had a star in it . . . it's hard to describe. It was hanging from the mirror . . . it was gold . . .

I stare at the name carved in the compass's back in small capital letters.

KEL ALLRED

A sound downstairs. Footsteps on the stairs. *Shit.* I shove the compass in my pocket and close the drawer. I step out of Justin's room at the same time the hall light goes on. I shield my eyes and when I lower my hand, Nora is there, standing at Ashley's door.

STAY OUT!!!!

"What are you doing here, Avis?" she asks coldly.

My body is suddenly too small to contain the heart inside it. It's the shock of being discovered, combined with the secret I'm now keeping. But no part of me is afraid. All I've wanted was to see her, and I'll take it even like this, in this place I'm not supposed to be and whether or not she wants to see me. She's in black jeans, a gray T-shirt, and a denim overshirt rolled at the sleeves. Her arms crossed, her hair in her eyes.

"I wanted the rest of my pictures back," I say. "They have to be here somewhere."

"Did you find them?"

I shake my head. "How did you know I was here?"

"The neighbors saw a light in the garage and called me," she says. "I knew it would be you . . . anyway. The police were here, and they turned the whole place over. If anyone has those photos now, it's them—"

"They don't, though."

"Then I don't know where they are. And I don't care. You should leave."

"Nora . . ."

"You should leave, Avis."

I sigh and make my way down the hall, the compass heavy in my pocket.

When I'm close enough to her, I stop.

I don't want to leave her like this.

I don't want her to let me leave.

She keeps her eyes off me. I reach out slowly and she doesn't react. My fingers near her overshirt, and then I grip its sides, moving myself even closer to her with a pull.

She turns her head from me.

"I'm so sorry," I say softly as she stares into the middle distance. "Nora, I am so sorry." I tilt my face up to hers. "I am so sorry all of this happened to you." Her lips quiver. She bites down, hard. "I'm sorry . . ." I reach my hands up, my fingertips a whisper at her cheeks. "Nora." And then she turns her head so her cheek comes to rest against my palm. She shuts her eyes tightly, grimacing, trying so hard not to cry as I stroke her face.

"You shouldn't have come here," she whispers. "You made me come here."

"I'm sorry."

"You made me—"

"Come here," I tell her, and I lace my arms under her arms, my palms against her shoulder blades, digging my fingers in. She buries her face in my neck and then her arms go around me, and all I've wanted was her arms around me. I close my eyes to the feel of her breath on me. She goes so still, just holding on—

And then, just as suddenly, she isn't anymore.

"Go," she says.

I'm almost at the landing when she reaches for me again. And then: the relief of her pulling me back, pushing me against the wall, her face close to my face, her palm at my cheek, hovering there as though she doesn't know how, exactly, she wants this to happen, just that she does, just that it needs to. My eyes search hers. She presses her thumb to the center of my lips before lowering her hand, and if this is the last kiss, I won't settle for sweet and fleeting, and I don't want her tenderness. I want her want. She gives it to me. She kisses me so hard, and it's a desperate kiss, her mouth as hungry against mine as mine is against hers, her body warm and flush against me, and I take it back: I won't settle for this either.

It will never, ever be enough.

She pulls away.

"Go," she says again.

Matthew's on the phone when I step into his office. He nods when he sees me, pointing to the chair in front of his desk. I don't sit down, instead focusing on the compass in my hand as I look at the gray sky outside. A storm is coming. It's close. After a moment, he seems to understand it's something important, why I'm here, and winds up his call to give me his full attention, tucking his phone in his suit's inside pocket.

"What's going on, Georgia?" I give him the compass. It seems smaller than it actually is in his hands. He glances at it, a spark of recognition. "Where'd you get this? Kel's been looking for it. He'll be thrilled to know it turned up."

"I found it at Justin James's house."

He blinks, stunned. "I'm going to need you to explain that to me."

Matthew's face is troubled as he listens, and as he listens, he turns the compass round and round. I tell him about Ashley, and Hulick, that she was planning to escape. That there was someone out there, a man, who was going to escape with her. How Liv saw Ashley leave a party with someone who matches Kel's description, with this compass hanging in the car's rearview, and I don't know how it

ended up at Justin's, but if it fits, if Kel was planning some-
thing with a girl as young as Ashley, it could only be bad for
Aspera. And when I say this, Matthew stares at me in a way
I can't remember a man staring at me before: less about how
I look and more as a response to something I've done. And
that what I've done is something that matters.

"You're absolutely right," he says. "It would be terrible
for us."

"What did he think he was doing with her?"

"Well, the thing is, this—I mean this *is* his," Matthew
says. "Even without the engraving, I could have told you
that. He keeps it in the Audi. Kept. He'd mentioned it was
missing. We thought one of the lower-level staff got a hair
up their ass about it because I don't let anyone personalize
resort cars, but Kel got so attached to that one, it was a little
running joke. 'His' car." He sighs. "Can I tell you something, Georgia? In confidence?"

"Of course," I say, my pulse quickening.

"Kel *did* give Ashley a ride home from that party." He
sets the compass on his desk as my mind works to process
this, but before it goes too far down a path I don't want it to
wander, he adds, "But it's definitely not how you think. It's
my understanding this party . . . it wasn't the kind of place
a young woman should be?"

I shake my head. "It wasn't."

"Well, he was there with a date who left without him.
Decided the whole thing wasn't his scene. Ashley saw him
leaving and asked for a ride and of course he gave her one
because it was the right thing to do. He took her home."

"But . . ."

I frown at the darkening sky.

"What?"

"I just don't understand why . . ." I rub my forehead. "If she was supposed to leave with someone that night . . . why would she go home?"

And why would she leave her wasted best friend behind if she was only going home?

"Maybe home was a stop along the way."

"So you knew this, and you didn't tell the police?"

"There didn't seem to be any point. As far as we all understood it, Ashley didn't disappear until two days later. Kel confided in me, but he did nothing wrong. I wasn't going to let a minor, insignificant detail like that put a spotlight on us and distract the authorities from the real investigation." Matthew drums his fingers along his desk. "There's something else . . . but I don't know if I should . . ." He looks at me. "It can't ever leave this room, Georgia."

The back of my neck prickles.

"I promise."

"You know the local police force avails themselves of the golf course," he says. I nod. "They're very good friends of mine. We play a few rounds. Of course we all talked about it. Toward the end, I got the impression they had their eyes on someone close to Ashley."

Jesus. "But did they say Justin?"

"Who else would it be?"

I bring my hand to my mouth, thinking of Nora, thinking of Nora desperately searching for Ashley's killer, the Ketchum Sheriff's Department circling her father the whole time . . .

"But is that what they said?"

"I won't repeat it exactly, because I've already said too much," he says, and that has to mean *yes*. "But let's think in that direction—what if Justin saw Kel drop her off? That means Kel was the last person to see Ashley alive before Justin killed her. When Justin realizes he's a person of interest, he starts looking for a scapegoat . . . though, I think he was always looking for one here, to be honest . . . he stopped by a few times after her death, you know that—"

"Oh my God," I whisper. "Nora—after we found out about Hulick, she confronted him. I think she must've told him everything she knew . . . the party, the ornament—"

"Which would put Kel into play," Matthew says slowly. "Justin wanted to implicate him."

The air is oppressive, strange, as we live out an untraveled branch of Kel's future. A future where he's pinned with the rape and murder of a thirteen-year-old girl, and he knows he didn't do it, but he can't get out of it because Justin James made it airtight, because Justin is a cop himself. Because Justin was her father and no father—no father would ever do something like what he did to his own kid. I imagine it; news crews descending on Aspera, a secret revealed to the world, no longer safe from its prying eyes. Scandal so woven into its fabric, members could never trust it after.

Matthew picks up the compass again.

"You know, if it *had* been Kel . . . clandestinely meeting with Ashley, that would have been catastrophic for us. And as far as you knew, that's what was happening." He studies me. "But you came to me."

"Of course I did."

He smiles faintly. "Like I said—you impress me, Georgia."

"Matthew, can I ask you something?"

"After this? Anything."

I take a breath. "If I impress you so much . . . why didn't you make me an Aspera girl?"

"That's what you want to be?"

"That's what I *should* be." My face gets hot, but I don't feel the truth of it any less now that I've said it aloud. "It's what I thought I'd be. That's what you wanted me to be when you picked me up on the road, right? So why didn't you make me one?"

"Georgia."

"Cleo said you had to be sure of me, but you must be sure of me now."

"I am," he agrees.

"But I'm still not an Aspera girl."

He quiets, pressing his fingers to his lips. "It's not that simple—"

"Is it because I'm not—I'm not good enough?"

His mouth falls open.

"Good enough," he repeats.

"You trust me, but I'm not an Aspera girl. What else could it be?"

"Of *course* you're good enough," he says. "Of course. How could you even think, for a second, that you're not?"

"My mom."

"Your—" He closes his eyes.

"She always said it was better to know who I am than who I think I'm meant to be." My voice breaks. "She always said I wasn't good enough be here."

The wind has picked up, bending the trees, and I realize I can't hear the storm in his office, can't hear the bluster of it, the angry rumbling of thunder overhead.

He's silenced the world beyond him.

What I do hear: his breathing.

My own.

My heartbeat . . .

His?

He opens his eyes.

"Come here."

I inch closer, stopping just before him.

"Georgia, if there's one reason I haven't made you an Aspera girl, it's because . . ." He sighs heavily. "Because, if anything, you're too good."

Too good.

"What does that mean?" I ask shakily.

"It means I'd never have an Aspera girl in my office. I'd never share a meal with her. And you . . . you come here, Katy Avis's daughter, and you defy all my expectations, and my worries, my fears. You don't hate me like she hated me. You're not just here to take. You talk to me like I'm—" He smiles a little. "Would you believe it gets lonely being who I am? People don't talk to me like a friend, a confidant, but you've shared things with me from your life that . . ." It's more than I can hide, the way it makes me feel, how good. "It means something to me. And I guess I was guarding that a little too selfishly . . . but when you have such an incredible thing, that's what you do."

An incredible thing.

"Oh," I say.

"The last I ever felt like that about anyone was . . ." I don't want to think about Cleo at the end of that sentence. "Am I wrong? Is it not special, what we have?"

Sheet lightning erupts across the sky, and it seems, briefly, like the brightest day. But the brightest day was this one: walking that road, furious with my mother who spent her whole life trying to keep my dreams from me, all because she and Matthew agreed in the end—I wasn't good enough for the things I wanted.

But look at me now, Mom.

I'm better.

"You, me . . ."

"And the road." He takes a careful step forward and brings his hand to my face, his palm clammy. "But then there's the other part . . ."

"What part?"

"What happened in here the other day . . ." There's a slight tremor in his thumb as he runs it along my skin. "I can't stop thinking about you. About how it shouldn't have happened and how, if I was any kind of man, I'd fire you just to make sure it never happened again."

"But nothing happened," I say. "You don't need to fire me."

"But it could have."

"No! Nothing could have happened—and it wouldn't mean anything anyway—because I—I told you . . ."

"You like . . ."

"I like girls."

"So it doesn't mean anything . . . because it can't," he

says, and I nod. I've never seen Matthew like this: so lost, almost small. He tries to reason it. "So when a thing like that happens—it's not really happening at all."

I nod again. "That's right."

"I just want to kiss you," he whispers and then shakes his head like he can't believe he said it. Then, almost dazed: "Christ, what you do to me . . . I really don't think this can work, Georgia . . . I can't ask you to work with me when I'm—I'm this . . . when I need this kind of release. I can't do that to you." He turns away, moving to his desk, suddenly businesslike. "I'll have Kel give you your pay. I had a bonus in mind. I don't want you to think you're not appreciated. Having you here was one of the better choices I've—"

"Matthew, please," I say urgently. "Please don't—" He keeps his back to me. "What if it's not . . . what if it's not something you're doing to me but what if . . . what if it's something . . . what if it's something I'm giving to you?"

He faces me slowly, his eyes wondering, waiting for me to continue.

"If it doesn't mean anything . . . if it's like it wouldn't even be happening . . ." My voice wavers. "I can give you release."

Just this once.

I see him working out the equation of us in his mind.

"Let's just try something," he finally says.

"Okay."

"Can I kiss you?"

"Yes."

He moves closer, almost shy, his gaze traveling from mine to my lips, staying there a moment, before coming to rest at my necklace.

He reaches out, taking the teardrop in his hand . . .

He pulls me forward by it.

He kisses me.

His kiss is a consuming thing, his lips needy against my own. My heart slams into my rib cage, and I'm suddenly aware of my hands, wondering where my hands should go. He draws back before I can figure out any one place, and I still feel his kiss in the bruise it's left behind, so painful, so desperate. Matthew exhales, running his hands through his hair, and then turns back to my body, all of it, staring at it, contemplating what to do to it next.

I press my lips together.

He slips the straps of my dress down, leaving my shoulders bare.

"Can I kiss you?"

"Yes."

He kisses both my shoulders, butterfly light this time, then pulls down the top of my dress, letting it bunch at the waist. He traces both sides of my collarbone with his fingers, then the seam of my bra, and he asks it again.

"Can I kiss you?"

"Yes."

He reaches behind me and unclasps my bra, helping it off, letting it fall to the floor. He takes a sharp, soft breath at the sight of my breasts. He kneels in front of me.

Matthew, on his knees for me.

He brings his mouth to my breast, his tongue exploring its contours, finding my nipple. He pulls at it with his teeth. I hiss through my own and stare up at the antlers woven around the light. He pulls my dress down, sliding it over my hips as his mouth works against my skin. His fingers come to the band of my underwear. He stops, waiting until I look at him. The afterglow of the light puts a neon hole in part of his face. He's sweating.

"Can I kiss you?"

"Yes."

He pulls my underwear down, kisses me there, licking me there, and my breathing gets fainter and fainter as his mouth explores that part of me, before finally pulling me to him, resting his head against my stomach, and I still don't know what to do with my hands. But maybe it doesn't matter so much what I do.

I don't have to do anything.

He's on his knees.

He takes in my nakedness, and I see his want in response to it, a demand. My stomach flutters. He rises, slowly, and guides me to his desk. He faces me in front of it and stands behind me. He pushes my hair from my neck and kisses it and then pushes himself against me until I'm flush against his desk, the front of my thighs against his desk, the urgency of his hard-on against me against his desk.

I feel the back of his hands as he unbuckles.

The toothy sigh of his zipper.

Lightning illuminates the fairway.

The sound of his belt hitting the floor.

He brings his mouth to my ear, his breath on the side of my face, and I feel dizzy, heady with how badly he wants this, me. What I do to him. The weight of him against me makes me stumble, a little. I put my hands down to steady myself.

"Lean forward," he says.

PART THREE

. . . .

I close my eyes, and there's a memory there:

I'm stood at the screen door, crying, my mother at my back.

She had a notion of my disappearance before it happened.

Where are you going?

And it occurred to me then, that I could go anywhere—

Anywhere, except the one place I'd wanted to be.

It was just a party.

But it wasn't. It was Nora James marching up to me in the hall—

It was Nora James, handing me a torn piece of paper—

You're invited.

It was me, invited.

There was something about her even then, that steely-eyed girl who always knew which way she meant to look, so it was no mistake when she finally looked in my direction. She put butterflies in my stomach. Or maybe not butterflies—butterflies were too fragile and fleeting. What Nora did to me was something else, something more. Something I couldn't name just yet, but something I wanted to know and be close to. But I didn't go to her party, and she wouldn't look at me in the hall the next day, or any day after that. She was always surrounded by other girls. Girl-stars turned girl-constellations, and there I was, staring up at them from the gutter.

I should have been her star.

Only thing a girl like you is worth to a man like Justin James is how good you can make him feel about himself.

But I didn't care about Justin James.

The first step was for Nora.

The key to that kind of running away is how far you get and how long you're out for. The white-hot fury powering me made me feel like I could walk forever. To start with, I circled Ketchum, and then I realized every eye upon me made me a sighting, gave my mother a path to trace, for Tyler to trace. To be successful, I had to disappear. When I reached the town limits, my fury hadn't abated, and I knew I still wasn't far enough gone. I kept walking, one foot determinedly in front of the other, the heat pressing in on me from all sides, pressing me forward, until, eventually, it started pushing me back. By then, it had been hours and the highway bled into a dirt road. My lips were chapped, my tongue parched, throat aching for water. There was the vaguest question in the back of my mind of whether or not I'd really thought this through, and then a car pulled up beside me, its window rolled down.

A man inside.

Are you the girl? he asked.

There could only be one answer.

More powerful than disappearing was being found. More powerful than being found was being seen. I sat in the car next to Matthew Hayes, listening to him tell a story where I was the main character. The whole town, looking for me. My missing hours had finally dug into my mother enough for her to send word.

She works for you, I told him.

Yes, she did, he said.

He spoke so well of her.

And then, of me: *You're beautiful, Georgia.*

I had no idea Katy Avis's girl was so beautiful.

He looked at me when he said it. He turned his eyes from the road, making sure I really understood. And I did. Just then, I did. I was suddenly aware of my body, the space it occupied between fading adolescence and aspiring woman-hood. My burgeoning chest. My bee-stung lips turned sud-denly suggestive. No one had ever called me beautiful like that before. I'd had the inkling that I was, in those leering gazes I sometimes found myself reflected in, or the way I'd glimpse myself in a mirror and lose my breath at what my image seemed to be hinting toward. But this—this was dif-ferent. The moment Matthew said it, it became true.

I was beautiful.

It was such a relief.

Come to Aspera, when you're old enough.

If someone else didn't discover me first.

When we pulled up to the house, Mom was waiting, and I could see what I'd done to her. I saw it in her puckered mouth, in her skin stretched tight across her knuckles as she held herself, and I was satisfied. The fight we had after was a simmering thing, the kind that finds the fracture in the glass and breaks the whole thing clean into a million pieces.

Matthew Hayes said I was beautiful.

He said I could be an Aspera girl.

I'm going to be an Aspera girl.

I barely held this precious promise before she ripped it from me. She told me not to be so stupid, to see the words for how empty they really were and how little I could mean them. How little I was, that I couldn't ever mean them.

It's better to know who you are than who you think you're meant to be.

Now I know.

Beyond the bathroom door, I hear the faint sounds of Tyler in the kitchen. Steam rises from the tub as I sit in its hot water, trying to remember how he looked at me when I came home. If there was something in his eyes that noted a difference. That's how I've read it in books, seen it in movies. Girls waiting for someone to see it on them, just so they can be sure. Except the kind of difference I want a witness to isn't the same because this isn't about what I've lost. I lean back, strands of blond hair floating in my periphery. I feel sore. I feel sore where Matthew put himself inside me, and some places where he didn't.

But I had him.

He was on his knees.

I push the outside of my legs against the sides of the tub, taking in as much of my body as I can beneath the surface. The view wavers with the water, but the most important parts, I can see. The curve of my hips. My breasts. I slip my hand between my legs, and it's in my head, the way he looked at me . . . My heart starts to race.

The way he looked at me—

Knock-knock-knock.

I jerk upright, the water sloshing against the sides of the tub, spilling onto the bathroom floor. The water is cold.

My body is cold.

I lean forward, nauseous.

"George." Tyler. "You been in there a while. You good?"

"Yeah," I say, shivering.

el steps inside my office, waiting at the door as I finish with a request. As soon as the phone is back in its cradle, he says, "Mr. Hayes told me what you did."

"Oh."

I haven't seen Matthew since—since I told him something needed to change for me at Aspera. It hasn't yet. I'm still in this office. Still working the digital concierge. I've spent the day stealing glances at the secret door, waiting for him to step through and tell me how it's going to be different, better, but it doesn't happen.

It's supposed to happen.

"I just want to thank you," Kel says.

"When did you notice it was missing?" I ask. The compass.

Kel has to think on it. "That last day. When everything went down."

Justin's last day. And then I remember—Kel's Audi, its door open, its light on. Someone had just been in it. My skin crawls at the thought of being in the garage alone with Justin because it had to have been him. He was there. Did he think I'd seen him? Is that what forced his hand and brought him to my house? The thought chills me, and

I try to shake it because why does it even matter now? Why should it all have to fit perfectly into place? There will always be one part of it that doesn't: that Justin would drug his own daughter into complacency and break any parts of her left to break before dumping her in the woods like trash, her skin a map of his fucked-up transgressions.

That bruise.

"I didn't know what to make of it when Matthew took you on. Katy Avis's daughter." Kel's eyes cloud over. "Everything she did—tried to do—threatened everything Aspera stands for. But you found out something that could've damaged Aspera—and me—and you kept it on the inside. I won't ever forget that."

There's something about the way he talks about it, her, that reminds me of the way Matthew does. There's a hurt there, a real indignation. Kel knew about my mother, but it occurs to me now he might've actually known her.

"You know her, Kel?"

The question seems to surprise him, revealing just how little there is I've been told about her time here. "We worked the executive floor together," he says and I stare, uncomprehending. Mom? On executive? "Well, she only cleaned it. But there was a time I thought us friends."

Her, on the executive floor.

Stealing from the executive floor.

"What did she take?"

"Take?" Kel blinks. "What are you talking about?"

"That's why she got fired, right? She was stealing from members." And if she was stealing from *executive* members . . .

Kel shakes his head, opening his mouth and closing it as

quickly when he registers the shock on my face. We stare at each other, and I'm afraid, suddenly, of what I'm about to learn. "Kel . . . what did she get fired for?"

"Maybe you should be talking to your brother about this."

"I can't. We don't really talk about it. I mean, he won't talk about it. She made him promise to keep me in the dark. Kel, please." He starts protesting, and I say, "I looked out for you. Now you look out for me."

He sighs. "Look, I can't tell you everything. Mostly because I don't know everything myself. I was pretty new to the floor, and your mom had been there a while, so it all sort of happened around me."

"I'll take anything," I say.

"It wasn't what she stole, Georgia," he tells me. "It was what she knew—what she thought she knew. It was black-mail."

A startled laugh flies from my mouth. Blackmail. It made more sense for my mother to be a thief, to think her tempted by Aspera's sparkling things. That was the closest to her I'd ever felt, because in some other life, I can imagine myself doing the exact same thing. But blackmail . . .

"No wonder you all didn't want to trust me," I say. "That's *insane*, Kel. What the fuck did she think she had on Aspera?"

"I can't tell you. But imagine it—unlimited access to rooms on the executive floor. Unlimited access to the kinds of powerful people who stay on the executive floor. There's no end to things you could find out or information you could come across, whether you meant to look for it or not.

It's the kind of shit you could sell for a lot of money on the gossip market."

"How bad do you think it was?"

"I mean," Kel says, "you have to contextualize it, Georgia. The kind of stuff I've seen from some members wouldn't mean anything if they were nobody, but the people who stay here have a lot more at stake. Greater images to protect. And Aspera prides itself on its discretion. Whatever it was, the Hayeses weren't going to give it anything less than Code Red treatment. I don't know what made her think she'd get away with selling us out, though."

"She didn't," I say. "She never thought that."

Because she knew who she was.

There was no one she was meant to be.

It wasn't Aspera she was selling out.

You've reached Katy Avis. Leave a message at the tone."
My eyes burn at the sound of her rough-hewn voice.
How it makes her almost alive again.

How it finds all those places inside me that reached for and recoiled from her.

Mom.

I hang up the phone, brush away my tears, and dial her cell again. It rings next to me on my desk, until the voice-mail picks up.

"You've reached Katy Avis. Leave a message at the tone."

It's your daughter calling.

"You've reached Katy Avis. Leave a message at the tone."

Your daughter, always calling.

G eorgia."

"Yeah?"

"She here for you?"

I turn to the windshield, my breath catching in my throat.

"I'm so sorry, Kel—some wires must have gotten crossed."

"No worries. It's my break no matter where I take it."

I get out of the Audi. Kel reverses up the drive until it opens wide enough for him to turn around and head back to the lodge. When he's out of sight, I face her.

Nora.

She stands next to her car, wearing torn denim shorts and a white button-down, half-tucked. Her hair is swept to the side, revealing a fresh-shaved undercut. She takes me in as I do her; my black flats and blue jeans, black tee. The ghost of our last fight hovers between us, the question of her, painful.

"Hey," I say.

"I found some things out for you."

"Like what?" I don't know what could be left.

"I asked around the sheriff's department and there's still no word on the rest of your photos, but they did catch the fuckers who took them."

"Oh," I say.

"I thought you'd want to know."

"Yeah. That's good."

"So can I give you a ride home or what?"

I nod, trying to keep my expression neutral. I get into the car, and she follows after me. She drives us from Aspera and I study her the whole time. Everything that's happened—it would be enough to make any girl fade away, but part of me feels like Nora's only become more of herself, even if it's not who exactly she had in mind. Her face and eyes are sharper than they've ever been, and I'd take every one of her edges even if it meant she'd cut me with them.

There's no part of her I wouldn't take.

She keeps one hand on the wheel, the other, palm open, at her side.

Squeeze my hand.

I'm just about to reach for it when she says something, quiet and sad.

"What?" I ask.

She swallows hard before repeating herself: "She always said I was the untouchable one."

When she pulls up to my house, she stares at it a long time.

"Show me what happened," she says, "and tell me everything."

We go inside and I tell her the way I remember it now.

All of it is red, the way I remember it now.

I see it through my own blood long before the moment my head hit the door. After we got back from the sheriff's office, Tyler sent me to my room while he tidied everything up. He righted the chairs, centered the table, cleaned the blood off the floor.

He missed the spot on the doorframe.

"How did he look?" she asks me, standing next to the chair Justin sat in, touching its back. I describe her father's corpse, because by then, he might as well have been one. Dead man walking. The terrible pall of his face. His rumpled clothes. The blood on his arm. She touches her own when I say this. Asks, "His arm?"

I nod. She shuts her eyes tight, committing it all to memory.

"Tell me everything he said."

And she wants it exactly as it was said, and every word I

say, she repeats with her fingers to her lips, as though it's not enough to hear, she needs to feel them too.

I never taught her fear. Never taught her where not to go.

"What do you think that means?"

"I don't know."

It's all above you.

"What does—"

"I don't know, Nora."

And then I think about all the things she doesn't know—Kel and the compass, her father a suspect at the very last; there's no percentage in it now, and I promised Matthew I wouldn't tell and I'll keep that promise. I just don't want to keep giving her nothing at the same time.

"He was out of his mind. He had my picture in his hand. And that's when it clicked . . . because there was only one place he could have gotten it." The memory of my panic wraps around me. *Wait, wait, wait, wait, wait! Listen to me, no, listen*—"I tried to get to my room. I was going to lock myself in. He grabbed me and—" I touch my forehead and nod to the doorframe. "Four stitches . . . anyway, Tyler came. Your dad ran. You know what happened next."

"Fucking coward." She walks to the kitchen window, leaning against the sink, trying to center herself. I'm glad I never told her what her dad did to the screen, that she won't look at it and see him there too. "If I'd ever found out, I would have shot him myself."

"You hear from anyone? . . . Your mom?"

"She didn't come for Ashley, she didn't come for him," she says. "And she's definitely not coming for me."

"I'm sorry, Nora."

"What's the point in being sorry." She lets out a bitter laugh. "For the longest time, I thought it was her, you know? Mom. I thought . . . her leaving was why Ashley was so fucking angry at the world . . ." Her grip on the counter tightens. "I didn't even think . . ."

"No one would."

"I want to know who she was meeting," she says suddenly. "Because I wish he'd come for her. I wish she'd got away. I wish I'd never known what happened to her and that I spent my whole fucking life wondering because anything would be better than this. Anything's better than what I know now." She brings her hand to her mouth. "All that time . . ."

I cross the room and slip my arms around her waist. I feel her tense and then—finally—relax into my hold. I rest my head against her back and she breathes in . . . out.

"It's not your fault."

"Yes, it is. And now there's no one left."

"I'm here," I say to her.

"Good." She exhales shakily. "Because that's what I came to find out."

I lower my hands to her hips. She turns around slowly, her cheeks damp with tears, and touches my forehead. She runs her finger along the scar, tracing its short path back and forth, then brings her hands to my cheeks, the heat of her palms warming my skin before she pushes my hair from my face.

She leans down.

Her lips, a perfect fit.

She kisses me so deeply, all my nerve endings come alive.

When she pulls away, I feel like I'm on fire.

She rests her head against mine.

I close my fingers around her wrists, feel the faint flutter of her pulse there.

The Aspera girls form an asterism in the lobby.

Asterism: a group of stars smaller than a constellation.

I'm learning new words all the time.

I hang back just to watch them, this rare glimpse. Even from a distance, they're everything I thought they'd be, their collective beauty washing over me like a wave. There are fewer than I'd imagined, six in all, the privilege of their title impressed upon me further still, making me long for it even more. The Aspera girl I've seen before, the brunette, stands at their center, though I wouldn't call her their heart. Each of them, in their own way, someone to want. Seeing them all together—you'd never take one at the expense of losing another. I don't know if Nora would be surprised or disappointed to discover they're not all white and they don't look like Cleo—but they are a certain type of beautiful the world readily defines. I think of her high, in my room. *The patriarchy's dream. The kind of beauty that's always leaving somebody behind.* I want to ask Matthew about that, if how they choose Aspera girls is less about who they're taking with them and more about who they're not.

Ask him why, if I'm the dream, I'm still not living it.

Kel strides across the floor to them. They unconsciously synchronize their turn to meet him, listening, rapt, to whatever it is he says. He refers to his phone repeatedly, pointing at one of them every now and then. After about ten minutes of this, the girls disperse in all directions. My eyes try to chart the paths of each, but most fade into their greater surroundings, beauty unto beauty. Except the brunette.

I follow her at a distance. She ends up in the executive elevator of course, and I reach the end of the corridor just as the doors close in front of her. I have that thought again but this time it's so angry it startles me: *I should be you.*

I don't understand.

I gave him what he needed.

It's supposed to be my turn.

The antlers on Matthew's office doors reach for me.

I feel light-headed for no reason I can parse, until I realize I'm holding my breath. This will be the first time we've seen each other since—since. But he called me at my desk, as if he could sense my growing frustration.

It's time we talked.

I tug the doors open and he's waiting for me. The sight of his desk steals me from this moment to the last we were together. I swear I can feel it digging into the front of my thighs, my breasts pressed against its cool surface, the heat of him on me, the scratchiness of his dress shirt at my back. Even the floor—even it sparks a memory. The way he picked up my clothes and handed them back, an item at a time, and watched me get dressed.

"I was talking to Cleo," he says.

Her name like a kick to the chest.

So it doesn't mean anything . . . because it can't.

So when a thing like that happens—it's not really happening at all.

"Georgia?" He cocks his eyebrow.

"Sorry." I clear my throat. "How's Miami?" My face reddens at the struggle to keep my voice steady, how impossible it is not to give myself away.

"Beautiful. I almost wish I was there." He gives me a look. "Almost."

"When's she going to be back?"

"She'll be here Friday for the summit. But what I wanted to talk with her about couldn't wait . . . Fact is, we agree with you, Georgia. If you're going to stay at Aspera after the summer, we're not going to keep you hidden away in that little room. And you've proven yourself many times over." I still, my heart poised on the edge of whatever he's going to say next. "So how would you feel about becoming my assistant?" Assistant? That's it? "Part-time. Kel would begin the process of training you following the summit. You'd take the role during the weekends, after school, holidays. It's fewer days in deference to your schedule, your education, but your duties and your responsibilities will be substantially greater . . . what do you think?"

I feel it, that anger rising in me again.

"From Aspirant to assistant."

He notices. "What's wrong?"

"How is that better than an Aspera girl?"

"I think you're misunderstanding me, Georgia. It's much better."

"*How?*"

"Because you *will* be an Aspera girl. But not just any Aspera girl."

And suddenly, I see myself across from Cleo on the terrace, my first day here. Her finger tracing a path from porcelain . . .

This is where you start.

To gold.

And that's where you're headed.

Not just any Aspera girl.

"Well?" Matthew asks. "What do you say?"

The Aspera girl.

W hat?" Nora asks me.

I'm watching her watch the road.

"Nothing."

"You sure about that?"

I wonder if, deep down, she knows how many times I've had to answer for her kisses. In my bed alone or in the shower, my hand between my legs. I wonder if, deep down, she knows how insatiable she's made me. If, deep down, she knows every time I've kissed her, it's like I forget this world in her, and how every time I kiss her, I feel found in this world. I want to tell her that even if today was a bad day like all the others, and for all the reasons it has to be, I'm determined to hold good things inside of it.

And there's nothing more than her I want to hold.

"No. What are you doing Friday night?"

She smiles in a way that makes me think, deep down, she knows.

"I have to deal with some . . . things about my dad. Then the Millers are taking me out for dinner after because they feel sorry for me."

"The Millers sound . . . nice."

"They've been good to me. Mr. and Mrs. Miller. Chell, and her new girlfriend, Caroline."

"Oh," I say. "That's nice too."

She gives me a sidelong look. "I'm free after nine, though."

"Then you should come over after nine."

"Sure."

We pull up to my house. I unbuckle my seat belt, and she grabs my arm, says, "Avis," and, "you know we don't have to wait until then, right? That you could be with me now?"

She leans against my bedroom door as I close the blinds. My head's buzzing, my heart thrumming as I face her. She meets me in the middle of the room and kisses me, a gentle announcement before making herself even more known; her mouth opening to mine, her tongue, tasting me. My hands hover at her hips, my fingertips tracing their lines before my arms come around her, my right hand resting between her shoulder blades, my left at the small of her back. Her muscles firm to touch. I bring my mouth to her neck, trailing my tongue over its delicate curve, tasting the sweet salt of her skin, pausing at the small gasp this elicits.

That I could do this to a girl.

For a girl.

I kiss her, nibbling her lip before pulling away, inch by inch.

I take my shirt off.

She stands back, her face flushed, no small amount of admiration for the sight in front of her, her eyes hungry, her desire a beautiful thing to witness, her desire making me something more than just a beautiful thing. She moves to me, pressing her lips gently to my right shoulder before moving to my left, then brings her hand to my breast and feels me, and everything about her is electric with want, amplifying my own.

She puts her mouth where her palm was and it's my turn to gasp. I moan as her tongue circles my nipple, making my legs go so weak. She gives me a brief reprieve, rising to meet me, touching her lips to mine, teasing and light. And then she *really* kisses me. She kisses me and I don't ever want her to stop, even with the promise of starting again. There's no distance I can tolerate between us anymore. Her hand comes to the back of my head, her fingers tangling in my hair as she pulls me close, our bodies pressed against each other, and then she has me against the wall, her leg between my legs, and I grip her bicep as I bear down on her, moving against her, feeling everything inside me lighting up, and I think of all her edges, how I'm inside them now. When it almost becomes too much, I make a small noise, pulling away, and then just as quickly return to her, crushing my lips against hers. I run the outside of my hand against the cut of her jaw, trace her kiss-bruised lips with my fingertips, focusing on the softness of them, the shape, until she takes my thumb in her mouth and gives it a little bite.

I reach down, touching the hem of her shirt.

"Will you take this off?"

She steps away, turning her back to me, lifting her shirt over her head.

She unclasps her bra.

Both fall to the floor.

She's incredible.

The broadness of her shoulders, the scattering of moles on her back, the sturdiness of her frame. The unapologetic way she holds herself, always and forever, demanding the world to take her to account. Even now.

Especially now.

I touch my lips to each of her shoulders, like she did me.

And I feel her shiver, like she made me.

I tug at the waist of her shorts.

She slips them off and faces me, and I take in the full view of her, my pulse racing. She's even more finely built than I knew, her abs visible in the bedroom's weak light, her breasts pert and lovely. Her boy shorts rest at her hipbones and, visible through the thin white material, her dark pubic hair.

"I want you, Avis," she says.

I kiss her, my hands at her breasts, feeling her harden to my touch. She sighs in that space between kisses. I leave a trail of them along her collarbone, and then I reach around her, cupping her ass. She murmurs out a laugh. I slip out of my shorts, my underwear, and then I pull her to my bed, and she tops me, straddling my hips, arching her back as she moves against me, turning my whole body into one desperate, feverish, demand of just her. Just this.

Us.

She kisses me and kisses me again, and then she moves her mouth to my neck as her hand drifts down between my legs, her fingers slowly, carefully inside me, her eyes on me as she memorizes my every little response to her touch: the hitch of my breath, my small uneven gasps as I reach for her, touching her, feeling her as she draws me out.

And the way she looks at me.

The way she looks at me—

come.

I feel like it happens fast. There's something affection-ate in Nora's eyes that says it might have. She lies down next to me and I fold myself into her, resting my head against her chest. I marvel silently over all the pieces of herself she's shared with me, and the pieces she's sharing with me still. The sound of her breathing. The rhythm of her heartbeat. Her sweat, the heat of her body. The hold of her arms.

"I liked that," I tell her.

She smiles, drawing circles on my side.

I close my eyes to the niceness of it.

"Was that your first time?" she asks after a while.

The question gives me pause, my body shying from it as much as my mind. I don't know why. I'm not embarrassed. I just don't know how to answer her. And I don't want to lie to her either. I push myself from her, rolling onto my back, my palm covering my necklace, the warmth of the moment leaving me.

"Avis?" she asks.

"Aidan Archer was my first kiss," I say.

"When he got you drunk?"

The warmth of the moment, gone.

But I don't know why.

"He kissed me." I make myself look at her. "And it was the first time I was ever kissed."

And if that's not a kiss, what else do you call it?

She doesn't say anything.

spera begins its preparations for the summit to-night, the staff orchestrating the discrete arrivals of Matthew's business partners and their entourages, directing deliveries without interrupting the peaceful flow of the lodge. It's like a dance: expertly and lovingly—and subtly—performed. I spend the morning working through requests, one eye ever on the clock because Cleo's back to-day and Matthew told me to expect to see her at lunch. When the concierge finally signals my break, I hurry to his office, knocking on the door before letting myself in, my eyes scanning the room. Kel sits across from Matthew at his desk but—

"Where's Cleo?"

"A slight delay," Matthew says. "She'll be here tonight."

My face falls. "But I won't be."

Kel's phone chimes. He glances at it, then Matthew. "One of your associates is en route. You might want to be present."

"ETA?" Matthew notices me tiptoeing from the room. "A minute, Georgia."

"Fifteen," Kel tells him.

"How's executive shaping up?"

"The event designer is finished, the florist just arrived. Bring—" Kel catches himself from revealing the member. "Your associate in here for a drink, and by the time you're done, the floor should be ready to receive them. Everyone else is on track to arrive. The tasting menu needs finalizing." There's something in the way Kel looks at Matthew, eyes admiring and a little wanting. "Only thing left to do is to make yourself presentable."

"Then we're in real trouble." Matthew grins at me. "You get all that, Georgia? That's what it's going to be like. Your job is to be as good as Kel."

"I think it's my job to make her better," Kel says.

"I like that. Give us a moment, would you, Kel?"

He stands. "I'll give you fifteen."

Matthew watches him leave. As soon as the door is shut, he opens his desk drawer and considers whatever's in there. He curls his finger, beckoning me to him. When I reach him, he holds up a red silk tie.

"Do you know how to tie these?"

"No."

"Well, today you're going to learn."

He lifts his collar up and puts the tie around his neck, letting either side of it rest against his chest, adjusting the length. He tells me to remember where, on himself, he's letting it fall. He tells me to take the wider end and cross it over the other. I do as he says, running my thumb over the silk as I await further instruction.

"Now bring the wide end under and up, and through."

The next part is more complicated, and he repeats himself twice before I successfully set the tie up for the final step, which he tells me is the most satisfying. When I pull the material through, achieving what he calls a Windsor knot, I understand what he means.

I smooth his collar down.

"First lesson as my future assistant," he murmurs.

"Did Kel do this for you?" I ask.

He laughs. "No." And then he grabs my hand, pressing it against his crotch, startling me. I feel the unyielding hardness there, and it shocks me into stillness. I search his face for an explanation. "But he didn't do that for me either." And then he lets me go, straightening his tie before moving past, gesturing for me to follow.

"I thought—"

But it comes out so quietly, he doesn't hear it.

We part ways in the corridor, and I detour into the bathroom and wash my hands. I stare in the mirror. My eyes wide, my mouth open, my cheeks pink with embarrassment. My throat tightens as I try to understand.

I thought—

The sun sets like a neon fire across the sky, as a storm moves in from the east. The sharp smell of ozone is in the air, raising the fine hairs on my arms, and it feels like the perfect kind of night to spend with a girl you really like. When Tyler comes home, I tell him Nora will be over, and he tells me he's taking a load off with some of the guys; just one beer, a shower, and the house is all mine. I toss an envelope at him from across the room and smile when he catches it easy.

"Should square us," I say.

"You kidding me?"

"I'm moving up in the world, Tyler." And then I tell him what it's going to look like past the summer at Aspera, that I'm going to be Matthew Hayes's assistant. I wait for him to congratulate me, to tell me that he's proud, but he's silent.

"What?" I ask.

And then he says, "I don't know about that, George. You got school."

"Who cares about school? This is an actual education."

"I'm serious. Coming off the summer you've had right

into junior year, there's a lot you're going to be juggling. You need one less thing to do—"

"It's not going to be Aspera."

"I thought you understood this was like, a summer-only thing." His voice is careful. "An exception but . . . temporary."

My stomach bottoms out, like I've been standing on a trapdoor the whole time and he just pulled the lever.

"Since when? You never said that to me."

He unlaces his work boots and kicks them aside, passing me for the fridge, for his beer. He presses it against his sweaty forehead, closing his eyes briefly.

"Can we have this talk tomorrow?"

"You're still trying to keep Mom happy. She's *dead*, Tyler."

"George—"

"I'm not giving it up. There. Good talk."

His upper lip bubbles as he runs his tongue over his teeth. "I know you think the sun rises for those two up there, but they threw Mom over after *years* of her busting her ass for them, and I'm not gonna let you stick around long enough for them to do the same to you."

"You mean when she blackmailed them?"

It's out of my mouth before I can stop it, but even if I could have, I don't think I would have. There's a point, I want to tell him, where her lies become his. That if he keeps telling them at my expense, I don't know what's going to happen between us.

"Who the hell told you that?" he demands.

"*You* should have!"

"I'm serious, George." He sets the beer down. "Who told you that? The Hayeses?"

"Someone she used to work with. Neither of them."

He raises his eyes to the ceiling, looking past it, as though he's waiting for a sign from her—but there's none.

"It's not what you think."

"Then what is it?" He doesn't answer. I raise my hands, grasping at air, trying to make him see what he's doing to me. "You never tell me fucking *anything*—"

"And why the hell would I? So the second you hear something you don't like, you end up at the Hayeses' for the night?" He steps forward, his face red. "You know that's when I knew—when I *knew* I made a mistake. I never should've let you work there in the first place—"

"No, you never should've *lied* to me in the first place—"

"*George!*" he yells—actually yells it. "You don't know what you're talking about."

"You can't make me give it up," I snap, and he gives me a disgusted look. "They *like* me, Tyler. And I'm good at it—"

"You know they liked her too? The Hayeses? You think they got time to learn everyone's name in housekeeping? Matthew Hayes knew hers. She was good at her job, just like you, and he liked her. So he bumped her up. You were about twelve. Top level. You think the pay got better or that she just went up one floor? I could tell you, but I don't think you really want to hear it." His face falls as my eyes fill with tears. "I don't think you've ever really wanted to hear it."

"That's not fair," I manage.

"Oh, I think it is. I think when it comes to her, you've made up your mind—" He breaks off. "And I think I really, *really* can't do this with you right now. So I'm taking a shower, and then I'm going out."

head to Mac's, to grab something there for Nora and me, and hope, by the time I'm back, Tyler is gone.

I need to talk to Cleo about it, him, and then I need her to talk to Tyler because I remember her, in our kitchen, the way she made it all so clear.

It's always better to dream.

If she told it to him like she told it to me, he'd have to see it.

He'd See.

The streetlights flicker on. Soon, the harsh lights of Mac's Convenience come into view. A small shape sits on the curb outside, her arms wrapped around her legs. She's familiar.

"Liv?" I call.

She raises her head.

It takes her longer to remember me.

"Oh," she says. "Georgia, right?"

"Yeah." She's in a thin tank top and shorts, shivering. She rests her chin on her knees. "It's kind of late, isn't it?" She gives me a look like, *not even,* but when I try to remember what I was doing around this time of night at her age, I know it wasn't this. "Are you okay?" She turns her face away. "I'm not going to bust you or anything, but at least let me know you're okay."

"I'm fine." A few cars go down the street. She cranes her neck as though she's expecting someone. "I was going to a friend's house, down on Williams. My ride's late . . . I don't know if they're going to show."

"You can't go back home?" The question earns me another look. "It's gonna storm. Williams is like, halfway across the city."

Liv rolls her eyes. "That's why I need a ride."

I look around, thinking. Thinking I don't like this. "How about I wait with you a little bit, see if your ride shows, and if they don't, I'll get you a cab or something, okay?"

"I'm not going home."

"Didn't say you had to."

She hesitates. "You'd do that?"

"It's either that or leave you out here alone."

And I won't leave her out here. Just because the threat of Justin James is gone doesn't mean there's not still the world. I sit beside her while we wait. She mumbles a thanks, then feels the need to clarify: "It really is a friend's house." And I want to believe her. The gutter is littered with cigarette butts and cracked plastic slushie cups. The bright pink lights of the store reflect in a pool of suspicious-looking liquid.

"Sometimes I wondered . . ." She trails off, then looks down the road, hopeful, but the car she's eyeing passes us by. She sighs. "Never mind."

"What did you wonder?"

"Nothing."

"Is it Ashley?"

". . . I just wondered if Hulick would've actually been good for her. I don't know. I mean, it wasn't a great place, I know, but like . . ."

"Rather her there, than this."

"Yeah. But it's not just that . . . Ashley never got over her mom. She really missed her. She always said Nora was the untouchable one." It's awful, hearing Liv say it. "It was because Nora just rolled with everything, you know? Like it never got to her."

"I don't think that's true."

"Well, even if it isn't, Mr. James never, ever gave Nora shit. *That's* the truth. But Ashley, he was always on her. But not like, not in a way that would make you think he was—" She breaks off, wiping at her eyes. "I can't believe it was her dad. Doing that to her."

"I don't think anyone can."

"Fucked up."

"Yeah."

And now Liv's started, she can't seem to stop, and I remember what Nora said about her parents, how they don't really know their daughter, and I wonder if there's anyone else in her life that means as much to her as Ashley did.

But if there was, I don't think I'd be the one she was saying all this to.

"I keep thinking I missed some signs. But, like, she *never* talked about him like that, not even when she was bitching." She sniffles. "And you know what else I don't get?"

"What's that?"

"Him wanting to even send her to some camp. Why would he do that? She could tell anyone there—why would he give her the chance, if he was doing all that to her?" She rubs her forehead. "Seriously, do you think I missed some signs?"

My mind reaches for anything to give her to make all of this less hard.

"You know, I was in Ashley's room after she died. And I saw her mirror, with all those pictures taped on it. You were the one in most of them. You were really important to her. So you need to stop thinking about what you might've missed and just think about how you gave her something she needed when she was alive. She was lucky to have you, Liv."

"I loved her," Liv whispers, almost to herself.

"I can see that."

She lets out a small sob, burying her face in her hands. Part of me wants to reach out to her, but I don't think she'd like it. It hurts, watching her cry. It takes time for her to collect herself, and when she does, it's only to raise her head to a series of cars passing by.

None of them stop for her.

"Maybe you should call a cab," she finally says, defeated. She gives me an apologetic look—then frowns. "Why do you have her necklace?"

I look where she's looking.

The teardrop against my neck.

Liv reaches out and grasps it.

"This is Ashley's necklace."

"This is mine."

"No, it's Ashley's. It was a secret."

I raise my eyes to hers, panic coursing through me.

"What kind of secret?" I ask.

ASPERA

Lightning flashes off the gate's golden letters. I look past them, up, dizzied by the sight overhead: dark clouds encroaching on a pool of shining diamonds. Stars. I reach out, as if I could make a ripple across the heavens and send them scattering down, and then I bring my hand to my necklace. A secret.

I trudge up the drive, steeling myself against the wind. The resort rises up to meet me, an ominous silhouette, lights illuminating its insides. I glimpse the lobby, and it's empty but it feels so watchful, as though it's seeing more than it reveals. I pass the lodge and head down the road that leads to the cabin as the sky complains; a low roll of thunder, a near thing. I quicken my pace. It starts to rain as the cabin comes into view. The lights in the windows tell me she's back. She's back and it only makes sense that a storm would herald her return. I scamper up the steps and knock on the door.

No one answers.

The rain falls harder.

I reach for the doorknob.

Unlocked.

I slip inside.

The heat is on, enough to take the chill off the air. The flatscreen is off, an artless void. The hallway leading to the hot tub is dark. The kitchen, dim.

All the light is coming from upstairs.

"Cleo?"

My heart on its tiptoes.

". . . Cleo?"

I wait a few minutes before I head up.

When I reach the landing, I listen.

There's a faint sound from the opposite end of the hall, the only part of this place I haven't explored. I creep toward it until I'm standing in front of Cleo's open bedroom door. When I peek inside, it's as though a soft champagne dream has met a post-travel tornado. Suitcase open on the floor, clothes scattered everywhere. Across the room, the bathroom door is just slightly ajar, and I hear the steady stream of water from inside. She's in the shower.

The scent of figs and orange blossoms is everywhere, and it calms me, reminds me that when Cleo is around, the world makes sense.

She'll tell me about the necklace, and it will all make sense.

I wait.

Is it strange to wait in here?

I can't bring myself to do it anywhere else.

I need her.

I follow the scent to her vanity and find her perfume. Dior. Her lipstick, that cherry red. Guerlain. I take the cap off and catch sight of myself in the mirror, my hair limp against my face, wet from the rain.

I look young.

Scared.

I press the lipstick to my lips without thinking, my eyes falling on the teardrop as I do.

A secret.

What kind of secret.

It was from the man she was meeting.

But no man gave her this.

I set the lipstick back on the vanity and glance back at the bathroom door.

Steam unfurls into the room.

It was his promise. She only wore it around me.

My phone chimes, that shimmery sound. Nora. Loud. Too loud. And suddenly, I don't want to be found here like this. I hurry out, tiptoeing down the hall. My phone shimmers again, and I duck into the nearest room, Matthew's room.

Just got to the restaurant.

Can't wait to see you.

I press the phone against my chest and exhale, and I'm about to text her back when I stop, aware of my surroundings.

The bathroom door open, its light on . . .

"Matthew?" I call softly.

But Matthew is on the executive floor. I check the bathroom, to be sure it's empty. His toiletries are scattered everywhere. Cologne and aftershave. The Viagra.

I back out and sit on the bed to thumb a reply to Nora,

when the shine of something catches my eye, just peeking out of his open nightstand drawer. I put my phone back in my pocket and pull it all the way open, and there, where Cleo's Polaroid used to be, a new set of photographs.

And in each photograph, a girl.

Pick me up at Aspera as soon as you get this. Hurry.

I send the text to Nora when I reach the bottom of the stairs, then I fold the glossies in half, tucking them into the waistband of my shorts, under my shirt, before I open the front door and step into the storm. The rain is sharp against my skin. I squint against it, barely able to make out the road back. By the time I get to the lodge, I'm soaked through. The lobby is still empty, silent but for the sound of my own frantic breathing, raindrops dripping from my clothes onto the floor. I press my hand against my abdomen, feeling the paper-crunch of my photos there. I'll hide in my office until Nora comes. I hurry down the hall, my pulse staccato. My shoes squelch against the floor, and when I look behind me, there's a trail of water and I don't know what I can do about it. I slow when the corridor to the executive elevator comes into view, cordoned off by a velvet rope.

I hear a moan.

Fuck.

I don't know what to do.

No one knows I'm here.

I want to keep it that way.

Another moan.

This time it's so desultory, I inch close enough to peer down the corridor.

The brunette Aspera girl.

She's halfway from the elevator, slumped against the wall, her right arm stretched across the floor. It moves back and forth weakly, searching for something, anything, to hold onto. She's a mess, but one of those gorgeous messes that reminds me of a Hollywood after-party, those girls who hold the scene up for as long as they can before the curtain closes over their eyes, ending the night. Her black dress spills around her like an oil stain, a slit up the side, so far up the side I can see she's not wearing any underwear. Her hair is messy and unkempt, in her eyes.

She's alone.

"Hey," I say quietly.

I step forward, forgetting the barrier, the rope hitting my thighs, its stands clattering. I glance back down the hall, terrified of the possibility of being caught, but no one comes. I turn back to her. She doesn't react, hasn't.

She's stopped moving.

"Are you all right?" I ask.

But she can't be. Couldn't be.

"Hey. You all right?"

Nothing.

I step over the rope and hurry to her, crouching in front of her. I bring my hand to her clammy face, tilting it toward me. Her head lolls like a ragdoll's, her makeup a smear across

her face, her mouth half-open. I push her back to get a better look and she *thuds* unceremoniously against the wall,
hard enough to make me wince and her eyelids flutter.

"*Hey,*" I say, louder now, and I pat her cheek none too
gently when I see her eyes falling shut again. My gaze travels
from her face to her twitching fingers.

A bruise staining the crook of her arm.

There was an injection bruise there . . .

"Mm." A thin, reedy sound.

When I look at her again, her half-open, cloudy blue eyes
bring her more into focus.

From a distance, she was tall and willowy, like a runway
model . . . this close, there's something . . . she's less formed.

Undeveloped.

I grab her arm, pressing my thumb into the bruise, trying
to bring her back to herself. It works, a little. Her eyes clear
for a second, and they look directly into mine.

"Help me," she whispers.

"Georgia? What are you doing here?"

I drop her hand. It hits the floor with a *smack*. I fumble
back as Kel strides down the corridor to us, frowning as his
attention shifts from me to the Aspera girl.

"She needs help," I tell him.

He kneels in front of her, dismayed.

"Just a little overserved. It happens sometimes." He glances
at me. "But you know all about that."

"Right." I nod and cross my arms, wincing when the
photos crinkle, hoping he won't notice.

"I'll take care of this," he says. "You can—what are you
doing here?"

"I wanted to see Cleo."

I don't know what else I could say.

"Does she know that?"

"I think she's busy, so I'm just going to go—"

"You should wait in Matthew's office."

"I can—"

"Wait," he says firmly. "In Matthew's office."

"Okay," I say in a tiny voice.

The Aspera girl moans a final time. Kel's eyes never leave me until I round the corner.

I press myself against the wall, balling my hands into fists. And then—

"Jesus. How did you even get down here?"

And then—

There's a sound—a soft whine, a subtle friction, like skin rubbing against the floor . . .

I risk a glance.

Kel has his hands hooked under the Aspera girl's arms.

He's dragging her back to the elevator.

'm halfway to the lobby before I hear someone headed in my direction. I double back quickly, slipping into my office, willing my heart to calm as I wait for the coast to clear. I dig the pictures out of my shorts and unfold them, spreading them across the desk, smoothing them with shaking hands, hoping, somehow, they've become any other photos, that I saw them wrong. I hold my phone over them, and its light glares off the girl captured in each.

Here, her arms crossed over herself.

Here, her bra straps loose at her fingertips.

Here, without a bra.

Here, from the side, her head tilted back in ecstasy.

And finally, the last, on the couch, leaned forward, legs spread.

I force myself to look away. Check my messages for anything from Nora. There's nothing. I glance at the window as a flash of lightning reflects the room in the glass, and in that brief moment, I see an open door, the secret door, the shadow of a man standing in it.

Matthew.

"Georgia," he says.

The red tie I painstakingly knotted this afternoon hangs

loose around his neck. He leans back on his heels, studying me, then he enters the room, the door from his office swinging shut behind him. For one brief moment, I can see him as he must have been when he was there on the road, standing over me—

The footsteps around my body.

His.

"Kel said you'd come."

"I needed to see Cleo," I say.

"Why?" he asks. I open my mouth, then close it again. Matthew raises an eyebrow, surprised by my caginess. "Come on now. There must be some reason to bring you out here in a storm like this. You look upset. Trouble at home again?"

"No."

"Then what's wrong? I know I'm not Cleo, but you can tell me anything."

"I want to know—" I bring my hand to my neck and hold the teardrop up. Matthew reaches for it, turning it over in his hand, running his thumb past the porcelain, over the gold. "I want to know why Cleo gave Ashley this necklace before she gave it to me."

His eyes meet mine. "Why would you think—"

"I know she had it, Matthew. I'm asking you why."

He sighs, long and drawn out, then shakes his head and stares out the window. More lightning branches across the sky before disappearing into the unforgiving night.

"Can I be sure of you, Georgia?"

"Yes," I whisper.

"We met Ashley at that volleyball game. She ended up confiding her troubles to Cleo, and you know how Cleo is.

How good her heart is. How much she wants to help. We offered Ashley a place to stay—like how we offered you a place after that fight with your brother. The plan was we'd try to reason with Justin, but we never got the chance, and he killed her before we could help. That's all. It was terrible. But that's all it is."

But the photos.

He sees the tears in my eyes and pulls me into a hug. His hold on me is crushing, asking me to accept what he's said, to move on. And there's a scent on him. Something past his cologne. It's like sweat, but not his sweat.

"You're shivering." He rubs my arms up and down. "Let's go into my office. It's warmer there. I'll have Kel bring you a change of clothes."

He ushers me toward the door, and as we pass my desk to get there, he catches sight of the photos scattered across it. The world drops out from under me. I step back from him, and he steps forward, staring down at them.

After a long moment, he turns to me.

"Let's go into my office, Georgia."

"If you're going to be my assistant," he says, "the only thing you really need to understand is the difference between what you need to know and the work you have to do."

He turns on the light, the antlers above throwing warped shadows, making the storm outside the window impossible to see, but I sense it there, raging beyond Aspera's walls.

"Then what do I need to know about Ashley?"

He motions me forward.

I stay where I am.

"Don't be afraid, Georgia," he says, hurt. "It's all right."

I swallow, my heart pounding, and go to him.

"We *did* meet Ashley at the game," he says. "And we offered her a place to stay. Refuge." His hand grazes the side of my face and then drifts slowly down. He presses his finger to my necklace. I twitch at the light pressure of his touch. He feels it. "She stole from us."

"She stole the necklace?"

He nods, still staring at it.

"She took advantage of one of our members. She overdosed in his room. And I couldn't compromise Aspera for her. You understand." He pauses, his expression darkening. "I need you to tell me something, Georgia. It's very important: Who else knows Ashley had this necklace?"

Liv. I lean against his desk, my breath coming out in short gasps, reaching for anything but her name: "Were you the one who hit me that day?"

"What do we always say, Georgia? It's you, me and—"

"And the member that did that to her? What happened to him?"

Matthew takes off his tie and lays it on the desk.

"What do you think should happen to him?" He unbuttons the first button of his shirt as the connections form and break, their threads tying themselves around me, holding me in place. I close my eyes and see a motel room, my photograph, my bike in the back of a trunk.

Matthew had them first.

But Justin was the one who died with them.

When I open my eyes, he's in front of me, his hands on either side of me.

"I should go," I say.

"You just got here."

"I know, but I shouldn't have. It's an important night—"

"And you're part of it now."

He presses himself into me, burying his face against my throat.

"Let's get you out of these clothes."

"I need to go home."

"You will. But before you do . . ."

He grasps at my shirt. I stare down at his hands, at how tightly he has my shirt in his grip, before slowly raising my eyes to his and the way he looks at me now isn't a way he's ever looked at me before.

Or maybe it's the way he's always looked at me.

"Can I kiss you?"

Y ou're needed upstairs."

"Thank you, Kel."

He zips up his fly.

Buckles his belt.

I'm on the floor, curled against his desk, my arms crossed over myself, trying to cover what parts of me I can, flinching as Matthew reaches out to touch the top of my head, a wordless goodbye. I close my eyes as they leave. I keep them closed, my heart beating weakly, until the door opens again, and through a blur of tears, I see her.

"Cleo."

I reach for her. She comes to me, crouches in front of me. She puts her arms around me and I try to push her away, and it's only when I've succeeded that I reach for her again, grasping at her desperately, crying harder now, sobbing.

"Georgia," she says. "Calm down."

"Cleo—"

"You're fine."

I gaze up at her.

She's so beautiful.

I wish, so badly, after all of this, she wasn't still so beautiful.

"You're fine," she says again. "You've done so well."

I turn away from her, acutely aware of my nakedness.

The ache between my legs.

The cold.

"Georgia."

She sits beside me, her silk shirt brushing my arm.

"Georgia. Say something."

"I saw an Aspera girl tonight."

"Did you?"

"She came down from the elevator . . . and she couldn't walk. She must have crawled . . . and then Kel came and he took her back up. But before he did that, she asked me to—" My voice cracks. "Help her."

I listen to the steady, even sound of Cleo's breathing, a contrast to my own stuttering breaths in and out.

"Those girls are nothing," she finally says.

"Help me," I whisper to her.

She doesn't reply.

My face crumples.

"He hurt me," I say. "Matthew."

"Georgia."

"He killed Ashley—"

"*Georgia.*"

I dig my hands into my hair, and I pull at it, trying to reclaim some sense of my body, if only through the hurt I can cause to it myself.

"I'm going to tell—" The words are feverish, lack direction.

Will I? I think at the same time Cleo asks, "Who? Who will you tell? The police? I can take you upstairs and you can tell them now." I lower my hands, numb. "You weren't hurt,

Georgia. This doesn't mean anything because it can't . . . it's not happening at all . . . isn't that what you told Matthew?"

"It was you," I mumble. "You told Ashley you'd save her. Kel took her from the party and brought her here, and you got her killed."

She presses her lips together a moment before she speaks. "Ashley wasn't like us. She was looking for something I couldn't give her, and she didn't want . . . she didn't understand the things I could. But you." Cleo reaches for my necklace and turns the teardrop around. "This should have always, only, been yours."

I rest my head back, staring at the ceiling.

The antlers hanging from the ceiling . . .

I close my eyes.

It's all above you.

"Justin knew."

"Georgia."

"If he knew . . . why didn't he . . ."

"There are rules. You'll learn them all, in time."

"Tell me."

"Members protect one another above all else."

I open my eyes.

"Justin was a member?"

"If protecting each other isn't a promise you can keep, it's the price you pay."

A motel room.

A gun to the head.

"You killed him."

"At first, he understood. We've protected him so long.

He couldn't expect us not to do the same for another. But then he decided he wasn't satisfied. It wasn't enough he knew what happened. He had to know who. He wanted them to pay. And what we wouldn't tell him, he tried so hard to find out. The compass led him to Kel. He was so sure it was Kel. He came to the lodge that day. I took him to Matthew's office to wait." She clenches her jaw. "That was my mistake. Matthew kept a photo of you there from your little modeling shoot. He was very partial to it. Justin found it and there was a confrontation." I remember standing outside the cabin. No one where they were supposed to be. The crack of gunfire in the air. The blood on his arm. "Well. You know what happened next."

"You killed him," I say again, fainter now, disappearing . . .

Cleo grasps my arm, forcing me back.

"But are you beginning to see? Do you see the amount of people it takes for a thing like this to work? The power necessary to make sure all the pieces fit into place just because we said they needed to? Matthew is untouchable. Even your mother understood that in the end."

I wrench away from her. "What?"

She reaches for my shirt, crumpled on the floor, and holds it out to me. I can't move. She presses it against my chest, and it falls limply into my lap.

"I told you, Georgia. I feel an affinity with you. When I met you, I knew you instantly, I *saw* you. You'll never be a girl crawling across the floor. You won't have to struggle. You won't have to hurt like I did. Because I care about you.

Don't you understand? I care about you so much I gave you Matthew."

"No. I don't—" I reach for the necklace, but she grabs my hand, stopping me. I try to pull away, but her grip is painfully tight. "I don't want it—"

"Listen to me," she says sharply.

I turn away, but she grasps me by the chin, makes me look at her.

I see myself reflected in her pale blue eyes.

"This is the way the world is. You know I'm right. So you get dressed and you go home and think about how I'm right, and then you see if you still want to take that necklace off." Her touch softens as she stretches her fingers across my cheek. "You have to accept this. You know you do. It's their world. There's nothing you can do about it. But with me, and with Matthew, you can have everything you've ever wanted. *Everything.*" She touches her forehead to mine. "And that's real power, Georgia. And it's better than any dream."

"Did my mother work a night like tonight?"

She brings her mouth to my ear.

"Every night is like this," she whispers.

collapse.

My legs splayed out in front of me, a bitter taste at the back of my throat. I stare at the road through the storm, pressing my hands into the mud, listening to the uneven sound of my breathing as I think of the Aspera girls, of all the things that are happening to them right now. I try to get back up again and I can't.

I can't.

A car is coming.

The rain falls sideways in the glare of its headlights. The world fades away, then slowly burns itself back in again, forming the blurry edges of a driver's side door as it opens.

A girl steps out.

Help me.

"Oh my God, Avis—"

I make a raw, animal sound as Nora drops to her knees in front of me. I slump forward, and she catches me, keeping me upright as I grab at her, my fingers clawing at her arms. I cry. I cry so hard I can't speak. She leans back, both of us soaked through, and pushes my wet hair from my face, trying to get a look at me. I can't look at her.

I can't.

"What's wrong? What's happened to you?"

My eyes find the woods.

Ashley.

Her, me, and this road . . .

"I'm hurt," I say.

"Where? Where are you hurt? Look at me. Please look at me," Nora begs, and I finally look at her, her worried face flickering in and out of focus. "I'm going to help you, Avis. I promise. Tell me what happened and I'll help."

There was a man at the mall, I whisper—

And what did he call me.

EPILOGUE

know it upsets you," Tyler says. "But I'm afraid it'll upset you even more if I—"

He sits across from me at the table, chewing his thumbnail, a nervous habit he doesn't often indulge in. The only other time I've seen him do it were those final weeks of Mom's life, before we moved her to the hospital and he couldn't seem to get a handle on her pain. I think about her as she was then, paper skin over bones, face sunk in, chapped lips pressed so firmly together like she was terrified. Like if she opened her mouth, she'd give it all away.

"Tell me," I say.

Tyler stares at me.

"George," he says quietly. "Did something happen?"

I wrap my arms around my knees, my toes hanging off the end of my chair, and shake my head. Tyler exhales.

"She knew she was dying. A long time before you ever did."

I close my eyes and bury my face against my knees.

"How long?"

"A year."

"A year," I repeat faintly.

"That's why she made her move against Aspera. Once she knew she was terminal, she didn't have anything to lose."

And still, somehow, lost everything.

"Okay," I say.

"Soon as she tried it, they were on her. She didn't let me hang around for the meetings she had with them, but one of the last times—they brought Justin James, just to let her know the law was on their side. That's what she said. She said no matter what, the sheriff's department was going to protect Aspera and that Aspera was bigger than this town." He pauses, and then he asks it again: "Are you sure something . . . nothing's happened?"

"Nothing happened," I whisper, my eyes still shut tight.

"She did it for you, George. She wanted to set you up. Get you the money to get out of Ketchum, so you could find a better dream . . ."

I raise my head.

". . . What?"

"When you got your teeth into Aspera, it scared the shit out of her because what kind of dream is that for a kid to have? She saw how desperate it made you . . . she wanted you out of here, wanted you to know there was something else—"

"She said I wasn't good enough for Aspera."

"That's because you're *not*," Tyler tells me, and I feel a vise around my heart, tightening to a shattering point. "Being good enough to work for them is *not* the same thing as being good enough *for* them. And by Aspera's standards, you're not." His voice breaks. "By Mom's standards, you were better."

"Why wouldn't she just tell me?"

"That's the thing, isn't it?" He struggles to stay in control. "At the time, she thought she was saying one thing, but you were always hearing another. She was ashamed—how did she put it." Tyler closes his eyes, pained. "She said she was ashamed of how imperfectly she loved you. She said it was better if she died with that regret, than to ever have you live with it."

I press my hands over my mouth. Tyler's chair scrapes across the floor as he pushes from the table and makes his way over. He wraps his arms around me.

"She wanted a world for you, George," he says, and I realize he's crying. "Just not this one."

My gaze drifts to the window and I can't see Aspera from here—

I'm sorry, Mom.

—but I can See it.

t's everywhere.

A vis . . . ? Can I come in?"

I close my eyes.

I don't want to be alone, but my voice is so far from me.

Nora slowly opens the door, lets herself inside.

She moves to my bed.

Lies down beside me.

"I'm sorry," she says. I bite my lip to keep from crying. "Avis." She presses her mouth against my shoulder. "I am so sorry that all of this happened to you." Tears trail down the sides of my face. "I'm so sorry . . ."

But what's the point in being sorry.

I grasp her arms.

"I'm cold," I tell her.

She holds me.

I open my eyes.

Light shifts across the ceiling.

The ceiling transforms to the sky.

Tree branches suddenly border its edges.

I turn my knee slightly, one pointing to the other.

I rest my right arm rigidly to my side.

Palm open.

Empty.

My left arm rests against my chest, my fingers reaching toward my throat.

Ashley stands over me, her face round and full, her cheeks pink, lips red, blood flowing.

Alive.

Hey, kid, she whispers. *You all right?*

I cough, choking awake, bolting upright, my mind foggy, realizing time has passed, realizing I fell asleep in Nora's arms.

"Avis?" she asks thickly, sitting up.

It's dark outside, moonlight filtering in through the blinds, thin lines of light stretched across us. My chest hurts so badly, crushed under the weight of the last forty-eight hours. I feel it, all of it—I feel it there and I press my hand to it and—

Oh.

"Talk to me," Nora says.

"It's their world. And there's nothing we can do."

She's quiet.

And then:

"One day it's gonna stop turning for them."

My heart stills.

"Where did you hear that?"

"It's how I feel."

"So you don't accept it?"

"No."

She sounds so sure.

"Not even after what it did to Ashley?"

"No."

"Not even after what it did to—"

"Avis."

She crawls over to me, comes to rest in front of me.

"Never," she says.

She brings her hands to my face.

I bring my hands to the necklace.

take it off.

Acknowledgments

Thank you to everyone who understood the necessity of Georgia's story and who worked so tirelessly, and who were so generous with their time and talents, to help me realize it. *I'm the Girl* would not be the book it is without:

Sara Goodman

Faye Bender

Jennifer Enderlin and Eileen Rothschild

Vanessa Aguirre

Brant Janeway, Alexis Neuville, Rivka Holler, Jeff Dodes

Meghan Harrington, Tracey Guest, Mary Moates

Kerri Resnick, Kemi Mai, Olga Grlic, Michelle McMillian, Anna Gorovoy

Tom Thompson, Erik Platt, Dylan Helstein, Kim Ludlam, Britt Saghi, Lisa Shimabukuro

Taylor Armstrong, Jennifer Edwards, Tim Greco, Sofrina Hinton, Meg Medina, Holly Ruck, Rebecca Schmidt, Talia Sherer

Emily Day, Amanda Rountree, Samantha Slavin

Lauren Hougen, Lena Shekhter, Eric Meyer, Elizabeth Catalano, Chrisinda Lynch, Carolyn Telesca

All at Macmillan, St. Martin's Press, Wednesday Books

The Macmillan Audio team, particularly Ally Demeter and Emily Dyer, and all at Macmillan Academic

All at Raincoast Books, particularly Fernanda Viveiros and Jamie Broadhurst

The Book Group

Susan, Marion, Megan, Jarrad, Cosima, River
David, Ken, Bob, Bruce, Lucy

Lori Thibert. Emily Hainsworth, Tiffany Schmidt. Somaiya Daud, Laurie Devore, Sarah Enni, Maurene Goo, Kate Hart, Isabel Kaufman, Michelle Krys, Amy Lukavics, Heather Marshall, Diya Mishra, Anna Prendella, Veronica Roth, Elisabeth Sanders, Nova Ren Suma, Kara Thomas, Kaitlin Ward. Whitney Crispell, Kim Hutt Mayhew, Baz Ramos, Samantha Seals, Meredith Galemore.

I'm grateful to Susan Summers, Megan Gunter, Diya Mishra, Anna Prendella, and Kara Thomas, for their invaluable insights at a critical juncture.

Special thanks:

All my family and friends
Michelle Cain, Meghan and Susanne Hopkins

The readers, booksellers, librarians, and gatekeepers whose enthusiasm and support of my work continues to make it possible.